Trinette Faint

W9-AGB-469

COLLETTE'S CALEB

COLLETTE'S CALEB © 2010 by Trinette Faint

ISBN# 1450539912/EAN-139781450539913

All rights reserved. No part of this book may be reproduced or transmitted in any form or by any means, electronic or mechanical, including photocopying, recording, or by any information storage retrieval system, without written permission from the author, except by a reviewer who may quote brief passages in a review.

This book is a work of fiction. Names, characters, businesses, organizations, places, events, and incidents either are the product of the author's imagination or are used fictitiously. Any resemblance to actual persons, living or dead, events, or locals is entirely coincidental.

Trinette Faint

TAKE I

1

"Did you get the *Chicago Style* tickets yet, Collette?" April asked her frazzled 27 year-old daughter over the phone from her oversized suburban Chicago kitchen to Collette's small hotel room at the Ritz Paris—a perk to being the personal assistant to Hollywood's latest hot, young, under 30 thirty actor, Caleb Christopher (at 29 and the star of the last four romantic comedy blockbusters, *Corrine, My Love, Come Back To Me, Rebound Robin,* and *You Have My Heart)* who recently added fashion designer to his resume. The reason for this trip was to show his second collection at Fashion Week.

Being an only child, Collette was very close to her mom, but sometimes the woman didn't know when to stop. She seemed to think that Collette could just snap her fingers and make anything happen. "Yes Ma, I finally got them yesterday. Didn't you get my message?" she asked, while she bounced up and down on her overstuffed suitcase to get it to close. She was now cursing all the shopping she had done, buying things she didn't need. Aware of the time, she still had to go to Caleb's room and make sure he was packed before the car arrived to take them to Charles De Gaulle to board their private Gulfstream 550 (courtesy of the film studio) to Chicago for his taping of the *Chicago Style Show* with Wanda Wallace. Although the plane would not leave without them, Collette still liked to be on time and did not want the pilot and crew waiting unnecessarily.

"Oh, was that you that called? Something is wrong with the ringer on my cell phone. Come to think of it, I did hear something rumbling around in my bag. Humph," said April. Two weeks ago Collette gave her mom the latest, sleekest user-friendly phone that Verizon had to offer, and she still had not figured out how to use it, even though Collette had a Verizon rep call her to answer any questions she may have had.

"Well, in any case I called you. *And* left you a message. They will be at Will Call for Pat and Cheryl. Learn how to use the phone, Ma," Collette said as she finally snapped the suitcase shut. "I have to go; the car is on its way. I'll call you when we land."

"Alright, well say goodbye to Paris for me! I hope you had fun."

"As always. I'll call you later."

"Okay, baby girl. Tell Caleb I said heeeeeeey! Love you."

"Love you too, bye," she said hanging up the phone. In the four years that Collette Sandrine-Anais Smith has been Caleb's assistant, she has been a more frequent guest of the Ritz Paris since Caleb entered the fashion world, but always felt it was too stodgy and rigid for her taste. When she was away from her cozy 450 square-foot fourth floor walk-up on 84th and Columbus, which was a lot more these days than she would have liked, she missed its warm décor of Indian eclectic with its hues of deep reds, golds, and oranges, mixed with subtle touches of plaids and toile prints of French country. Her ever-burning Diptyque Feu de Bois and Feuille de Lavande candles always enhanced the often stale Manhattan air with aromatic melodies that matched the sounds of 70s soft rock that she often played. Collette's unique design aesthetic was unique in that that these contrasts were reflective of her personality and contemporary bohemian chic style of dress.

"Knock, knock. You decent?" Collette said as she entered Caleb's large suite that overlooked both the Place Vendome and the private garden out back. Very ornate with its canopied bed, 18th century style furniture, and numerous objets d'art, the room contrasted his casual attire of broken-in classic Levi 501s that managed to be long on his lithe 6'1 frame. He wore a heather gray Hanes t-shirt under a navy J Crew zip-up cotton hoodie.

"Yes, I'm almost ready, come on in," he said from the bathroom, gathering his toiletries.

"I see you got everything packed up to go," she said, surveying the expansive room.

"Yes, Collette, I know you don't believe it, but I *can* do some things for myself." He smiled as he walked past her across the room and knelt next to his luggage. A mixture of pine and citrus left itself in his wake. Collette inhaled.

"I guess I should have showered earlier, my toiletries are all wet," he indicated as he went to pack them. Collette retrieved a dry towel from the steamy bathroom that had wet towels strewn about on the floor. His scent enveloped her senses again.

"Oh, it's okay. Here, I can just dry these for you quickly so the rest of your stuff doesn't get wet." She knelt next to him and went to take the toiletries from his hand and noticed a bit of moisturizer on top of his left brow. "You missed a spot," she said. She rubbed it into his pale skin with her thumb; his emerald eyes momentarily resting on her pink sapphire necklace nestled in her cleavage. She was glad she wore her newly appropriated floral print Cacharel wrap dress from Galleries Lafayette.

"C, what would I do without you? I mean, really."

"Nothing, I suppose. Just kidding. Let's get moving. We have to go." He looked into her brown eyes for a moment longer than she expected and she felt herself blush. She doubted he could tell through her cinnamon-hued cheeks.

"Are you blushing, C?" he teased, making it worse. Self-conscious, Collette quickly rose to her feet.

"No, don't be silly. I don't blush, I'm black, remember," she teased and he stood next to her.

"Indeed you are, but I think you were blushing. Look, I see it right there," he said, as he lightly touched her cheeks. At 5'11 it was easy for him to look into her eyes.

"Stop it!" she said as she slapped his hand away in mock anger. "Let's get moving. There's probably going to be traffic."

"OK, you're the boss. Let's go." He relented and gathered his things. When they entered the hallway, the bellhop took their bags to the waiting car. They walked in silence, save for the gold bracelets that jingled on her small wrist.

"I saw you *bluuush*. I saw you *bluuush*," Caleb sang as the elevator door closed. The bellhop tried to conceal his laugh as Collette chided back, "Oh shut up you!"

An hour later they boarded a very plush Gulfstream V that was nicer than most apartments. Its large leather seats that fully reclined with real pillows and cashmere blankets made it so much more relaxing than flying commercially. It was also easier than dealing with crowds and security at airports along with the tourists and paparazzi that always seemed to find him. With everyone having a BlackBerry or an iPhone if he so much tripped on his shoelace, you could bet it would be all over TMZ.com or People.com in an instant. As much as Collette loved working for Caleb and would do absolutely anything for him, the whole celebrity thing was getting harder and harder to manage. Quite honestly, she didn't know how much of it she had left in her. Lately she had been dreaming of leaving the business altogether and returning to school for writing for a better work/life balance. Of course finding love was on her agenda too. Until then she would continue to be the best assistant she could be and make sure that all of Caleb's needs were met. Besides, she actually enjoyed being around him, which was a good thing since they spent so much time together. A handful of times he'd flirted with her but she never took any of it too seriously. Mostly because all his girlfriends looked like clones of each other—brunettes or red heads, and all aspiring slashes—model/actress/whatever, so she really never took any of it to heart. Although she didn't think any of them were good enough for him, because they were all opportunistic in some way, she just did her job and stayed out of it.

Four years was a long time to work in this sort of job. She always said it was like having a husband you didn't marry and a child you did not give birth to. She certainly experienced all the downsides of constantly being on the road, never being able to complete writing courses, dealing with people whose motives were unclear, and not knowing who her true friends were. But the biggest challenge was maintaining a lasting relationship. She'd had a few prospects here and there but after cancelling dates at the last minute because of her erratic schedule, they stopped calling. Or once they found out for whom she worked for suddenly they had a script Caleb just had to read.

The closest she had gotten to anything resembling a boyfriend was Spencer James. He was a tall, handsome 33 year-old English TV star, largely unknown in America, who was Caleb's co-star in his current film, *Midnight Moon*. Caleb played the romantic lead, again, as in all his films, and Spencer was his rival who threatened to steal the girl who Caleb thought he loved. The handful of dates that she had with him did not constitute a relationship in Collette's book, but so far he was the only one who understood her line of work. He did not put unrealistic expectations on her. It also made her feel good that he was completely gaga for her, although she did not necessarily share the sentiment. She had been taking it slow the past two months. There was no need to rush. As Collette settled into her plush leather seat preparing for the flight, she rifled through her bag looking for her iPod and reading material.

"Great bag. Lisel give that to you?" Caleb asked. He was referring to the gorgeous supermodel Lisel Wright, who opened his show yesterday in a raw silk canary yellow gown with a diamond studded v-neck down to *there*. It caught the light as she strutted to the throbbing music. Lisel's dark skin made the beautiful dress pop on the runway, and her performance was received with thunderous applause. After the show she saw Collette backstage. As a gift, Lisel gave her a gift from her handbag line.

"Like it? It's great, huh. She gave it to me after the show. She is a sweetheart," she replied, twirling it around.

"Yeah, it's cool. Maybe I should start doing bags," he said. Their flight attendant poured him a Blue Moon, which he gulped down like there was no tomorrow. "Ahhhhh.... this beer is fucking great. How on earth did you find it in Paris, Collette?" His grateful eyes sparkled from under his jet-black eyelashes.

"Oh, I've got my ways…" she smiled at him.

She didn't need to bother him with all the details of just how she got the famous Denver beer to Paris. Born and raised in Denver, she knew how important it was to make sure his fridge was stocked with it. When possible, she even had it FedExed to wherever they were. All it took was a phone call to the marketing head of Blue Moon and at the mention of Caleb Christopher's love for the product, and suddenly it was being delivered by the caseload for free every other week. This, along with the Diet Coke, the Fuji water, and anything he wants from Perfect Organics. They were all too eager to give Caleb Christopher, celebrity actor/designer the goods for free. Naturally, Collette also got the goods too—a very nice fringe benefit of her job.

"You never cease to amaze me, C," he said. The sun drenching the cabin illuminated his wavy black hair and pale skin. He kicked back on the sofa and buried his head in one of the many scripts his agent sent to Paris the day before.

Collette accepted a beer from the flight attendant and dove into the latest issue of *Vanity Fair*, turned on her iPod and relished the pure joy of her turned-off cell phone. Thirty minutes later after she had fallen asleep, the flight attendant went to cover her with a down comforter, only to be intercepted by Caleb offering to do it himself. He watched her sleep for a few minutes before returning to his seat.

2

Nearly ten hours later they arrived at the Ritz Hotel in Chicago, both very exhausted. The last few days in Paris had been non-stop interviews and press leading up to the show. It amazed Collette how eager the press was to ask the same questions over and over again. *"So Mr. Christopher, are you enjoying Paris? How is this line different from your debut line? You're so busy with acting, why become a designer?"* Blah blah blah blah blah! It was all so mind numbing!

In Collette's room on the eighth floor, she was welcomed with the most spectacular views of Lake Michigan and was greeted with a dozen champagne roses on the living room table.

> *Dear Collette,*
> *I am sure you fared well in Paris. Very much*
> *looking forward to seeing you soon.*
> *Love, Spencer*

As she adored the view and the roses, Caleb paced anxiously in his room two doors down. Every time he got

15

up to leave the room, he would change his mind and begin pacing again. He picked up the phone and dialed Collette's room, only to hang up at the first half ring. He tossed the note on his table that said a Ms. Amber Skye had come by looking for him, and ignored her call when his cell phone rang. He was not in the mood for her easiness, as she had made herself available to him once before when he was in Chicago. He couldn't stop thinking about how cute Collette was when she was sleeping on the plane. Knowing she was dating Spencer bugged him, but he also did not want to begrudge her happiness. He was surprised at how it really got under his skin that Spencer was the beneficiary of her fun-loving side. He was primarily only exposed to her professional side. Collette had been with him a long time and was a great assistant, but more and more he was starting to see her in a different light.

Although for the better part of the last year he had tried to ignore it, she had gotten into his head and left him with unsettled feelings towards her. There were plenty of women around to satisfy him, he was a young, hot celebrity after all, but as he grew up, these dalliances grew more shallow, and Collette was quickly becoming the only woman with whom he truly enjoyed spending time, even if she was his assistant. As his nerves got the better of him, he took a shot from the mini bar and chased it with a Guinness. Before he lost his resolve, he headed for the door.

Exhausted from the flight, Collette quickly scanned the 40 messages in her inbox—half being friend requests from Facebook. Working for Caleb and being in the pseudo public eye, it was easy for all those friends from high school to find her. Among the others were from Julie, his publicist sleeping two floors below, about various media requests, a few forwarded joke emails from her mom that she would trash without reading, a message from her best friend Lou in Paris with photos attached of her latest boyfriend, and a message from Spencer with a request to call him when she arrived at the hotel. She ignored all of the friend requests, sent Lou a message of approval of her new beau, and was about to reply to Spencer's email to thank him for the flowers when she heard a knock at the door. She saw Caleb through the peephole and quickly ran into the bathroom to apply lip gloss and fluff up her hair before opening the door. She felt her face go hot and hoped she wasn't blushing again. Much to her chagrin, this blushing was happening more frequently than she would have liked.

"Hey, what's up? Is your room okay?" she asked. He stood there with dried red dots peppering the bottom of his t-shirt, undoubtedly from Gino's Pizza from an hour ago. He looked like a boy hoping to get picked for the kickball team at recess. "Caleb, you alright?"

"Oh, yeah sorry, just tired I guess. You mind?" he said as he entered her room, lightly brushing past her. He helped himself to a beer from the mini-bar, turned on the TV and started channel surfing on the couch as if he were settling in for the night.

"Okay…what's up? Something you want to talk about?" she asked. He stopped on a National Geographic special about an African safari. She sat on the edge of the bed across from him and thought her heart was going to jump out of her chest.

"I totally want to do one of those someday. Wanna go?" he garbled through big crunches of the chips that filled his mouth.

"Yeah, maybe. Listen, Caleb, it's almost midnight. Aren't you tired? You've got Wanda first thing tomorrow."

"Not really. Wanna beer? They don't have Blue Moon, but they've got Guinness...." he said, opening one for her, his eyes hoping she wouldn't refuse.

"Why are we watching this? Isn't *Letterman* on or something?"

"Probably," he said. They watched a lion feast on a zebra for dinner. It seemed tame in comparison to the way Caleb devoured his potato chips. She could barely watch either spectacle.

"Did you want to talk about something? Everything is set for Wanda. Your parents will be in the green room and I told the producer how excited your mom is to meet her, and...."

"Collette."

"Huh?"

19

"Relax. I know you're on top of it. Don't worry about it, it's cool." Collette was so tired and had difficulty processing what was going on. For all the time they spent in hotel rooms, they had never hung out like this. Was something changing? Did she want this? She didn't know. She felt her cheeks flush again and remnants of his pine and citrus scent tormented her.

"Okay then."

"We never do this."

"Do what?"

"This. Hang out. Chill."

"I'd have to disagree with you there, mister. Considering for the last four years I've seen you pretty much every day of your life on the average of about ten hours a pop. I think we hang out a lot."

"I *know* that, C. I mean just *chill*. You know, like friends." She thought there was something else on his mind but he was hard to read. She did notice, however, that he seemed as nervous as she, but his smile put her at ease.

"Like friends. Okay," she said, confused. "Well can we hang out tomorrow, I'm exhausted. We just got off a ten-hour flight, remember." He showed no signs of leaving. What could she do, but give in? She started drinking her beer and before long, being the lightweight she was, the buzz became a perfect remedy for her nerves.

"Look, if we're going to hang out then I can't sit here and watch this. Gimme the remote," she said. He hid it behind his back making her reach around for it. She found herself sitting on his lap playing this little game, both of them laughing in hysterics as he tried to keep it away from her. Caleb further toyed with her by using one hand to drink his beer and the other to keep the remote away from her.

"What's wrong, C? Can't get it?" he taunted, as he circled it around her waist within his hands. When it slipped from his fingers she managed to grab it. She was about to get up and return to the bed when he pulled her back down to his lap.

"Sore loser, eh, Caleb? Nah nah." She felt her hands grow moist and bit on her lip to calm her nervous laughter.

She grew more nervous as his smiling eyes calmly looked into hers.

"You're so beautiful, Collette. I have so much fun hanging out with you." His emerald eyes twinkled.

"Um. Thanks. You're not so bad yourself—for a boss, that is." She took a huge swig from her beer and got up to get another one before sitting back down on the bed. *Murphy Brown* on was playing on *Nick at Night.* She loved this show and was grateful to find something to distract her from what was quickly becoming a precarious situation.

"So, let's see if this place has anything stronger than beer…" he said with a devilish twinkle in his eye as he went to the mini-bar for round two. Producing two Grey Goose nips, he poured two vodka tonics and sat down next to her and watched the antics of Murphy and Miles in the newsroom. They were both engrossed in the show and Collette didn't notice that he had refilled their drinks twice by the end of the thirty-minute episode. By now they were in hysterics at *The Cosby Show* and enjoying their running commentary to the show. An episode of *Roseanne* followed and they continued working their way through the mini-bar. They had finished off the bag of chips and was chomping their way through the chocolates and biscuits, leaving crumbs and bits of chocolate all over the bed.

"What's that on your shirt?" Collette pointed to the red dots on the bottom of his shirt and when he went to look she flicked his nose up with her forefinger, sending herself into a fit of laughter.

"You got me, C. I'm glad you think that was funny because you are in for it now," he said. He began tickling her. She pleaded for him to stop but was laughing so hard she couldn't get the words out. Caleb's soft fingers nestled into her ribcage making her cry with laughter and he took in the curves of her body as she thrashed about. She was still wearing her pink sapphire necklace that sparkled as it moved about her cleavage. Eventually, he found himself on top of her during this tickle fest while Collette grabbed a pillow and tried to distract him. She used one hand to tickle him and one hand for pillow defense. He was now laughing so hard his resolve weakened and they both engaged in a half-assed pillow fight. They carried on this way for the better part of ten minutes before he held her and stared at her. She burst into laughter again when she noticed a big chocolate stain on the top of his t-shirt.

"Shit! The chocolate!"

"You look good with a little bit of brown on you." She laughed at her own wit, doubling over in laughter again.

"You think so?" he said, softly touching her cheek. Her laughter ceased.

"Uh, yes. Yes, I do think so. Don't you?"

"Absolutely. But first I have to pee." Collette's laughter was infectious, she had Caleb doubled over again. But his laughter stopped when he noticed the roses on his way to the bathroom.

"Spencer," she replied.

"Spence? Humph."

"What's that supposed to mean? He's a nice guy."

"If you like the stuffy English type," he snorted.

"Now you're just being mean. He's a nice guy, Caleb. Besides, he's your co-star which makes him the only guy I see besides you all the time, so who else am I gonna date? Huh? Smarty Pants." She chided him from across the room.

"I just didn't think you guys had hit if off is all," he said.

"We've had dinner a few times, that's all. So relax willya?" she slurred.

He made his way to the bathroom and she attempted to unpack her suitcase pulling out her horde of girlie products a few minutes later when…

"Ouch!" sounded from the bathroom.

"Are you okay?!" She ran to the bathroom and could not help but laugh at the sight of him on all fours. He was underneath the sink rubbing his head like a five-year-old ready to cry.

"I dropped the soap and when I went to get it I whacked my head under the sink."

Collette was now crying she was laughing so hard.

"It's not that funny, Collette."

"See, that's what you get for talking about my properly English boyfriend, Spencer James."

He stood up next to her and took her Hello Kitty product bag out of her hand. His hands were soft and moist.

"*Hello Kitty?*" he said dangling in it the air revealing her tampons, Advil, heating pad, face mask, a bra, and zit cream before she snatched it away.

"It came with my pajamas. Don't ask!" Attempting to leave the bathroom, she tried to walk past him unsuccessfully. He blocked her every step.

"So now he's your boyfriend. You didn't say that before." His green eyes pierced her.

"I was joking, Caleb. He's not my boyfriend. Jeez! But in any case it's almost three in the morning and …." she stammered before realizing he had cradled her boiling hot cheeks in his hands as he pressed his lips against hers. In the years that she had worked for him she'd listen to her girlfriends fantasize about it, read about it in the tabloids, been asked about it a million times, and now it was happening to her. Knowing that this was going to change everything, her lips did not have a problem responding. Rummaging his hands through her curly Afro and nibbling on her ears and neck he whispered, "Your skin is so soft, I love your hair. And you're blushing again. You're absolutely adorable, Collette."

"Oh my," She pulled back. She needed a dose of reality.

"I'm sorry, C. I couldn't help myself."

"Uh, okay. Um…" she stammered. Her judgment was clouded by all the drinks she had and although she didn't want to risk her job, she also didn't want to miss this moment either.

"Goddamit, C, I'm such an ass." He retreated from her. "It's just that…" His eyes cast downward as he tried to find the words.

"Yes?" She searched them for anything.

"It's just that, I don't know, I like you," he said looking at her.

"You do?" Shocked by her sense of relief at his admission, she returned his gaze.

"Yeah, I do. I just have so much fun with you."

"I have fun with you too, Caleb."

"Yeah?" he asked.

"Yeah. Especially tonight." She couldn't believe she had been so bold, and for the first time felt completely at ease with him.

"Well, let's get back to the fun then," he said as he kissed her again.

She was lost in his kiss for what felt like forever and took pleasure in his intoxicating scent. She kissed his neck while he moved his hands lightly underneath her bra strap. Her dress had fallen off one of her shoulders. He kissed her exposed shoulder and made his way across her clavicle and lightly squeezed her backside, and she did the same. He unzipped her dress and it fell to the ground revealing her matching La Perla ivory lace demi bra and panties on her thin but curvy body. Her pink sapphire shone brightly around her neck.

"Oh, Collette," he said as his finger made its way from her cheek to her breast. She quietly watched as he removed his t-shirt, revealing a smooth chest with a small amount of black chest hair. His six-pack was firm and Collette stepped toward him to feel her chest on his. "Collette, you are so beautiful. I've always dreamed of this moment."

"You have?" She looked up at him with wide, eager eyes.

"Of course," he said. He began kissing her again, this time with more intensity than before. He removed his pants, fully exposing himself to her. He was not wearing underwear. This revelation was shocking, but she was pleased all the same. Her pleasure intensified as he explored her breast with his mouth. "Come on," he said. They moved toward the large marble shower built for two.

"Caleb, I don't know. Should we? I mean, I'm your assistant," she said trying to talk herself out of it.

"C, it's me. There's nothing to worry about," he said, kissing her again.

"I just don't think…"

"Well then don't, Collette. Don't think for once and just be in the moment." His tongue worked its way around her long neck.

"Caleb." She stepped back.

"I'm sorry. We don't have to if you don't want to. I'm being an ass."

"Believe me, it's not that I don't want to, I am just not sure that we should," she said.

"C, we don't have to do anything you don't wanna do. It can stop right here. And don't worry about your job, you know I can't live without you," he said. His smile melted her like every other time.

"Oh fuck it, come here," she said. "Like you said, let's just be in the moment and not over think things. Right?"

"My thoughts exactly. Hang on a sec." He went to the mini-bar and came back with two nips of Bailey's Irish Cream. "Here's to being in the moment."

"To the moment!" she said, as they both emptied their bottles.

The hot water steamed up the bathroom and he pulled her into the shower, hungrily kissing her. He let her bra straps fall over her shoulders and gently tugged at them with his teeth while he removed her panties. She turned away from him as he undid her bra hook and cast the garments aside. He poured shower gel on her and rubbed himself on her to create a foaming lather of lavender-scented essence. She washed his hair after he washed her body, sprinkling him with kisses throughout the process. After their shower he took her wet body into the bedroom where their lovemaking was as intense as the shower had been. The clock read 4:00 a.m. They fell asleep, exhausted in each other's arms.

***

"Hullo?" Collette groggily answered her phone as Caleb slept soundly next to her.

"Collette, it's Julie. It's 8 o'clock. Are you still asleep? The car is here."

"Shit! I'll be right down," she said.

"And have you seen Caleb? He's not in his room. I tried calling and knocked on his door," she said.

"Caleb? Nope, haven't seen him. I'll see if I can find him and will be down in ten minutes."

"Hurry up!" she said.

Collette's Caleb

Collette jumped up and opened up the heavy blackout shades. The sun poured through the room, waking Caleb.

"Close the shades," he said rolling over.

"Caleb! Get up! The car is here. We have to get going or we're going to be late." She surveyed the messy room. One would have thought she'd had a party based on the mini-bar explosion. She would have to leave housekeeping a very large tip.

"Mornin' C," he said. He pulled her back into the bed and kissed her on the lips.

"We have to get moving, Caleb. We don't have time for this."

"Jesus, look at this room," he said observing the mess. "I'm sorry. We'll leave a nice tip."

"Okay. I told Julie we'd be down in ten. Up, up!"

"C, relax a minute," he said, pulling her back under the covers.

"But…"

"It'll be fine. Wanda can wait a few minutes. It's not live anyway." His smooth voice relaxed her and she allowed herself to be held.

"Alright. I'm going to make you deal with her producers if we are late," she admonished.

"Fine. Say, last night was awesome, C. It really was." Memories of the evening flooded back into her brain; the drinking, the shower, the lovemaking...

"Yes, it was."

"I like you a lot and I know you work for me, but I don't want anything to change with us. You know?"

"No, I don't know, Caleb," she said. Her heartbeat intensified.

"I mean, I don't want anything to change. I want us to be able to work together still and not be affected by what happened. I mean, what would I do without you, C?"

"You mean you want me to still be your assistant and just forget last night ever happened?" She turned facing him. Her eyes searched for clarification.

"No, honey, that's not what I mean. I just am not ready for a relationship, is what I mean." The moment he said it he felt like an ass. In the sober light of day he just blurted out what he said so many times before to other women because he didn't know what else to say.

"Who said anything about a relationship? Believe me, I've seen the girls you date and I know that you are not ready for one," she said more harshly than she would have liked. She thought about the questionable women he had dated in the past. They were all pretty enough but all were uneducated, ambitious in the social climbing sense, and were more or less starfuckers. Collette could never understand why such a smart guy would date such dimwits, but she'd managed to hold her tongue.

"What's wrong with the girls I date?" he asked.

"Nothing. Look, you don't have to spell it out for me. Last night was great and let's just keep it at that."

"See, that's all I was trying to say."

"Well, we agree then."

"Agreed."

"Now let's get moving before we are too late."

After he got dressed and left the room, she quickly scanned her BlackBerry and saw an email from Spencer received last night at 1:00 a.m.

> *"Hope you received the flowers, love, and are not too bloody tired. Tell that Caleb character to give you a break every now and then. Sweet dreams."* Spencer

Spencer's innocence triggered a flood of tears and in a hung-over fog she took a hot shower and cried harder at the sight of her wet underwear on the floor. As she tried to scrub away the night, she became more and more upset as she replayed Caleb's noncommittal words in her head. She didn't know what she expected Caleb to say after the night they'd just had, but she didn't expect him to say that.

Back in his room, Caleb quickly showered and took some Advil for the pounding in his head. He looked at himself in the mirror as he shaved and a disappointed face looked back. Although he really liked Collette he didn't think a relationship with her was realistic or even possible, and he didn't see the sense in pretending otherwise.

Collette made it to the lobby 20 minutes later than she promised and Caleb gave her a pleasant hello as she entered the lobby, which struck Julie as odd. Collette thought it was inappropriate that Julie was planning to go to Wanda dressed like a stripper. Her heels were so high she looked like she was about to tip over and her obviously fake boobs looked extra perky underneath her fitted sweater. She was also heavily made up and had tendrils falling all over her face. Collette's face was puffy and she wore a large pair of black Ray Bans in the dim lobby. She downed a can of Red Bull, the only thing left in the mini-bar, and her large bag was overflowing with papers, makeup, a sweater, and whatever else she threw in before her mad dash out the door. Her beige Gap safari shirt was buttoned wrong and one sleeve was rolled up and the other was not. Her pale pink skirt was twisted, the slit off kilter somewhere between the side of her body and the front. Collette returned Caleb's concierge-like greeting with a tight smile before getting into the large SUV that awaited them. As Caleb climbed in after Collette, Julie wondered why at 8:20 a.m. he had numerous chocolate stains on the backside of his jeans, but again she kept her curiosity to herself. They sat in the second row, Collette looking out one window and Caleb looking out the other, while Julie thought it best to sit up front.

The ride to the show was painfully quiet, save for the 70s music that played softly in the car—its lyrics referencing a lothario and his childish love 'em and leave 'em ways. This further punctured Collette's heart. Apparently, the driver—an unassuming middle-aged woman named Sherry Lynn with a long braid down her back—had an affinity for 70s pop as well. Typically, Julie would have used the time in the car to brief Caleb, which she should have done a few days ago to give him ample time to prepare, but the air was so thick that she simply handed him a sheet of paper with the questions he should be prepared to answer. The rest of the car ride she remained quiet.

3

"So how is *Midnight Moon*, the current film that you're working on, different from your previous romantic comedies?" Wanda asked Caleb.

"Well, I'm obviously playing a different character and the title is different," he said, distracted. It left Wanda and the audience unsure of how to respond.

"I understand that, but how is it different?"

"Hmm. Well Toby, my character, is dealing with his feelings toward Susan, his love interest, in a way that my previous characters have never had to do."

"Meaning what, exactly?" she said leaning in.

"Um," he looked at the floor for an unusually long time. "He is emotionally conflicted because he has to figure out if he really loves her or if he just wants her because his best friend has her."

Collette watched from the front row of the audience and swallowed hard at the lump in her throat. Caleb's eyes remained cast downward and again Wanda and the audience were thrown a bit off.

"Well THAT'S a tough one! Good luck with that! Right girls?" she said to the audience of teenage girls who all started to cheer. A few yelled out, "Yeah, good luck with that!"

"We'll be right back with more of Caleb Christopher!" Wanda roared. Girls were screaming so loudly that Collette thought her head was going to burst. During the four-minute break, Caleb signaled for Collette to join him backstage. When she did the audience realized he was talking to her and not them, those sitting closest to her pointed and wondered aloud who she was.

"C, are you alright? I know this morning was, well this morning, and I just want to make sure that we're cool."

"Yeah, I'm totally fine. Don't even worry about it," she said a little too chipper as her mouth formed a tight smile.

"Good, because I was worried," he said with relief.

"Don't. Now you better get back out there."

"Ok, thanks C. You really are the best," he said. He kissed her on the forehead before breaking into a light jog back to his seat as he waved at the girls, basking in the attention. The stage manager signaled that the show would be back in 5,4,3,2, and…

"You've got quite a fan base today, Caleb," Wanda said, pointing at all the screaming girls. Again, Collette's hangover kicked in to high gear.

"I guess so! Thank you all for coming, I appreciate it." He gestured to the crowd as they continued their screams.

"So, Caleb, you know I have to ask. Not because *I* want to know, but because *they* want to know," she said.

"Fire away!"

"Who was the young lady you were talking to over the break? She's cute…"

The camera panned to Collette who looked exactly like she had a hangover and was plugging one of her ears to muffle the audience screams. She removed her hand quickly once everyone turned to look at her with glowing eyes.

"Oh her? That's my assistant, Collette."

"Well, I will say that you guys looked very cute together back there."

Caleb's face turned tomato red. This was not on his list of questions. Collette felt like she was on fire, burning live for all to see.

"Oh now, Wanda, don't go starting anything. She's my assistant that's all. But thank you for the compliment," He fidgeted with his hands.

"Awww, you're blushing. That's cute! Guys, Caleb Christopher is blushing!" The frenzied audience started up again. Collette looked around in disbelief. "Do you have anyone special in your life right now? Again, this is for them." Wanda was clearly enjoying herself and the audience ate it up.

"Thanks for asking but I think I'm going to pass on that question," he said.

"Okay, got it. Sorry ladies!" A collective sigh of disappointment sounded from the audience.

Ready for another commercial break Wanda addressed the camera, "We all know Caleb Christopher as a hot actor, but he is also a fashion designer. We are going to talk to him about his recent show in Paris when we come back," she said. B-roll footage of him on various red carpets played over the music. He was with a different woman in every shot and in one of the photos Collette could be seen in the background looking fondly at him. His arms were wrapped around some girl's tiny waist as they posed for the cameras.

The show had been a success and Caleb quickly vanished backstage with Wanda as Collette went to find Pat and Cheryl, her mom's best friends from church. Before Collette saw them, she heard them. They were talking loudly to the security guard making sure he knew they were not going *anywhere* until they said hello to Collette first. Even though the security guard was much larger than them, he was no match for their determination. He continued to escort the rest of the audience out leaving Pat and Cheryl be.

The last time Caleb was on Wanda to promote one of his films, Collette couldn't get extra tickets for them, so this time her mom made sure she hounded her until she got these. Three weeks ago when she told her Caleb was doing the show she called Collette very early in LA on the one day she was actually able to sleep in until nine. They had finally finished shooting nights on Caleb's film, and she was sleeping like a baby in her posh room at the Four Seasons in Beverly Hills. Thinking it was some major crisis with Caleb, Collette picked up the phone on the first ring when it startled her awake at 6:23 a.m.

***

"Hullo?" she gargled into the phone careful to keep her head under the covers of the fluffy down comforter.

"You asleep still?" April brightly asked, with the sound of something loudly frying in the background, undoubtedly smoking up the kitchen.

"Who is this and what is that sound?" Collette asked knowing full well it was her mother.

"Don't get fresh with me, girl. I'm still your mother."

"Ma, it's 6:30!"

"It is? My clock says 8:30. I've been up for at least an hour and I'm making your daddy some breakfast," April said, as she sipped her cup of coffee while making a breakfast of bacon and scrambled eggs.

"Your clock says 8:30 because you're in *Chicago*. I'm in LA," Collette said trying to keep the edge out of her voice.

"Well I'm sorry. I thought you'd be up. I called you the other day in the morning."

"The other day I was in New York and it was 9:30 for me."

"Oh, so it's two hours behind out there?"

"Yes! Ma, I'm really tired."

"Okay, movie star. Look, I'm just calling to remind you to get those Wanda tickets for Cheryl and Pat. Collette, are you listening to me?"

"Not really. I'm trying to sleep."

"You can go back to sleep in a minute. I just wanted to remind you about the tickets."

"Ma, why'd you promise them the tickets? I will try but I don't know if I can get them."

"Girl, you work for Caleb Christopher, you can get whatever you want. Now, I'm tired of them hounding me after church every week asking for those tickets. Especially that Pat, 'Did you get the Wanda tickets, girl? You know I just got my purple suit out of layaway and can't wait to wear it on TV! I got shoes too!' She's been getting on my last nerves," April said, removing the bacon from the skillet.

"Pat in a purple suit? I hope she doesn't plan to color coordinate her makeup too like she does with everything else." Pat was like Collette's aunt and she loved her dearly, but it was sometimes embarrassing to be seen with her. If she wore a yellow shirt, you could bet her eye shadow was yellow, along with her earrings, purse, and shoes. She was so sweet and always had fresh baked cookies or cupcakes. You could never tell her she looked like Big Bird. Now she wanted to go to Wanda looking like Barney.

"Collette, I know you're busy and that boy has you goin' everywhere, but it would be really nice if you could get those tickets for them."

"Okay, Ma. I'll see what I can do," Collette said. "That's my girl! Call me when you get them. Love you. Oh, and Cheryl's niece still wants an autographed picture of Caleb.

Tell him to sign it 'Love, Caleb'. She'll like that. I told her you'd give it to her at the Wanda show."

"What?"

"I know you sign all them pictures anyway, so just make sure you make one out to her. Her name is Jacqueline and it's spelled..."

"Can you just email it to me? I wanna go back to sleep," Collette nearly cried into the phone.

"Alright, baby girl. I'll call you later. Love you."

"Love you too. Bye," Collette said, as she rolled over and tried to fall back asleep.

After putting the security guard in his place, Pat and Cheryl continued talking to an older woman they'd met seated next to them in the audience. She stood about 5'4 and had a soft, round face with friendly grey eyes surrounded by deep crow's feet. Her silver hair was in a bouffant style that made her look like Collette's high school lunch lady.

"Yeah, my friend's daughter is his personal assistant, his *PA*. Girl, she goes *everywhere* with him! It's so glamorous and exciting. London, New York, Paris, Rome, LA, girl everywhere."

As Pat talked to her new friend, Collette navigated the crowd to find them. She knew they were somewhere in the middle but had a hard time locating them because there were so many screaming girls, and people kept stopping her to ask her what it was like to be Caleb's assistant. She was polite to everyone who stopped her even if her responses were short and sweet, to their chagrin, as they wanted dirt and gossip. They pressed on for more details, which she would not give, and was delighted when she heard Pat call out to her and forcefully excused herself as she pushed her way through the crowds and followed the sound of Pat's voice ten rows up.

"Collette! Up here," she loudly summoned.

As she bolted up the stairs through the crowd, she looked upwards to see Pat doing her best Barney impression waving wildly. She wore a bright purple suit with a carefully coordinated purple ruffled blouse and long dangly purple earrings. Every curve was trying to find breathing room in all that polyester. Her purple eye shadow was streaked as if her eyes were about to take flight. Cheryl, a petite 5'2 in heels was more conservative in black slacks and an ivory sweater.

"Oh my God! Can we get a picture with you?" asked a group of five girls that blocked Collette's path. She had made it nine rows up before becoming ensnarled in this group of teenagers. "It must be *so cool* being Caleb Christopher's assistant," one of the girls said as they all started to scream madly. Collette tried to smile but unintentionally plugged her finger in her ear.

"Guys!" one of the girls said to the group. "Sorry, Collette, will you pleeeease take a picture with us? Pleeeease?"

"Sure."

The girls threw their arms around her, enveloping her in their Caleb Christopher love, while someone took the photograph. Faster than she could have thought possible, other girls quickly gathered around and started taking their photo with Collette. The flashes contributed to her headache and she tried to push her way through them as they descended on her, peppering her with questions. They were persistent when they received no responses because Pat grabbed her hand and yanked her away.

"She's with me, step aside. Move! Get out of our way!" she said, as the crowd parted for them. "Let's go down here," she said as she marched Collette to the other end of the aisle past the security guard, who darned not say a word, into a cleared out nook.   "Thanks, Pat, that was absolutely crazy. Hi, Cheryl. So nice to see you guys." She kissed them each on the cheek as their new friend looked at Collette like she was a superstar herself.

"Yes, and thank you so much for these tickets." Pat said giving her a bear hug, which released a highly offensive amount of Jean Nate body splash. Collette could feel the scent attaching to her shirt and knew it would take a special dry cleaner to get rid of the scent.

come. It was nothing," she muttered. After

rever, she finally released her and gave her a

bag of homemade chocolate chip cranberry walnut cookies.

"Thanks Pat, this is really sweet," Collette said. She was

genuinely touched. "Oh, hi, I'm Collette," she said,

extending her hand to their new friend.

"I'm Ruth," she said shaking her hand eagerly and

aggressively. "It's so nice to meet you. They told me all

about you. It sounds so exciting. I can't believe my luck, I've

tried to get these tickets for three years and I can't believe I

got to see Caleb Christopher and meet you!"

"Good for you, Ruth," she said, trying to extract her

hand from the woman's grip.

"Oh goodness, I'm sorry. I'm just so excited I guess!"

"It's okay. Really, it's nice to meet you."

"So how did you get this job? I mean, I live in Indiana

and I just can't even imagine!" she said, speaking a mile a

minute.

"Well, I guess you could say I was in the right place at

the right time. I was working on a movie as a production

assistant that Caleb was in, and one day I was assigned to bring him to the set and we started talking and he told me he needed to hire a personal assistant and was I interested. I always thought he was nice and he was getting pretty famous and it was obvious that he needed some help so I said sure. And that was about four years ago."

"Wow! Collette that's so exciting!"

"Maybe a bit, but it's a job like anything else," Collette said, noticing the time. "Oh, here, Cheryl, I have the photo for your niece. I hope he spelled her name right." She pulled the photo from her bag.

"Oh, he signed it *love*. She's going to absolutely die!" squealed Cheryl.

"Girl, where did you get that bag? It's fierce! And look at those heels. Oh, to be in my twenties again." Pat said.

"I got it in Paris the other day."

"See I told you she goes *everywhere*." Pat said to Ruth.

"So, how is it working for Caleb Christopher? He's so cute. How do you stand it?" Ruth asked giggling like a schoolgirl. Every ounce of her body moved with her.

"He's great to work with, but it really is only a job."

"Only a job?" Ruth nearly screamed, drawing a little too much attention to herself from the other guests leaving the set. "I would just die if I could be around Caleb Christopher every day."

"Well, he's a nice guy, but it really is just a job. Look, it was nice meeting you, but I've got to get going."

"I guess you don't want to keep Caleb Christopher waiting!" Ruth shrieked.

"Nope, guess not."

Collette hugged Pat and Cheryl and found her way back to the green room where Caleb was drinking a Diet Coke and talking on his cell. She sat down on the couch next to his dad who was reading the newspaper. Dave, a theater director in Denver, was a fit 6'3 man with salt and pepper hair that nicely complemented the green eyes he passed on to Caleb.

"Hi, Dave. Did you enjoy the show?"

"You should be asking Anna. I think she has Wanda cornered over there." He said pointing across the room to

Caleb's mom, the playwright looking every bit the Talbot's ad, talking Wanda's ear off.

"That's awesome."

"There were sure a lot of girls in the audience. All that screaming, I thought I was going to go deaf."

"Tell me about it. It's like that everywhere. That's your boy!"

"Well, I don't know how you do it. You're here one day, LA the next, New York after that. It makes me tired just thinking about it."

"It's not so bad. It's fun. And besides he's easy compared to a lot of other actors out there." As she spoke, she overheard Caleb trying to have a private conversation.

"...Yeah, too bad you couldn't make the show. It would have been good to see you, too, Amber... I know... we got in late last night and I didn't get a chance to call you ... yeah, I was in my room all night, but turned the ringer off my phone..."

"Excuse me a second, Dave." Collette needed to get to the bathroom before her head split open and before hearing another word of Caleb's conversation. She rummaged through her bag until she found her Advil and Midol. Cramps and a hangover on the same day had to be some kind of record, Collette thought. She chomped down two of each and stuck her head under the tap to chase them with what she hoped was drinkable water. She splashed some on her face and stared in the mirror and found herself doused in tears. Although she was sure Amber was just one of the many groupies that found him everywhere they went, it didn't ease the pain. Trying to put on a brave face, she decided if Caleb wanted this "Amber," then he could have her. She was not going to risk her job over a pop tart and tried to put their liaison out of her head. She reapplied her lipstick and headed out of the bathroom.

When she returned, she found Julie listening intently as Anna gushed to Dave about her chat with Wanda. Caleb was on his third Diet Coke and was finally off the phone.

"Ready, C?" he said.

"Yep, let's go!"

"You're awfully chipper."

"Oh, Spencer sent me the cutest text message. He said hi. I really can't wait to see him," she lied.

"Oh," he said as he covered his eyes with his dark Gucci shades.

"You ready Anna and Dave? I'm starved. Let's go get some lunch," she said as she locked arms with them. They walked past Caleb talking amongst themselves.

"Come on, Hollywood. Let's go." Collette called back.

4

Sherry Lynn was waiting outside the Cadillac Escalade in the secure underground parking lot and opened the door for them when they approached the SUV.

"So where we headed?" she asked. When she started the car a medley of the 70s greatest hits was playing. "Oh I'm sorry, let me get that," she said, ready to turn off the music.

"Oh, it's okay, Sherry Lynn. It's nice actually," Collette said making her feel more comfortable, as a mix of female singer/songwriter voices echoed through the car. Collette sang along, to the delight of Anna.

"You know this stuff? It's from my generation." Anna asked, joining Collette in song.

"Yes, I love 70s music. I was born in the wrong decade I guess."

"You hear that Caleb?" she said to her son in the front passenger seat. "Collette knows *real* music."

"Yes, Mom, I know she's great," he said. He gave Collette a soft smile, which made her self-conscious when he held her gaze for a moment before Anna spoke.

"Those girls he dates don't know good music like this," she said to Collette.

"Well, I'm sure they have other qualities." She tried to sound bright and cheery all while pushing Amber out of her mind.

"If they do I don't know what they are," she said to Collette in a low whisper. They shared a laugh.

Sherry Lynn waited patiently for directions until they finished speaking.

"I'm sorry Sherry Lynn, what do you suggest?" Caleb asked.

"I know of a great Chinese place if you want something like that. Or I can take you anywhere else."

"Nope, Chinese sounds good. Guys?" Caleb said to no one in particular.

"Sounds good!" Collette replied a little too overzealously.

"Fine with us," Dave said from the back row seated next to Julie.

Collette and Anna sang through a few more songs on their way to lunch, which actually made Collette feel better. As hung over and exhausted as Collette was, she was glad for their sing-a-long because it kept her mind off Caleb's conversation with Amber.

In the back of her mind Collette was thinking about how desperately she wanted to talk to Lou right now. Her best friend since their college days in Boston, she was raised in Paris, New York, and Miami by her late French father, Henri-Paul, who had been an extremely successful restaurateur of one of Paris's most exclusive eateries, Le Bistro Lou, and another one in Miami, named Plato, a Latin-themed restaurant, which was an ode to his American wife Pauline and her Miami roots. For twelve years while Henri-Paul oversaw the restaurants, Pauline was the head of public relations at the Fashion Association of North America before trading the fashion business for the restaurant business full-time when Henri-Paul died suddenly four years ago. She and Lou now oversaw the restaurants and Lou split her time between New York,

Paris, and Pauline's residence, Miami, managing their empire. Lou's schedule kept her on the road as much as Collette, making it difficult for her to connect with her friend at times.

Her desired conversation with her would have to wait. They arrived at the exclusive China City Restaurant 13 floors up on Lake Shore Drive and were quickly whisked away to an absolutely stunning private room with shiny hardwood floors. Their mahogany circular table displayed etchings of elephants and gold leaves and thick white candles adorned the middle. Displayed on the floor-to-ceiling windows were the thickest, most luxurious chocolate brown velvet curtains Collette had ever seen. The hostess opened them so they could take in the breathtaking view. Collette gave Caleb the same tight smile she gave him in the hotel lobby earlier when he sat down next to her and much to her annoyance kept "resting" his leg on hers under the table.

The manager arranged for a variety of dishes to be sent to the table, of which he said were on the house. The feast arrived within fifteen minutes. Not being able to even look at alcohol, let alone drink it, Collette sipped on a ginger ale while Caleb drank a beer with his meal. Anna passed her the garlicky green beans and the question she least wanted to be asked was put on the table.

"So, Collette, you seeing anyone special these days?" Anna inquired.

"Not really," she said. She passed the beans on to Caleb.

"She's being modest, Mom. She's dating Spencer James, the English chap." Caleb said, in his most condescending English accent.

"What? You're dating *Spencer James*?" asked Julie. Collette always thought if she weren't his publicist she could have easily been the type of girl, physically at least, that Caleb would have dated. Her overly eager response didn't faze her. After all, he did meet her in a bar and hired her on the spot.

"No, it's not like that. Caleb, see what you've started." She nudged him in the arm.

"Well, Collette. Tell them what it is like then." Caleb said with a straight face. He put his fork down and stared at her square in the face. Forget the ginger ale, she now had a sudden urge for a stiff drink. "He even sent her flowers," he said, in a low whisper.

"Oh, son, leave her alone. Lordy knows she doesn't have the time anyway running around with you," said Dave coming to her defense.

"Thank you, Dave." Collette winked at him and addressed Julie, "Julie, it's nothing. We just had dinner a few times," she replied.

"Now, Collette, you know you guys are more than that." Caleb pursed his lips. Collette was silent for a moment before speaking.

"Actually you're right, Caleb," she said. Addressing Julie across the table, she said, "He's a great guy and I do like him. More than anyone I've liked in a really really long time." She smiled seeing Caleb's eyes nearly pop out of his head next to her. "I feel really lucky and I have Caleb to thank for it. I mean, we met on the set of his film and boy, there were sparks from the get-go," she said. Caleb choked on his beer.

"Well, that's just great." Anna said.

"Good for you, Collette. He seems like a nice fellow," Dave replied.

"Wow, I just never heard you talk about him, but good for you," Julie said, stunned.

"Well you know, I guess I'm just a private person, but thanks to Caleb, again, I guess you all know now."

Caleb looked like someone took the air out of his balloon as he could have sworn she was glowing as she talked.

"Thank you, Caleb. You are simply the best. What ever would I do without you?" she asked, as she leaned over, looked directly into his eyes, and kissed him on the cheek.

"Well, let's raise a glass to Collette's new love, Spencer James!" Dave said. They all raised their glasses.

"To Spencer!" Anna said, leading the clinks all around. Collette then purposefully rested her leg heavier against Caleb's and giddily kissed him again.

"Thanks again." she said.

<u>5</u>

"It's okay, honey. Stop crying. It's okay." April said to calm her daughter. After the lunch debacle, Collette called her mom and told her dinner was off tonight and that she was taking the rest of the day to relax. April, sensing something was wrong in Collette's voice over the phone, appeared at her hotel room within the hour with a bouquet of orchids, peach roses, and baby's breath. When she entered the room and noticed Spencer's roses, and said "I see someone beat me to it," Collette just lost it, and had been ruining April's shirt with her streaked mascara and blush for 20 minutes now.

"No, it's not okay." Collette said, through uncontrollable sobs.

"Well, what's wrong? Is it what I said about the flowers? I know you love them, that's why I brought them, honey. I didn't mean to upset you." Collette held her mom tight while April stroked her hair.

"It's not you. Caleb's a jerk."

"What? What are you talking about? You guys get along really well. What did he do? You just tell me girl, and I'll go get him. He ain't my son, but I'll still whip him if he hurt you." The thought of April giving Caleb a whipping made her laugh.

"Oh, Ma."

"What's wrong, Collette. Don't be crying over your boss like this. What happened?"

Sitting up to blow her nose she said, "He embarrassed me at lunch today. And everybody was there. His parents and Julie."

"Girl, that ain't everybody. What did he say?"

"He called Spencer my boyfriend."

"So? You are going out with him, aren't you?"

"Ma, you're missing the point. He embarrassed me."

"How Collette?"

"He just did is all. He gets on my nerves sometimes!" she said as she walked to the window and watched the tiny couples walking by on the street below. "I didn't say anything about him and that airhead Amber."

"Oh, I think I understand."

"Understand what, Ma?" she said turning towards her.

"Collette, are you sweet on Caleb?" She placed her arm around her shoulder, which she quickly yanked away.

"What? No. Ma, please. Why would you say that?"

"Cause I'm your mother, that's why. And I was your age once, Collette."

"Oh, here we go."

"Well I was! I was sweet on your daddy for a long time, before I had the nerve to do anything about it."

Collette's parents met when her mom was 20, right after she had lived in Paris. She had managed to graduate college early and the day after graduation she took the car her father had given her as a graduation gift, sold it, and moved to Paris where she spent most of her time painting tourists' portraits on the Champs-Elysees. After four months there, she moved to New York and got a 9 to 5 at NYU's medical school as a secretary to one of the doctors. One day Hampton Smith, one of the medical students, called to make an appointment with her boss. Upon his arrival, April realized they had attended high school with each other in Chicago.

"Hampton Smith. I thought that was you on the phone." she said as he hugged her. He had been her secret crush in high school and let herself be embraced by his 6'4 frame.

"April Robins. Wow. Is it really you? Oh my goodness. Look at you!" he said as he twirled her around. "What are you doing here?"

"Well, I work here." He stood back and they looked at each other.

"No, I mean in New York?"

"Oh, well, I went to Paris after college for awhile till I ran out of money, then came here to avoid going back home and here I am!" Hampton's teeth were as white and straight as they ever were. Her stomach was doing cartwheels and she only hoped he couldn't tell.

"Paris? Wow, April. I always knew you'd do something big like that. What'd you do there?" His eyes were blazing into hers and she wondered where Mrs. Hampton Smith was.

"Oh, this and that. What about you? Are you here in New York alone?"

"I guess you could say that."

"Oh, well, that's nice. I'm sure you're quite busy."

"I was a little too busy for her."

"I'm sorry."

"Don't be. She didn't really want to be in New York anyway. Say, where you livin'?"

"East village. You?"

"Uptown. Harlem. It's up there, but I take the A train and it's pretty quick. Say, what time is it?"

"Oh my goodness, your appointment. I'm sorry. Look at me taking up all your time. Let me tell Dr. Cross you're here." She leaned over her desk to buzz him while his eyes spied her backside. She spun quickly around to catch his deep brown eyes staring at her.

"Um. You can go right in. Great seeing you."

"Maybe I'll see you again. Dr. Cross is my mentor this term."

"I'm sure we will see each other again." She made sure when he arrived at his next appointment three weeks later she was as dressed up as much as her meager salary would allow. She wore her best perfume and when Hampton emerged from the elevator looking good as ever, she looked in his eyes and slipped her number in his hand without saying a word. He was mesmerized by her confidence and they had their first date two days later. Four months after that they were living together in his tiny apartment. They stayed in New York for five years until a job at St. Joseph's Hospital took them back to Chicago.

April had told Collette this story a thousand times, but this was the first time she felt April was trying to draw a parallel with her and Caleb.

"Jeez Mom. Daddy? Is that what you are comparing this to?"

"See."

"No, I mean, what? No, Mom. He just upset me is all. I don't know why you're taking his side anyway."

"Honey, I'm always going to be on your side. Remember that. Just be honest with yourself, that's all. If you like him, then you're going to have to do something about it. Just like I did something about your daddy. Ha!"

"I don't like him like that Ma. You don't get it."

"Oh I get it"

"No, you don't. He made me look like an ass today."

"Why? Because he stated the obvious? You're dating Spencer, so I don't see what the big deal is."

"He had no right to blab to everybody. I don't go around blabbing his business to everybody."

"That's because he's famous, the media does it for you."

Frustrated, she flopped back on the bed and buried her head in the pillow and screamed, "Why are you taking his side?"

"Girl, get up and stop acting like a baby. Now, I told you I don't see what the big deal is, but you obviously like Caleb or you wouldn't be actin' like this. You're gonna have to quit your job or do something, but you can't be goin' around cryin' every time he says something you don't like."

"Quit my job? What?" she replied rolling over facing her, as the sun peeked through the clouds in the windows behind her.

"Look, Collette, I have been your mother for 27 years and I hate to see you like this. You weren't this bad when that Jason character stood you up on your third date. He never called you again but you didn't seem to care. You just brushed it off because I don't think you really liked him anyway. "

"I did care. I cried for two days."

"More like two minutes, Collette. I believe you and Lou went out later the next night and you met Oliver."

"Oh yeah, Ollie."

"Yeah, Ollie. And you didn't even care when you saw him out with his ex girlfriend. And was your boyfriend Collette!"

"We were only together for two months, Ma. It wasn't that serious."

"You didn't have a problem calling him your boyfriend, and you've been seeing this Spencer for like two months or something and he has not evoked this kind of reaction out of you. But Caleb says something stupid at lunch and you are all a mess. Trust me, Collette, this is different, you *care* about him. I know he's your boss, but it's okay to admit it. Stranger things have happened," she said taking her hand.

"Now stop crying, or else you're going to make me cry. Let's fix up your face and go out. Daddy is downstairs waiting for us."

"Daddy's been downstairs the whole time? Why didn't he come up with you?"

"From the sound of your voice on the phone earlier, I knew this was a woman's job and he needed to stay downstairs. Now come on, get yourself together, you're leaving for LA in the morning and it's already three o'clock."

In the lobby Hampton was pacing back and forth like something heavy was on his mind. Looking up at the sound of the elevator opening, he walked quickly towards them, a smile breaking out on his handsome brown face. He tightly squeezed his daughter and she felt some of the sadness slip away.

"Daddy!"

"How's my baby girl? Your mother tells me you didn't sound so good earlier."

"Oh, it was nothing. I'm fine."

"Nothing, huh. If you say so."

"She's fine, Hampton, let's get a move on before it starts to rain again." She took his hand. If their hands drifted apart, even momentarily, they would soon be clasped together again. It was as if they both had magnets buried within their palms.

***

Amber sat on her daybed in her parent's modest Skokie, Illinois home, looking out the bay window onto dewy lawn with her pale blue eyes. A beautiful leggy redheaded 22 year-old, she still lived in the bedroom she'd grown up in, having never changed the décor of teddy bears and balloons on the walls. As she sat there and looked around the room, she found these childhood reminders stifling. In a fit of frustration, she threw her pillows across the room, which knocked down the bottles of nail polish on the bookshelf filled with her favorite childhood reads.

As generous as her parents were in letting her live in their house rent-free, even with their antiquated rules—no boys (probably had something to do with those 2 abortions in high school), and no parties (could be because of the parties she had in their home when she became pregnant both times). She also had to be home by midnight (they only gave way on this when she was working) and knew she had to get out from underneath them. With no career path because she hadn't gone to college like her older sister, which her dad took every chance to remind her of, and a modeling career that was going nowhere, she spent too much of her bartending earnings from Azure, a popular Rush Street bar, in other bars. It left her with no savings to leave or do anything else. She wanted to walk the runways in New York—the only place where she thought she could realize her dreams, but she had no idea of how to get there. None of the guys she met while bartending could help her and certainly the duds her parents introduced her to from their church were useless as well. They only talked about getting married and starting a family. This made Amber recoil.

Upon hearing that Caleb Christopher was having a launch party at Azure in celebration of his clothing line being picked up at the Chicago retailer Marshall Fields, Amber pulled all the strings necessary to make sure she would be working it. She had to sleep with the sleazy owner in the back office to ensure this, but she was okay with it. She'd slept with him before in order to get assigned to the best shifts and didn't find this to be any different. She figured if she drank enough beforehand she could numb herself from feeling anything.

On the night of the party she wore her shortest skirt, a midriff bearing tight shirt, and spent $400 on a pair of red patent leather four-inch Jimmy Choos to be sure to grab and hold Caleb's attention. She felt this would be a life-changing moment and knew she needed to be ready. The party was a happening mix of models, publicists, marketing execs, and athletes. Everyone was trying to be heard over the loud music and drinking copious amounts of champagne, but there was no sign of the man of the hour. Maybe he wasn't going to show. Rumor had it he was not the brains behind his clothing line, but some guy named Roberto. At least this is what Amber read on a gossip website or heard from some other unrealiable source. She didn't care either way, but was getting pissed that her one opportunity to meet him and maybe get a modeling job out of it was looking like it wasn't going to happen. And her feet were killing her to boot. To make matters worse, she didn't even think Caleb was all that attractive, which annoyed her even more. The fact that she was willing to do whatever was necessary for her one shot with someone she thought was just so-so, who also had the nerve not to show up really rattled her chain. She seemed to be the only one who cared that he wasn't there, because it didn't seem like anyone else did; they were more concerned with posing for the photographers or swaying to the music.

After about three hours, the party was winding down and the crowd had thinned out considerably. Amber was bent over a table clearing away empty glasses when she heard the few remaining guests call his name and address him enthusiastically. She turned around to find him staring at her as he boldly approached her. She was surprised at how simply he was dressed for his own party. He looked like he had just rolled out of bed with his disheveled hair, jeans, haphazardly buttoned down shirt, and Chuck Taylor gym shoes.

"Why are you cleaning this table? I mean, look at you. You're the hottest thing in here," he said, reeking of alcohol.

"Is that so?" she responded. She handed the tray of glassware to a passing busboy.

"Yeah, it's so," he said, taking her in with his eyes. She found his audacity a turn on even if he wasn't necessarily her type. She generally preferred blonds, but overlooked this minor detail and kept her eye on the prize.

"Well thanks, I guess, umm..." she said, pretending as if she did not know who he was.

"Caleb. Caleb Christopher," he said. He kissed her hand. "And you are?"

"Amber. Amber Skye," she said. His lips felt good against her skin.

"Amber. How was the party?" he asked. "I hope I didn't miss anything worth seeing."

"I don't think you missed anything at all," she said, seductively tossing her hair. "But if you were supposed to be here earlier you should have showed up on time."

"Ah yeah, well," he laughed.

"Everyone's gone," she said indicating the near empty room.

"My dinner ran late but I got here as fast as I can. I'd like to make it up to you. We can go have our own party," he said in her ear, letting his lips brush against them as he spoke.

"I don't know. I'm kinda tired..."

"C'mon, Amber. Let's get outta here," he said, speaking closely in her ear again. Amber felt a hot flash run through her body.

"Oh, alright. Nothing worse than seeing a grown man beg. Let me get my things and meet me outside. Now," she said. She did her best runway walk past him to the bar leaning over to retrieve her bag. Caleb, the busboy, her manager, and the other patrons watched as she sashayed outside into the cool air, not bothering to finish working her shift or collect her earnings. She knew she could cash in on something far greater than the $300 she was promised to work the party. She and Caleb made their way to his hotel room where she would stay for the next three days.

She became somewhat of a living legend at Azure and took every opportunity to tell her customers and co-workers that she was Caleb Christopher's girlfriend. Never mind that he didn't remember her name after he woke up the next day. He had a hangover so severe he stayed in bed for most of the day, while she lounged in a bathrobe ordering room service. After that night, six months rapidly flew by and she even stopped sleeping with her boss because after having Caleb, she just couldn't go back to him. Over the course of those six months her phone calls and messages to Caleb went unanswered which did nothing but infuriate her. She still had no savings and her modeling opportunity never transpired.

Lying on the couch in her house one day, she saw on television that he was going to be on Wanda. She would finally have her second chance. Figuring he was probably going to be in town the night before the show's taping, she called him a few times and texted him a few more in hopes that he could meet up with her. In the press he'd been linked with a few women, but Amber knew those girls meant nothing to him, and surely he would call when he got to Chicago. But he didn't.

When she finally reached him on his cell, and he told her that his phone had been turned off the night before. Her mind raced with ideas of how to see him again. She didn't think he was still in town and wasn't sure if he was going back to New York right away, but she did remember him saying all those months ago to look him up if she was ever in town.

6

Amber felt her heart quicken as she gazed at the Manhattan skyline through the grimy bus window. She felt like a kid in a candy store, on this, her first, visit to New York. As the bus rolled down FDR Drive, a smile inched across her face as she closed her eyes and replayed her tryst with Caleb in her head. It didn't matter that she never heard from him again, or that she didn't know if he was in town or not, she only knew that if he were ever to be truly hers, she would have to step up her game and be more aggressive. Caleb was ripe for the taking and she would not let him, or a modeling career, slip away again.

"Hey babe!"

"Amber?" Caleb questioned as he rushed through the lively Chinatown streets, instantly regretting having answered his cell phone. He was on his way to dinner with Trey Xu, a director with whom Caleb rallied hard to schedule a meeting. He was hoping to star in his upcoming action movie and Caleb needed to convince him that he could do more than romantic comedies. He had been mentally preparing for the meeting all day and could not afford to be late. His agent told him to arrive early, as Trey was known to be punctual and didn't wait for more than two minutes for anyone.

"Who else would it be? Of course it's me. Guess where I am?" She said smoking a cigarette as she shivered outside of Port Authority in the early evening light. She surveyed her surroundings and moved her duffel bag closer, waving goodbye to some of the passengers she met on the bus from Chicago. It had been a long ride and she was glad that she had finally arrived to claim what was hers.

"Uh, where?" he said crossing the street with the restaurant in view.

"New York!" she said with delight. "Can't you hear all this traffic and stuff?" Oh it's so exciting here! I can't believe you never invited me here before." she said.

"What are you doing *here*?" he asked stopping dead in his tracks. He was nearly run down by a determined nanny pushing a stroller past him.

"What do you mean what am I doing here? I came to see you, silly!"

"What do you mean, you came to see me?" he asked, sitting on someone's front stoop letting his shaking head drop into his hand.

"Oh, don't be mad. We couldn't get together in Chicago a few weeks ago, so I hopped on a flight to New York. My parents don't even know!" she said, stomping out her cigarette.

"What the hell were you thinking, Amber?"

"I know you wanted to see me again and I didn't know when you were going to be back in Chicago, so ... "

"Amber, you should have asked me first. I have a lot going on and don't really have time to hang out. I'm really busy right now." He looked at his watch anxiously.

"Well I thought you'd be happy to see me. I mean, I haven't seen you in like six months or something and you never return my phone calls anymore."

"It's not that I'm not glad to see you, it's just that like I've told you before, I don't want a relationship and you can't just drop in on me like this."

"Well what am I supposed to do? Huh? Tell me that. I come all the way here from Chicago to see you and you don't even want to see me because you 'don't want a relationship?' It's fucking bullshit, Caleb," she said, lighting up another cigarette.

"Look, I'm sorry, I didn't mean to get upset, but you can't just do this Amber. I mean, really. We only spent one weekend together in Chicago. I told you I was busy and didn't want a relationship. Can't you see where I'm coming from?"

"Honestly, no I can't Caleb. We really connected and it was so fun staying with you in your hotel room the whole time. It was awesome and you know it. I totally felt a connection and know you did too," she said exhaling a plume of smoke. A group of middle-aged people with fanny packs and stark white sneakers talked loudly as they walked past. *Tourists*, she snickered to herself.

"I'm not saying it wasn't fun, but seriously, Amber."

"Seriously what, Caleb? Do you want to see me or not? I've already been here for two days and met some cool people and I can hang with them. They're standing a few feet from me and invited me to crash with them if you don't fucking want to see me," she said, standing alone.

"You've been here for two days? Where have you been staying? And where did you meet these people?" he said, noticing Trey walk into the restaurant five minutes early. He was hoping to have been the one to arrive first. Shit.

"Oh, what, now you give a shit? You're unbelievable Caleb. You really are."

"Alright, just stop this bullshit, Amber. I don't have time for it. You can stay with me for a few days but that's it. You'd better call your folks and tell them where you are and that you're safe. Jesus."

"Oh, all right. No need to get all *parental* on me and shit. Why the fuck do you think I left?"

"Just tell me where you are," he said, checking his watch again. He could see Trey curiously looking around the restaurant for him.

"Some place called Port Authority in Times Square," she said knowing full well where she was.

"Port Authority! What the fuck, Amber. What the hell are you doing over there? You shouldn't be over there by yourself at night."

"Well, that's why I called you."

"Get in a cab and meet me at The SoHo Grand on West Broadway and Canal. I'll be there in an hour. Wait for me in the lobby there."

"What, you can't meet me now?" she pressed.

"No, I can't meet you now! Shit Amber, I'm fucking busy right now. You really should not have done this. Just get in a fucking cab," he said, continuing to watch Trey who had sat at a table and appeared to be ordering something.

"A cab? I don't have any money left."

"Jesus, Amber. You don't have any money?"

"I probably have like 20 bucks, but that's it." She said as she fingered the wad of 100s in her bag she took from the back room safe at Azure yesterday, before hopping the bus to New York. She'd memorized the code after watching her boss open it a few times after their sordid lovemaking.

"Just get down here before you get yourself killed. I'll give you the money back."

"See you soon, babe," she said, as her smile grew wider on her manipulative face.

7

"No fucking way. You slept with Caleb?" Lou whispered as they got pedicures at SoHo Nails. Collette felt bad for the woman who scraped the streets of New York off her heels.

"Yes, and keep your voice down please. I've been a mess ever since."

"Why am I now just hearing about this Collette?" she said, as she flipped through *US Weekly*.

"Um, hello! I've been trying to reach you for like, two weeks since I've been back."

"I know, sorry I've been so crazed. I was nuts in Miami with Plato and I've been helping my mom with some PR stuff here in the city. You know I still love you though." She smiled at Collette. Her big brown eyes begged for forgiveness.

"Yeah, yeah it's okay. I know you've been busy."

"You want me to come over tonight? We could watch a movie and have a bottle of wine or something."

"I wish I could, but I am supposed to see Spencer and I have to meet up with Caleb's casting director to look for models for his print ad. Seriously, it's the last thing I feel like doing."

If Collette was not mistaken, she thought the pedicurist was breaking a sweat. She gave her a weak smile and shrugged her shoulders, to the displeasure of the pedicurist.

"Oh my God! Spencer! Did you guys break up? How was it on set when you went back to LA?" Lou squealed. She nearly dropped the magazine on the pedicurist. "I'm sorry!" she said.

"No, we didn't break up and he's still being so nice to me. When we got back he had flowers waiting for me in our trailer. It was sweet, but I don't know."

"Flowers waiting for you? Again?" That's sounds so awesome, C. We all dream of that. You're lucky."

"I know I should feel lucky, but I guess I mostly feel indifferent. I don't know. I like him, but I am not sure I like him like him. Ya know?"

"Yes, I do know what you mean. But it sounds like Caleb really rattled your chain. Does someone have a crush on her boss?"

"Don't be stupid. Of course not. I've just been doing some thinking about Spencer is all."

"That's all? Umm hmmm," she said as she resumed flipping through her magazine.

"Yes, that's all."

"All I'm sayin, C, is that I've know you for a long time now and I think I know you pretty well. If you like Caleb just tell him. It's not like he's a loser or anything. But try not to hurt Spencer's feelings. He's been really sweet to you."

"I'll see how tonight goes. Maybe I just need to be alone for awhile."

"You want me to come with you to this casting thing? I can bring Big Macs for us and we can watch the models salivate!"

"Thanks anyway, but I'll be ok." Collette smiled to the pedicurist as she put her feet back in the warm water. Lou hurriedly closed the magazine and went to put it on the table beside her.

"You done with that? Lemme see it."

"I'm going to save it for later. It was a really boring issue," she said, as she rammed it in her bag. "I'm getting hungry. You?"

"What is wrong with you? I wanna see the magazine," she said. She tried to reach around Lou unsuccessfully. Both pedicurists eyed them curiously as did some of the other patrons.

"Collette, really, why do you want to see this trash? Honestly!"

"Give it to me Lou. What's in there?" she asked. When she reached for it she splashed water all over the place.

"Oh alright, here! Just take it before you get us thrown out of here." Lou tossed it at her.

She quickly flipped through the gossip magazine and on the *They're Just Like Us!* page, was a photo of Caleb holding the hand of a redhead while they waited in line outside for a seat at a café. Collette's eyes grew wide with disbelief as she looked at another shot of the two of them sharing a kiss, and a third shot of the redhead feeding him French fries. The caption, in bold print for the world to see, read: *Caleb Christopher and his main squeeze, aspiring actress and model, Amber Skye, enjoy a romantic late lunch at the Second Street Café in New York's West Village.*

Meanwhile Caleb was annoyed and agitated. His phone kept ringing and he did not want to answer the call. He recognized the number and knew the caller had left a few voicemails over the past few days, so he knew why he was calling. Still, that didn't make him want to deal with what was on the other end of the line.

"Look, Roberto, I told you already I don't have time to talk about this," Caleb said into the phone. He paced the newly refinished hardwood floors of his expansive downtown loft. "I don't care if *Veector* wants to do it!" he snapped.

The muted sage walls were decorated with photography by Maureen Sullivan and Trinette Faint, and the pinewood coffee table was littered with empty Diet Coke cans, beer bottles, Chinese food containers, and dirty ash trays—signs of Amber's impromptu gathering with some new friends she met at a bar the night before. The leather sectional had a large cigarette burn, and one of the walls bore an imprint from a dirty basketball, a result of the Blue Moon and Jagermeister-fueled dodge ball game he and his friends played the other night.

"Because we had an agreement, that's why, or have you forgotten about that? I told you no fashion TV shows!" He yelled into the phone. His pacing increased. "I really have to go. I can't deal with this right now."

He hung up and sat on the couch with his head in his hands. Unable to sit still, he resumed his pacing, back and forth past on his 73-inch wall-mounted flat screen TV. It was on mute. Trying to cool off, he sat in a chair by one of the loft's many enormous windows, cranked it open and looked down 11 floors to the streets below. The city sounds enveloped and soothed him. Reaching for a cigarette that peeked out under a copy of Amber's *US Weekly*, he opened the magazine to the page she'd bookmarked and was reminded of his romantic late lunch. Underneath this magazine he was disturbed to discover a note from Collette giving him the details of the model casting today for his fall collection. Last night he thought he misplaced the note when Amber said she hadn't seen it either. "Shit," he said springing from the chair, and bolting out the door.

<u>8</u>

"I'm sorry, what's your name again? I don't see it here," Patrick, the flamboyant casting director said looking up through his square-framed black glasses to Amber. Collette looked at another portfolio, as they had been doing for three hours now still not having found what Patrick was looking for. They didn't have the time or energy for crashers at his casting.

"It's Amber, Amber Skye," a syrupy voice said. "I'm from Chicago, which is probably why I'm not on there, but I just moved here." Collette thought her ears betrayed her as she looked up and saw Amber in person for the first time. If Collette's eyes were weapons, they would have sliced her all over the floor. An audible gasp released itself from her mouth. Patrick was taken aback by Collette's sudden personality change and questioned her state of mind, asking her repeatedly if she was okay, looking at her as if she were crazy. Amber stepped back from this suddenly deranged woman.

"I...um...I'm ok. Sorry," she said to them both. Patrick returned his attention to Amber.

"Who did you say sent you, Amber?"

"I didn't say, but my name is Amber Skye. Why don't you write it down so you don't forget it."

"Amber, we are very busy here and since you're not on the list I'm going to have to ask you to leave," he said, indicating the long line of girls who were sent by their agents.

"Excuse me?"

"Thanks for coming. Next," he said, waving the next model to the table.

"I was trying to keep our love private, but I am Caleb's girlfriend, idiot, and he sent me."

"What?" Patrick said. Collette felt her entire body redden.

Amber flung her shiny hair over her shoulder and it landed in the crease of her breast. She made sure to squeeze them together with her upper arms as she leaned over.

"You heard me. Call him if you want. He's probably still in bed waiting for me to come back home."

"I don't think I should ... " he stumbled.

"Patrick, is it? You're starting to waste my time. Why don't you just send these other low-rent models home. I don't have all day."

"I can't do tha—"

"Caleb would not appreciate my being treated like this. Do you want me to call him myself?" she interrupted, penetrating her icy eyes into his. Dramatically straightening up, she tossed her hair over her shoulder and lightly licked her lips as she threw a glance in the other models' direction, ensuring that they were watching her little show.

"That won't be necessary, dear. Do you have a book?" Patrick wearily asked.

"A book? Did you not hear me? I *said* I am Caleb. Christopher's. Girlfriend. What are you a moron or something?" she asked practically shouting. The other models were silent with disbelief.

"Very well then. Why don't you take a seat over there on the couch and relax," he said, pointing across the room. Amber's long legs carried what couldn't be more than her110-pound body, across the room. She sashayed in her red patent leather Jimmy Choos as if she were on a runway. When she sat down she applied lip gloss so shiny Collette was nearly blinded by it. She lit a cigarette and blew smoke at the 'No Smoking' sign on the wall.

"You're going to actually look at her, Patrick? After the way she talked to you?" Collette asked, her face burning hot.

"She came all the way down here. I can at least see her," he said.

"Because she says she's with Caleb?" Collette's high-pitched tone surprised even her. She noticed Amber smirking.

"What is the big deal, Collette?" he whispered. "She's your boss's girlfriend and we need to keep him happy."

"I don't believe this. I have to go," she said, frantically packing up her things. Her armpits dampened the material of her Pucci print dress. She made a mental note to switch back to Secret, obviously that natural crystal rock shit didn't work. Her folding chair nearly toppled over as she yanked her cropped denim jacket from it.

"But, what about the rest of the girls? This is going to take me all night, Collette."

"Seems as though you've already made up your mind. Good luck." With no other way out, she walked across the room past Amber, her Teva's flopping in her wake. Amber's eyes followed her across the room. She's mocking me, Collette thought. Tears formed in her eyes when she heard Amber say, "Bye, bye," with a dismissive wave of her French-manicured hand. She exhaled a plume of smoke, and dumped the ashes on the floor.

***

Caleb raced downtown to the Tribeca studio where the casting was being held, certain that Amber would be there. Riding in a rare slow-moving cab that seemed to catch every red light, he wondered to himself exactly how he would get her out of his house. In the nine days since she had arrived unannounced, she did nothing but talk about how much she wanted to model and how being there was her destiny. Her talk about them belonging together thoroughly freaked him out. To top it off, she'd also cleaned out his liquor cabinet. He had to admit that some of the drinking had been fun along with the crazy sex, but it was time she headed back home to Chicago. Or at least out of his house. She certainly was not the type of girl with whom he envisioned spending so much time. He also didn't like the way she was trying to forcibly integrate herself into his life. She tried to tag along to all his meetings and professional engagements, which he had not allowed, so she was on her own when they were not together hanging around town or in a bar. During one of her outings he searched her duffel bag and found a bus receipt from Chicago that left him confused as to why she'd lied about when and how she arrived. This discovery led another significant finding—a wad of cash—which he found in a pair of her dirty jeans. Angered, he was tempted to keep it. Though he knew she didn't steal it from him, he didn't really want to know where she got it from.

Collette had been keeping her distance, only speaking with him over the phone and by email. At least it required little effort to keep them from meeting, but Caleb had a feeling Collette would not be happy if she found out Amber was there. Although he sensed that she was upset with him about Chicago, he didn't press it and she remained the consummate professional she was and continued to keep his best interest in mind. He knew he owed her an apology about Chicago and only hoped that she would accept it.

As his cab finally pulled up in front of the studio he grew sad and was without words as he saw Collette's cab pull away. Her long dress was caught in the bottom of the door and he watched her shoulders heaving, while her hands wiped away heavy tears. Caleb entered the studio and saw Patrick speaking with Amber.

"Hey, babe!" she excitedly greeted him. "I got the job!"

9

"Collette, you alright, love?" Spencer asked through her apartment intercom downstairs as Collette had a breakdown upstairs. Her apartment was infused with scents of lavender and spice. A dreary song played from her computer. Collette had repeated it four times in the last hour.

"Yes, sorry, I'll be right down," she managed to reply hoping she had not given anything away. She tried to hold back a wave of tears that had been plaguing her since she left the casting two hours ago. Though she knew makeup would be no help in the state she was in, she fixed her smudged mascara by adding more (which is never a good idea) and applied her favorite MAC Underworld lipstick. She couldn't keep Spencer waiting another ten minutes. Through a quick glance out the window, she saw that he had a single rose and a look of worry on his face. She took a deep breath, turned off the iTunes on her computer, drank the last of her wine, and headed out.

"Collette, you look beautiful," he said, giving her a hug. When he handed her the small box of chocolates with the rose, she started crying again. "Oh honey what's wrong? I could tell by your voice on the intercom that something was wrong. What is it?" His soft grey eyes consoled her, registering genuine concern and care. She never noticed how beautiful they were and his full lips and blond hair nicely completed the package of his handsomely chiseled face. Being 6'3 with a cute accent didn't hurt either.

"Oh gosh I'm sorry. I'm just a mess," she said, wiping her tears with the back of her hand, further smudging her "waterproof" mascara. "The last scene in *Pretty Woman* when she's on the ladder and he comes back for her … I just lose it every time," she sputtered, accepting a handkerchief from Spencer. She gave her nose a healthy blow feeling lower than she had in a long time.

"You're sure nothing else is going on? You seem pretty upset," he asked, eyeing her suspiciously.

"No, that's it. Look, I'm sorry. I didn't mean to ruin the night. Let's get outta here," she said. She took his hand and led him down the street.

"You didn't ruin anything, love," he said, kissing her on the forehead. "It's sweet. I just didn't take you for such a romantic."

10

Twenty-two year-old Roberto Carnellos always felt destined for greater things and had no problem working for them. A personable boy from Belize, he grew up on the island of Ambergris Caye, where his tall, sun-kissed body was maintained by working numerous trades—as a fisherman, a Pedi cab driver, and as a sailing and snorkeling instructor. As a kid he often accompanied his older brother Miguel on his popular tours of the Mayan Ruins (a very humid three hour roundtrip bus ride on a non-air conditioned school bus). His brother charged the thirsty tourists a hefty $2 for bottles of water that they were told were included in the cost of their ticket. His brother encouraged this activity, and helped himself to half of the profits, of which there were plenty. By the time Roberto was 15, Miguel had him bartending on the tour bus, inflating the price of Belize beer and watered-down rum and cokes.

In addition to making easy money on the tours, he was exposed to a world that was otherwise foreign to him. In his conversations with tourists, he would ask about the places they came from, absorbing their stories like a sponge. Their worlds opened up his mind to the possibility of living somewhere else. New York, with its tall buildings and diverse culture, seemed the seemed the most exciting option. One day while he was on a break from bartending, he overheard a tourist talk to his companion about a dress he designed for a celebrity. Roberto initiated the conversation that would change his life.

"Excuse me, sir," Roberto said.

"Yes?" the man replied. He was thick and bald and pleasantly surprised to be interrupted by such a beautiful boy.

"You know celebrities?" His eyes gleamed.

"You could say that. Yes," the man replied, removing his hand from the knee of his young but paunchy companion.

"Sir?"

"Umm hmm?"

"I'm sorry, sir. I don't mean to bother you, I just never met anyone who knows celebrities. My name is Roberto

Carnellos," he said, wiping his sweaty hand on his shorts before extending it.

"Roberto, huh?"

"Yes sir," he said. The man slowly shook his hand, with a welcoming gaze.

He turned to his friend and said, "I like this kid. He's got spunk." Roberto's smile lit up the bus and he shook his hand more eagerly than he'd intended.

"Your name, sir?"

"Victor."

"Just Victor, sir?" he said, his pronunciation of Victor sounding more like VEEC-TOR. He smoothed his black hair away to show his model-like face.

"Yes, just Victor. Say, how old are you, Roberto?"

Miguel spied his brother being too friendly, and quickly approached him. Roberto introduced him to his new friend.

"Roberto, don't bother the nice man. How about another drink, sir?"

"It's no problem at all. I was enjoying talking to him, and yes, I'll take another drink. But put some rum in it this time, will you?" Miguel went to make the drink and Victor signaled for Roberto to sit down in the empty seat across from him, where he could fixate on his legs. "Roberto, this is my friend Julien," he said. Julien reached out his hand.

"Nice to meet you, Julien. I'm 15, sir. You live in New York, sir?"

"Yes, but please call me Victor," he said.

"Victor, yes. What do you do there, Victor?" Miguel returned with his drink and looked at Roberto before walking away. "My brother, sir. I mean Victor...um, so what do you do in New York?"

"I'm a fashion designer."

"Wow a fashion designer! I wish I could make clothes. That's exciting Victor."

"It's a lot of work, Roberto. But it's a nice living," he said, as he wiped the sweat from his brow. Julien fetched a handkerchief from his bag and dabbed Victor's moist forehead.

"I want to go to New York one day Victor. I meet a lot of people from there on the tours."

"Well you should definitely go then," he said crossing his legs.

"Yes Victor I will. I swear! Can I talk to you there?"

"Of course, Roberto. I'd love that. My shop is at 565 Madison Avenue," he said. Julien angrily nudged him before Victor replied, "What? I'm just being nice. Relax already."

"Oh, thank you Victor. I will come and I will find you. I swear it!" he said.

"Please do Roberto. Please do," he said. He watched Roberto stand and walk away, his sweaty shorts outlining his tight butt.

11

Collette had managed to put the whole Amber and Caleb thing out of her mind and had a great time with Spencer. The night started with pizza and Chianti at Italian Ville, her favorite hideaway in Little Italy, followed by an adventurous subway ride uptown to Times Square. On the subway platform, Spencer performed his robot-like dance moves to the beat of three kids drumming on empty buckets. Collette, finding this terribly funny rooted him on. Once in Times Square they decided to be tourists and take a double-decker bus around the city. They followed this bus ride with drinks at a local dive bar in Hell's Kitchen, where they danced from an old jukebox whose musical selection did not go beyond 1989. Spencer's uninhibited dance moves inspired those drunk enough to get on their feet and join him, as he twirled Collette around to the likes of all things 80s. The night was the perfect tonic for Collette and when they returned to his modest SoHo apartment, he put on some music and laid out a spread of Cheetos and beer— the only thing he had in his tiny kitchen.

"Hey, who is that? I like it," Collette asked of the pop-infused jazz Spencer played as she freshened up in the bathroom.

"It's The Storti Band. Jazz Fusion. Glad you like it," he said appearing in the frame of the bathroom door. He kissed her on the forehead. "I had a great time tonight, Collette."

"Me too," she replied.

"I hope we can do it again real soon," he said, as he took her head in his hands and kissed her with great ferocity. He gently leaned her against the wall while his mouth nibbled down her neck. She took off his sweater and admired his toned chest. They scrambled to the bedroom, tripping over the rest of their discarded clothing in the process, before passionately falling into bed.

Sleeping peacefully four hours later she continued to ignore the buzz of her cell phone that seemed to be going off every three minutes. Not wanting to wake Spencer and thinking it must be urgent, she gingerly got out of bed and tiptoed into the living room. "CC" flashed on the screen of her cell phone that was cast aside on the floor.

"Caleb, what's wrong? Is everything alright?" she groggily whispered.

"Collette, I'm sorry to call you so early, but I need to talk to you."

Earnestly, she fished out a notepad and pen from her bag, preparing for anything. Clearly something was very wrong because he sounded wide awake an unaware that it was 7 a.m. "Is it your parents? Is everyone alright?" she asked. She heard a loud strange noise coming through the phone. "Say, where are you? What's that sound?"

"It's Amber."

Annoyed, she put down the pen and paper and walked back to the bedroom door to check on Spencer.

"Amber? Not like I really wanna know, but what is she doing?" she asked, as she closed the door to Spencer's room.

"Snoring. She gets like this when she's had a lot to drink. Apparently she was out celebrating last night. It's so loud I am on the couch."

"Oh, you poor thing. Good luck, I gotta go," she said about to hang up.

"C, wait. I can explain."

"Is this what you called me for, Caleb? It's seven in the morning and I am trying to get some sleep. I'll see you on Monday. I have to go."

"What do you mean, 'You have to go?' Where are you right now?"

"You have some nerve, you know that? Calling me with this Amber shit. Where I am is none of your business, and if you don't mind, I'm going back to bed now. I don't have time for this."

"You're with Spencer aren't you? Goddamit, Collette!"

"Excuse me? I was not the one in *US Weekly* playing suck face enjoying my *'late afternoon lunch'*."

"I know, Collette, I'm sorry. It's really not like that. Just let me explain."

She angrily whispered into the phone, "What is there to explain, Caleb? You couldn't see her in Chicago, so you made sure you saw her here."

"Chicago? What? How did you ..."

"Never mind. Look, what you do is your business and what I do is mine. Let's just forget about Chicago altogether. I mean it's what you wanted, remember?"

"Come on Collette, now don't say that. Just let me explain."

"You don't need to explain anything, Caleb. It's all forgotten. Now why don't you go make your girlfriend some pancakes or something. I'm hanging up now."

"Collette, come on let me—" the sound of the dial tone shut him up as he slammed the phone down on the table.

For five minutes Collette stood, resting her forehead against the wall. She wondered how she got into this mess, and more importantly, how she was going to get out of it. Before turning off her phone and returning to bed, she read a new text message.

C, I'm sorry. She means nothing to me.
She just fucking showed up and is ruining
everything. I'm trying to get her out.

Called because I need to talk to
you about Roberto. He's
been picked to do the show Real Runway
and some guy is threatening to talk to the press
and I need your help. Please call me. Love, CC

Exhausted and exasperated, she turned off her phone and crept back into bed, returning to the safety of Spencer's arms.

***

Over a liquid lunch at a Tribeca eatery later in the day, Lou had to practically lift her jaw off the table after Collette filled her in on everything. She broke down in tears at the retelling of the casting session with Amber and with her going out with Caleb. Lou kept the mimosas coming as she listened to her saga with a sympathetic ear.

"Oh honey, don't cry over that dipshit. She doesn't mean anything to him, you must know that."

"I know, but, but … I just don't know why it bothers me so much," she said, wiping her eyes.

"Have you ever thought that maybe you are jealous of Amber because you like Caleb? You guys do spend a lot of time together. It's like he's your play husband or something."

"Ugh. Don't even say her name."

"Sorry. But think about it. Since Chicago you haven't been the same and I've never seen any guy get to you like this." She playfully nudged her friend. Collette smiled.

"Well, he made it clear he doesn't want a relationship or anything so there's nothing I can do about it," she said, downing half her drink in one big gulp.

"See, you do like him! It's okay to have feelings for him, Collette. It's probably natural in your situation. You're closer to him than his mother."

"Yeah, maybe...but, I just don't get it. What's he see in Amber? She's nothing but a starfucking groupie," she said, blowing her nose.

"He's just probably just fucking her like he did those other floosies is," Lou said. I'm sorry, C, but he probably is. But you know he's not going to marry her or anything. He's a smart guy and probably doesn't even really like her. You said that's what he said, right?"

"Yes, he kept wanting to explain, but I wouldn't let him. I was at Spencer's and couldn't deal, ya know?"

"Yeah, I guess, but you should hear him out. Speaking of Spencer, what's up with him?"

"He's so sweet, Lou, and I feel like a shit treating him this way."

"He does seem to like you an awful lot."

"I know and I like him too, but he's just not—"

"What, Caleb?"

"Yes."

"You said he left for London today, so it sounds like a good time for you to figure things out and see what happens. How long is he gone for anyway?"

"About five weeks. The shoot for his BBC show is for four weeks and he is going to spend a week with his parents and sister. He's taking them to Italy for a vacation."

"What a sweetie."

"Yes he is, that's for sure. He wants me to join him in Rome so he can introduce me but I told him it will depend on Caleb's schedule."

"Oh, boy. He's got it hard for you, C. We should all be so lucky to be the object of affection of two hot guys."

"One hot guy, remember."

"Oh, he'll come around. You'll see."

"Maybe, but I certainly didn't plan on this and do not recommend it. I have to work out my shit with Caleb while he is gone, but I have no idea what I am going to do."

"You'll figure it out. What's up with Roberto? What's the deal with him?"

"Girl, we are going to need some more drinks for this one," she said, flagging down the waitress with every intention of ordering their third round of mimosas, but opted for a bottle of champagne instead.

<u>12</u>

After saving enough money for a plane ticket from Belize and showing up at Victor's shop four years from his fateful meeting on the tour bus, Roberto had worked hard to become a menswear designer of note. Victor was surprised to see him and quickly made room for him, making an upset Julien take him shopping for more than the lightweight sweater and khakis he showed up in. Julien's personal effects were strewn all over the large Upper East Side apartment and he made no apologies for them. He moved a pile of his stuff off the bed in the guest room that Roberto would be staying in. Victor had told him to remove his belongings from the closet as well, which he scornfully did, not hiding his emotions from Roberto as he did so.

Victor took him under his wing and gave him a job in his store as a part-time sales associate. He paid for his night courses at The Fashion Institute of Technology, impressing Victor with how quickly he was learning the basics of design. Roberto's ambition was boundless; he ran errands for Victor and kept his apartment spotless. It didn't take longer than a month before Julien was completely out of the picture. Most shocking to Julien was when Victor calmly told him that he was no longer in love with him and asked him to move out, only giving him two weeks to do so.

Roberto accompanied him to fashion and art events and was soon a fixture on the town, showing up on *Page Six* frequently. It was at one of these fashion events where he met Caleb and approached him about dressing him. More specifically, it was a disco themed party and everyone who was anyone in fashion was in attendance.

Caleb's agent had accepted the invitation on his behalf as he had been looking for another creative outlet for his star client. Caleb asked Collette to go with him to check it out. She happily accepted and spent most of the night on the dance floor towering above everyone in her wedge heels and vintage Diane von Furstenberg dress.

"Thanks for the offer, but I'm a Gucci guy," he said taking a swig from his Heineken, just delivered to him by a rail-thin cocktail waitress with full lips and an Afro wig. His eyes followed her as she walked away.

"Really?" Roberto replied looking him up and down at his baggy jeans, t-shirt and baseball cap slowly sipping his Cosmo.

"Only when I have to dress up, obviously," he said laughing at himself.

"Obviously. Well it was nice meeting you, Mr. Christopher." He said as Victor tugged at Roberto's arm trying to get him to pose for a picture.

"You too. And please, call me Caleb."

"Very well then, Caleb," he said.

"Um, actually, can I talk to you about something else before you go? Not right now, but later?"

"Of course. Anything. Just give me a minute." He snuggled up to Victor and posed with him smiling into the camera, his white silk suit competing with his white teeth. Victor looked up, admiring his prize lovingly, his arm wrapped tightly around his waist.

As the party wound down around 3 a.m., Collette was having a ball on the dance floor with Victor while Caleb wrapped up a conversation with Roberto in a corner booth.

Collette didn't realize how long they had been talking because Victor, in reliving Studio 54, kept her on the dance floor with every disco song that played. Eventually her feet could not hold up any longer, so she sat down for a break while Victor started shimmying with another girl on the floor. Across the room she saw Caleb and Roberto toast their drinks and shake hands.

"So it should be very simple, Roberto," Caleb reiterated.

"Exactly!"

"You'll make out handsomely creating my designs and I'll get another career. It's perfect."

"Wonderful, Caleb! I'm very excited!" he said as the waiter, who had managed to stay in close proximity to them all night, cleared away his four empty martini glasses along with Caleb's empty beer bottles.

"I'm glad, Roberto. My agent's been bugging me to do something like this for a while now, so I think it's fate that we met tonight. And you sure you can do women's wear?"

"Oh yes, Caleb. I can have Victor help me. The girls love his stuff. All the Hollywood people wear it."

"You sure he won't mind?" he asked cautiously.

"No he won't. He's been wanting me to work with him anyway so this will be perfect! He likes making money Caleb, so it will be good. Okay?"

"Okay, Roberto. Sounds good." he said gazing at Collette across the room chatting up some newly made friends at the bar. When she laughed, her whole body laughed. It looked like she was having a great time.

"You are very lucky, Caleb," he said noticing Caleb watching Collette. "She is so nice and pretty too. You should keep her. Victor likes her too."

"Yes, I know. She is great and I am very lucky," he said, snapping out of it. "Anyway, my agent's been pushing for me to do something like this and I said to him, 'Dude, I don't know the first thing about designing anything,' and he goes, 'Don't worry about it. You live in New York, there are designers everywhere, just go find a shmuck to do it for you.' Not that you're a shmuck or anything…"

"Oh, honey, I know. I can't believe it! I'm going to be designing for Caleb Christopher!" he said loudly.

"Shhhhh ... .remember, you can't tell anyone besides Victor, obviously. And more importantly since you'll be under contract with me you can't do any of those TV fashion shows or anything. At least until the contract expires. My agent insisted on that." he said, as if talking to a slow-witted child.

"Okay Caleb, I promise not to tell and will keep the contract," he reassured as the lights slowly started to come up.

"Excellent, Roberto. I am glad we understand each other."

Julien had gone through a pack of cigarettes and a bottle of gin while he waited for Victor and Roberto to emerge from the party, intending to woo Victor back. He was also going to tell him that he knew about Roberto's secret deal with Caleb; he'd paid his spy to generally hang around them all night, looking for any information. As Roberto and Victor left the party, Julien startled them both when he blocked their path and threw his arms around Victor. Victor pushed him off as Roberto grabbed his hand.

"Jesus, Julien you're drunk. Get a hold of yourself. I told you it was over, he said pushing him away.

"But honey come on. Don't say that. You don't mean that." he pleaded, standing in front of them.

"Julien! It's been nearly a year now. Victor is mine now. Why don't you get out of here and go fix yourself up or something."

"*Veector* is mine now!" he mocked him. "Don't tell me it's over, Victor. Please honey. I miss you." His eyes begged for reciprocity.

"Julien, don't do this. We had our fun. Now you take care. We have to go."

"Yes, we have to go. Sorry you feel this way," Roberto chimed in.

"You're not fucking sorry, you goddamn asshole! We were fine before you came along." He lashed out to strike Roberto's face but lost his balance mid-swing, his fist smashing against the brick building. He fell to the ground holding his bloody hand. The paparazzi captured the entire scene, Julien's eyes like a deer in headlights while Victor and Roberto looked on in horror.

***

"Tell me what's going on with Roberto," Collette said over the phone to Caleb. She had just woken up from a much-needed nap following her liquid lunch with Lou. For as much as she did not want to talk to him, she did work for him and had to deal with his self-inflected drama.

"Some guy named Julien left me a cryptic message saying Roberto is going to go on that fashion show *Real Runway* ...."

"So," she interrupted.

"I'm explaining Collette."

"Sorry, go on."

"Anyway, this guy calls me yesterday and tells me this and I'm thinking, 'Yeah whatever', then he starts on about how he knows Roberto is designing my line and I am a fake and he's going to tell the press and destroy both of our careers. I was like, 'What the fuck, and who the hell is this guy?'.

"Are you serious?"

"You think I'd make this shit up? I don't know what I'm gonna do, C."

"I don't know what you're gonna do either. I told you you should not have made that deal with him."

"Jesus, Collette I know okay? You were right for chrissakes. Now help me here, I don't fucking know what to do. Can't you call Lou's mom or something?"

"Calm down, Caleb. This seems like another one of your choices that you later regret. I mean, really! Why the hell did you need to have a line anyway? Your acting career was fine."

"Christ, I don't know. Everybody else had something else going on and I was trying to keep up, I guess. It was Sean's stupid idea and he even found Roberto. That's why he made sure I went to that stupid party and told me to ask him there. He said he was talented and could pull it off. He said doing a fashion line would be a good idea because it would keep me in the press. I don't even know why I went along with it."

"I don't know what the hell you were thinking, Caleb. That agent of yours will tell you to do anything because you're his little cash cow. You have certainly financed his place in Beverly Hills and all those cars in the garage."

"Shit, C. What am I gonna do? I don't know shit about designing any fucking thing and if this guy does talk to anyone I'm beyond screwed."

"Did you talk to Julie? Maybe she can help you." It was doubtful that his publicist had the contacts he needed in the fashion world to find out who this Julien character was. She was fresh out of college with two years of work experience: one as an assistant to a publicist at a small agency in her hometown somewhere in Oregon, and the other as the bartender at Hooters in Las Vegas. It was at this Hooters where Caleb met her and after she over served him by about five drinks, and listened to her pitch herself, he hired her on the spot. He thought she would be more "qualified" than Katherine, his 60-year-old publicist who had guided him through the early years of his fame. Apparently, Julie represented newer, fresher ideas.

"Christ, C, Julie can't help me. She doesn't fucking know anybody!"

"I think I mentioned that that wasn't such a good idea either, Caleb."

"I know Collette! Fucking A!"

"Look, I'm just saying you have to start thinking for yourself. I've done more for you in the past three months than she has during her entire time with you. Just get rid of her already and call Katherine."

"Yeah, I guess so. So can you call Lou for me?"

"Let me see what I can do. I'll call you later."

"Thanks. And C?"

"Yes?"

"I mean that. Thanks for everything. I don't know what I would do without you."

"I'll call you later."

<u>13</u>

"AMBER SKYE, CALEB CHRISTOPHER'S MAIN SQUEEZE! THEY'RE IN A NEW YORK STATE OF MIND! ONLY PEOPLE HAS THE EXCLUSIVE!" On the cover of *People* magazine was a photo of Amber running one hand through her hair and the other cinched tightly around Caleb's waist. He, on the other hand, was using his free hand to shield his face, as Amber's eyes made love to the lens. Collette's heart sank as she caught up on Caleb's latest jaunts about town on the pages inside. There was a day of them shopping in Williamsburg, every inch of her leg peering out from underneath her über-short skirt; another photo of them in line at the Roosevelt Island Tramway (on their way to visit one of his college friends the byline said); another one of him looking annoyed; and yet another of her draping herself all over him. Lastly, there was a shot of them leaving St. Nick's Jazz Pub in Harlem, her hair shining under the streetlights, his looking a bit disheveled. As Collette poured over the photos, she tried to count her blessings for Spencer. He'd only been gone three days and had already

sent her flowers and called her every day. After a few more crying fests, and after Lou's convincing argument that he wasn't worth all the fuss, she thought that Caleb could date a circus freak if he wanted.

Two days later in the car with Caleb on their way to his fashion shoot, her cheeks warmed as she read Caleb the card that accompanied Spencer's flowers, watching his face redden at every saccharine word. Her glow quickly faded as they waited at a red light to pull into the studio lot at Chelsea Piers where she spotted Amber outside smoking and talking to a young, gawky boy weighed down with walkie-talkies, duct tape, and other paraphernalia that hung from his tool belt.

"I *said* I'll be in in a minute. Can't I have a goddamn moment to myself?" Amber shouted.

"I'm sorry Amber, but we're already behind schedule and they asked me to come get …" the production assistant tried to explain.

"Are you deaf? Did you *not* just hear me tell you I'll be in a second?" she said, gesturing with her cigarette, silencing him.

"But, but, they said—"

"I don't care what *they* said, I'm telling you what *I* said. I'm *Amber Skye,* Caleb's *girlfriend,* in case you don't know, you moron, and when I am *finished* smoking, I will be in," she said, turning her back on the stunned assistant who gave up and went back inside. Her eyes looked as if they were rolling back into her head when Caleb and Collette's car pulled up.

"Hey, baby," she greeted him. She peppered him with kisses and jumped all over him as he got out of the car. Her joy was short-lived when she saw Collette exit the car.

"Hi, Amber," Collette said extending her truce-yielding hand.

"Amber, this is Collette, my assistant," he said, eyeing her strangely.

"You're, you're the girl from the casting! Caleb what's this all about?" She crushed her cigarette under her foot, suddenly not so happy.

"Look, Amber, I'm sorry about all that. I was having a bad day."

"Babe, she was such a bitch to me and she's your assistant?"

"Amber, baby, Collette is the nicest person in the world, you must have misunderstood something."

"I misunderstood something? You should have seen her! I can't believe you're taking her side, Caleb."

"I'm not taking anyone's side here, I wasn't even there, for chrissakes. Just calm down. Whatever happened there is over, you're here aren't you? So relax already." Agitated, he apologized to Collette and she followed him inside. Amber lit up another cigarette glaring at Collette as she resumed talking to Caleb about his obligations for the rest of the day. Collette watched with some satisfaction as Amber puffed away her temper tantrum.

The shoot went largely without incident and Collette managed to stay as far away from Amber as humanly possible in the large studio space. Collette kept Caleb busy returning phone calls he was overdue in making; some of which were to *In Style* about his latest collection, to his agent to discuss the Trey Xu project, to his business manager to discuss the latest investments made on his behalf, and to his mom to say hello. Collette then got him to fulfill her numerous autographed headshot requests for various charity auctions, fans, etc. Sitting in a small office in the studio, they overheard the photographer praise Amber on her moves as she posed with delight, thrusting her hips to-and-fro in synch with the rock songs she requested they play.

"So, I think I want to take a vacation," Collette said after he signed the last photo.

"Um, okay. When and where?"

"Rome in a few weeks," she said casting her eyes downward.

"Rome, huh? Who are you going with?" he said, leaning in towards her from his chair.

"Spencer," she said, not returning eye contact.

"Wow, that's romantic. Guess I have to give him credit for that," he said, leaning even closer to her, as she inhaled his scent.

"Yeah, I guess you do." Collette said softly as he took her hand in his while she made eye contact with him.

"C, let's have dinner tonight and talk."

"I don't know, Caleb..."

"Come on. We need to talk." He squeezed her hand and wiped the tear from her cheek that materialized. "Don't cry, sweetie."

"I'm sorry. I just—"

"Shhhh," he said pressing his finger to her lips. "Can I pick you up tonight at eight? We'll go wherever you want to go."

"You don't have plans tonight with Amber?"

"Believe me, this is much more important." They looked over to see Amber wildly flailing about.

"Okay, Caleb. Okay." She acquiesced as he squeezed her hand.

"Why don't you take off and I'll see you in a few hours."

"Okay, I guess you made those phone calls so you're good for now," she said as she stood and gathered her things. He gave her an extended hug good-bye and softly kissed her cheeks gradually making his way to her lips.

"Till eight."

"Till eight."

Waiting for 8 o'clock to roll around felt like an eternity to Collette. It was only three o'clock and she wondered what she was going to do for the next five hours until her dinner with Caleb. She was a bundle of nerves and had absolutely no clue what she was going to do about anything. Although she cared deeply for Caleb, she liked Spencer and thought meeting him in Rome might be a good idea since Amber was showing no signs of leaving. Collette needed a break from the whole thing. She also didn't know if she was going to call Lou's mom or not. Pauline was so busy and she didn't really want to bother her with some drama Caleb brought on himself. Besides, she thought it was time Caleb started making better choices and grew up a bit. She switched off her phone and decided that the first thing she would do was to bypass the subway and take a walk to clear her head. The city was bustling with crowds and noise as always, but Collette felt as alone as ever. Her sort-of boyfriend was out of the country, her parents in Chicago—though she honestly didn't feel like filling them in on this—and her best friend was on a plane to Miami to meet up with her boyfriend for a few days of fun. On her own, she would have to sort this mess out. She took her time and walked in a daze up Eighth Avenue, unsure of how far she would go. Never having walked from Chelsea to the Upper West Side before, she decided to go with it until she felt tired. Walking in a funk up the busy street, she nearly collided with a gaggle of young teenage girls getting off a bus laughing and talking to each other. She envied their innocence as they brushed past not noticing her, and yearned for her life to once again be as simple as theirs.

Collette continued on and as she neared 34th Street her fog had not lifted. Being almost run over by a policeman on horseback snapped her back to reality. Feeling like she should probably take a break before she got herself killed, she entered a tiny greasy spoon on the corner where she sat at the counter and was pleasantly greeted by a middle-aged waitress named Flo.

"What'll you have?" Flo asked as Collette settled in at the counter. Collette could tell by the deep wrinkles in her face that she was at least 50, but was trying to look 40 with the massive amount of makeup she wore. The heavy eyeliner, clumpy mascara, and pink lipstick did not do well to turn back the clock.

"Oh, just a cup of coffee. Thanks." She smiled at her.

"You got it," she said, turning over the mug and fetching the pot of burnt coffee that she had to yank to lift off the burner. Collette saw this (and smelled it too), but didn't have the energy to protest or complain. Instead she added an extra pack of sugar to it and stirred, watching the crystals dissolve into the black abyss.

"Looks to me like you need more than coffee, if you don't mind me sayin'," Flo offered. The diner was a throwback to the 50s and Collette was the only customer despite the massive crowds outside. Maybe everyone else knew to go to Starbucks across the street for a good cup of joe.

"'Excuse me?"

"I'm sorry, honey, but you're looking like someone stole your puppy. I don't think coffee is going to fix what's ailin' you." Her warm, motherly manner moistened Collette's already sad eyes.

"Is it that obvious?" she replied, as a teardrop landed in her cup.

"What's his name?" Flo said, making Collette laugh as she offered her a Kleenex.

"How'd you guess?" she asked, accepting the tissue from her new friend.

"How'd I guess? You kiddin' me? I saw you across the street over there about to get run over by that horse, and that cop didn't even pay you no mind. You were walking like you were all spaced out and didn't see it comin'. How could you not see that big ole' horse comin' at you like that? I saw that and knew something was wrong. You surely gave me a fright watching you."

"Yeah, I guess I was kinda spaced out."

"You had that love-sick look on your face, kinda like now."

"Oh...I uh ... "

"I don't mean to be buttin' into your business, but you seem to be hurtin' pretty good."

"Seems like you know me pretty well, huh, Flo?" she asked, looking at her nametag.

"Flo. Flo Jackson," she said extending her hand.

"Hi, Flo. I'm Collette," she replied shaking the woman's calloused hand.

"Such a pretty name for a pretty girl. Now who has got you all up in arms like this? He don't deserve you, honey, if he made you feel like this."

Although Collette did not know this stranger, she was comforted by her and was glad for the chance to talk to someone who knew nothing about the situation.

"It's a long story, Flo."

"You got somewhere to be? I don't. Besides, you're my only customer right now." She warmly smiled at her. "Here," she said, fishing out a silver flask from under the counter. "I keep this here for special occasions. Sometimes folks need a little something extra," she said, as she poured the two of them a drink. Collette swallowed the indistinguishable dark liquid and started talking.

14

"Look, I told you we'll be there," Amber aggressively said into the phone from her dressing room at the shoot, as she packed up her things. Caleb had left shortly after Collette, about two hours ago, claiming he had to get home to make some phone calls. She thought it was just a lame excuse. Amber didn't entirely believe him because she'd seen him on the phone earlier but said okay and that she was looking forward to going out later for drinks, suggesting going to Tribeca as the location. He responded by saying he couldn't hang out tonight, but he'd call her later. She knew she could get him to change his mind. All she had to do was walk around in her teeniest thong when she got home and he'd be putty in her hands.

"Are you sure, because we are short a few guys today," snapped the gruff male voice on the other end of the phone.

"What do you mean you're short tonight? You have paparazzi all over the city," she said. She was talking to Bruce, the head of Celebs One, the city's leading paparazzi agency.

"Yeah, usually we do, but I got my two best guys on some other stuff and I don't wanna take em off someone else if you guys are not gonna show. I mean, they're trying to keep up with Joan Rider and all those damn kids. They're in the city for something or other—" he said referring to the star of cable television's latest reality show documenting her raising her flock of kids.

"What the fuck, Bruce? You're comparing me to *Joan Rider*? She's a fucking nobody," she said, raising her voice.

"Yeah, you tell that to my guys who can sell her photos for enough fucking money to pay for their kid's private school in the city. Now, look, I'ma ask you again, Amber. You sure he's gonna be there?"

"Of course, Bruce. Come on. He's been everywhere else I told you," she said gently into the phone. Calming herself down, she ran her fingers through her hair in the vanity mirror.

"Yeah, but never at the time you say. You've been keeping my guys around too long and they've been losing money, Amber. When you tell me one o'clock I expect him at one o'clock. So when you tell me tonight at eight o'clock, I expect him then, not at 11."

"Bruce, you can trust me. I will be at the bar at the Tribeca Grand with Caleb at eight o'clock tonight. He'll go wherever I wanna go," she replied reassuringly.

"Alright, if you say so."

"Just make sure you leave my money in the usual place. I hate going to Port Authority, but those lockers are the easiest place to get my shit. This time, I'd like my five grand in smaller bills. You know, tens and twenties. It looks suspicious if I am carrying around anything larger. I don't know what you guys were thinking last time giving me all those c-notes."

"Damn, girl, you are cold!"

"Yeah, whatever," she said, examining her fresh manicure.

"I'll put my best guys on it. Say, what should the spin be this time?"

"How about, 'Caleb's girlfriend, Amber Skye, top model, named the face of his clothing line. They celebrate with a night out. Could a proposal be next?' Yes, that would be cool!" she said excitedly, unaware that she had raised her voice again.

"Say, do you really like this guy, or are you just playing him?"

"I like him enough. I mean, I can get a lot out of him and get a modeling career. Who wouldn't want that? Besides, I'm sure I'm not the first person who hooks shit up for you like this," she said, closing the door to her dressing room. She had not noticed that it had been wide open before, but doubted anyone could hear her because all the crew were still upstairs on set cleaning up.

"Naw, I'm not saying you are, but damn girl. By the way, that picture my guy got of you in that short-ass skirt ... .I swear if I didn't already have a piece at home I would be comin' after your ass myself. All the time that is. Your shit looks good. I'm getting excited just thinking about it. Damn."

"And you remember that. You have your guys there and there could be something sweet in it for you," she purred seductively, reapplying her lip gloss.

"I hope it's as good as the last time. I don't care if it was in that skank-ass hotel in Hell's Kitchen. That was hot, for real though."

"It'll be better than the last time. I'm completely bare now, if you know what I mean. Just like you said you liked it," she teased.

"Shit, keep talking like that and I'll have to come find your hot ass right now."

"You just get your guys there tonight for our drinks and I'll come find you for dessert," she said, as she abruptly hung up on him, rolling her eyes as she slammed the phone shut.

Jesse, the production assistant, could not believe his ears as he listened to Amber's every salacious word through the thin dressing room door. He had snuck away moments before she entered her room. He sat in the empty dressing room that connected to hers for a quick break to nurse the headache that her demanding behavior had given him over the course of the past few hours. He hadn't meant to spy on her conversation and thought he would just listen for a minute before making his presence known. But he was so pulled in he sat in an oversized chair, listening with his mouth agape as she left saying to herself, "Men, they're so fucking easy."

The crew always said you could hear a pin drop on the other side of that door and that day, Jesse had certainly heard much more than a pin.

<u>15</u>

Julien felt both silly and immature in the light of day for leaving Caleb that message about exposing him as a fraud. He knew he should not have had that fourth gin martini but couldn't stop himself. Of course Caleb's number was unlisted, but he was able to get his publicist's info and told her that he was calling from the wardrobe department of his last movie and needed to speak with him directly. He was surprised that she was so clueless and actually gave it to him.

Since being dismissed so unceremoniously from Victor's house, his life had taken a turn for the worse. He gained 15 pounds thanks to a diet of Chinese take-out, Tanqueray, and Ben & Jerry's. It also didn't help that the only place he was able to afford was a small studio in Battery Park. He'd begrudgingly found work as a concierge at the new W hotel in Hoboken—which he was lucky to still have after the unflattering photo of him in the *Post* ambushing Roberto and Victor after the Who's Who of Fashion party. It just didn't seem fair that after all those years of being with Victor and helping him with his business, that he'd dump him once

Roberto showed up. He should have seen it coming by the way Victor eyed him like a cheeseburger on that bus in Belize. He'd find a way to get back at them, he thought to himself as he listened to opera music on his iPod. He stomached a cold egg and cheese sandwich on the Path train on his way to work, and decided his vengeance would have nothing to do with Caleb.

<u>16</u>

Dear Collette,

Missing you tons here in England and am looking forward to seeing you soon and introducing you to my mum and sister.

Lots of love,

Spencer

Collette read the postcard that greeted her when she finally made it home. She'd helped Flo finish off that flask and told her everything about the mess of her life. Flo listened and gave her Kleenex when she cried and reminded her that her life was too short to be entangled in such a mess. Collette owed it to herself to do what she needed to be happy. After three hours of Flo therapy she got herself together and hopped in a cab to get ready for her big night with Caleb. She was more sure of what she wanted to do than ever.

"Hey there! How's your trip?" she asked to Lou on the phone. Her friend had made it to Miami and called to check in.

"Going good so far. I think we'll have a good time this weekend. We may even go to the Bahamas if we have time," Lou said, lounging poolside at a swank hotel while her boyfriend Pedro fetched their drinks.

"Oh, that would be nice. I'm so jealous!" she said as she lit a few candles.

"Tell me what's up with you? What's going on with the men in your life?"

"Well, I'm seeing Caleb tonight for dinner," she said.

"Good start ..." Lou said.

"But I got a postcard from Spencer today. I might just go see him to see what happens. I mean, Amber is still being, well *Amber*, and I don't want to get hurt if he's not gonna break up with her," she said, plopping down on her unmade bed.

"Just go to dinner tonight and then decide. Rome isn't for like a month or something anyway, right?" she said, accepting both a kiss on the cheek and a margarita from her South American beau.

"Yes, I guess I have a little bit of time. I feel like I want to be with Caleb, but he seriously has to grow up first."

"Well just tell him that, C. I mean, you tell him everything else."

"I know, but this is different."

"It is, but it isn't. He trusts you so much Collette and I wouldn't be surprised if he loved you too. Just tell him exactly how you feel and stop worrying about Amber. She's got nothing to do with anything and is just a stupid fucking groupie. I'd bet he'd send her ass packing if you told him to."

"Maybe you're right," she said laughing in spite of herself as she got up and put Spencer's postcard in a drawer atop a pamphlet from the University of Colorado Writing Program she requested a few months ago.

"Okay, I gotta run. Call me later and tell me what happens."

"I will have fun."

"Love you lots, C."

"Love you too."

Collette hung up the phone and dove into her mess of a closet to find something to wear for dinner. While changing in and out of various outfits, she realized she forgot to ask Lou a question. A text would have to do.

> Forgot to ask. Pls call me 2mrw abt ur mom. Need to ask her something about Caleb. xoxoxo

<u>17</u>

Caleb got out of the shower and stood in the living room brushing his teeth while watching the stats on *ESPN*, thinking to himself how pleased that he would finally have a chance to really talk to Collette. He was ready to disclose his feelings for her and try to move forward. The most exciting information he wanted to share with her was that he planned to officially end things with Amber tomorrow and get her out of his house. If she was the major obstacle with Collette, then it was a no-brainer. Thinking about it, he didn't know why he'd been such a jerk to her in Chicago, and he did not want to lose her to Spencer, especially since he felt she wasn't really into him anyway. It was 7:15, and he only had 15 minutes to get ready before going to get her uptown. He'd made a dinner reservation at Le Monde, a French bistro on Broadway and 112th, and planned for a night of music afterwards at the hole-in-the-wall Smoke Jazz Club around the corner.

He was disappointed to see that Amber did not have plans of her own when she used her keys and walked in the door. In any case, he was just glad that she would be out of his house tomorrow, and that he would have fun tonight with Collette. Collette was right. He did need to take control and grow a pair, and that was just what he planned to do. The way Amber talked to Collette at the shoot was unacceptable and he was embarrassed by the grumblings he overheard of her diva-ish behavior. Caleb also suspected Patrick gave her the job at the casting, but Amber was so excited and he was so distracted from missing Collette in her cab that he hadn't questioned it.

He started to make things right when he left the shoot shortly after Collette and called his business manager right away to see to it that Julie received a good severance package when he fired her tomorrow, and called Katherine to beg for her to come back, which she happily agreed to. She had every right to say she told him so, but didn't, which made Caleb appreciate her all the more. He explained that her first job was to find out about Julien. Her second job was to call the photographer from the shoot and ask for a reshoot. He would even pay for it himself. He did not want

Amber representing his brand. In fact, he didn't want any connection with her at all.

"Hey, babe," Amber said as she slinked toward him dropping her things at the door.

"Hey," he mumbled, not looking at her with toothpaste secreting from his mouth, focused on the witty sports ads.

"Mmmmm you smell good," she purred in his ear. Her hand rested on the front of his towel, which he promptly moved and walked into the bathroom. "What's wrong? Should I join you in there?" she asked, following him into the bathroom as he began rinsing his teeth. He ignored her as she tugged on his towel and swatted her hand away while his head was under the running water. "Babe? Come on?" She tried again. He was taking longer than usual to rinse his mouth so she tried another tactic. "Cay-leb," she sang, as he lifted his head up and wiped his mouth on a hand towel.

"What're you doing?" he asked. She pulled her dress over her head and removed her bra. She was still in her heels and her thong when she eyed him hungrily.

"I'm wantin' you. That's what I'm doin'," she said, attempting to press herself against him.

"Come on now, stop it. I have to get going." he moved past her, leaving the bathroom.

"What? Where are you going?" she asked, running after him. She tugged off his towel and revealed his flaccid self.

"I said no, Amber. Christ." He retrieved his towel and quickly entered his bedroom and closed the door behind him.

"Come, on baby. I thought we could celebrate tonight. The shoot went really well. Hmmmm," she coyly said. She let herself into the room and sprawled out on the bed in front of him, as she rolled around and exposed the backside (or lack of) of her underwear. "I mean, we can start celebrating right now," she said, as she turned and wrapped her legs around his naked hips.

"I said no. Now move."

"What the fuck Caleb? I wanna go out tonight! Come on baby, I want to celebrate the shoot and go have some fun," she begged of him. She tried to wrap her legs around him again, which he swatted away.

"Stop it, Amber!"

"I know you don't mean that, Caleb. Just relax, I'll make you feel good," she said, quickly sliding back on the bed and taking him in to her mouth. She was pleased at her performance when she felt he was starting to enjoy it. Suddenly he shoved her head back violently against the bed, and it nearly missed the footboard.

"Goddamit, Amber! What the fuck about *no* do you not understand?" She had never heard him yell before and was taken aback. He'd always liked it when she went down on him and didn't understand what his problem was.

"It's that bitch Collette, isn't it? You're fucking her aren't you? Fuck! I shoulda known it!"

"I want you out of my house," he said, picking up her things and tossing them out of his bedroom.

"What? What are you talking about? Come on, I was just kidding!" she said. She scrambled to pick up her things as he tossed them.

"I'm not kidding, Amber. I want you out. I've had enough of your shit."

"*My* shit? *What* shit? What the fuck are you talking about Caleb? I mean, where the fuck am I supposed to go?"

"You should have thought about that before you hopped that bus here and stole all that money in your bag. I don't know where you got it, and frankly I don't care. I just want you out."

"Bus? How did you—"

"You still had the stupid bus ticket. Real fucking smart, Amber. I can see why you still live at home."

"Caleb, you don't mean that. Come on! I've done nothing but be here for you and love you and clean and cook for you since I've been here. You know I'd do anything for you!" she said, feeling tears streak her cheeks as she stood there with a pile of clothes in her hands.

"You cook? Yeah right, and I've been tripping over your mess since you got here. So you can stop your fucking crying because I don't give a shit. Call up some of your new 'friends.' Just get out of my house."

"But ... but ... I don't get it. What did I do?" her voice quivered.

"Hmm, let's see. For starters, you treated my assistant like shit, which is a big no-no. Then I overheard practically everybody complain about your behavior on the shoot. Oh and of course Jesse, the poor production assistant, took the brunt of your bullshit today. Then let's not forget how you just dropped in on me here like a fucking crazy person."

"What? I didn't—"

"Oh, but you did. See, Jesse thought enough of me to tell me about your little conversation with Bruce, whoever the fuck that is. You remember him right? He's your little paparazzi connection. I was starting to wonder how those guys knew my every move."

"Wha—"

"Jesse overheard your entire conversation Amber," he said, watching her cry. "Oh what? You don't have anything to say? Well apparently you had a lot to say to him. So why don't you just go fuck him, again apparently, and go pick up your fucking whore money at Port Authority. Isn't that where he usually leaves it for you? Right after you tell him every place we're gonna be so you can get your stupid fucking picture with me in those shitty rags? Huh? Why don't you just go ahead and call him. See if I care."

"But, but, I didn't mean—"

"I'm sure you didn't. You just can't stop yourself from being a fucking whore can you? That's worse if you 'didn't mean it.'"

"I'm so sorry, baby. I never meant for…" she said, moving closer to him.

"I'll bet you are sorry. Now if you'll excuse me, I have to get ready."

"Where are you going?" she asked. She tried to touch his face, but he pushed her away.

"None of your goddamed business. Now if I have to tell you again I'm going to call the cops. Now. Get. The. Fuck. Out. Of. My. House," he said, walking away from her as she sobbed. "Here." He threw her duffel bag at her. He then threw all of her toiletries into a plastic garbage bag and tossed that too. "Don't forget this shit. Now get out." She grabbed her things and wailed loudly as she got dressed before quietly closing the door behind her.

<u>18</u>

Collette wondered what was keeping Caleb. It was nearly 8:30 and he hadn't called to say he was running late. She couldn't fathom what the hold-up could be. Spencer had called her as she was getting ready to see that she got his postcard, which resulted in her promise to call him back later. She said she was running late to the movies. He said he was shooting crazy hours and she could call him any time and that he'd keep his phone on. She liked him, but didn't see the use in him calling to confirm that he got his postcard, for crying out loud.

It was 8:40 and still no Caleb. She was about to turn on the TV when she heard someone bounding up the stairs. A few moments later there was frantic knocking on her door. Caleb looked out of breath through the peephole and was yelling her name. "Collette, open up! It's me!" he kept saying.

"I did it. I kicked her out, it's over," he said grabbing her by the hand as she opened the door.

"What? Are you ok? Your face is so red. Do you want some water? How'd you get in the building?"

"I ran in when someone was coming out. Collette, honey, I'm so sorry. Will you please forgive me? I've been a complete ass. Please forgive me," he begged as he squeezed her hand.

"Well, I can forgive you for being late, I suppose. I was starting to think you'd forgotten," she said, allowing herself a smile.

"I'm so sorry about that. I had to take out the trash. Honey, please forgive me. For everything." His eyes begged as she smiled brightly.

"One other thing," he said dropping to one knee.

"Caleb, what are you doing?"

"Collette, will you marry me?"

"What!"

"Please say you'll marry me. I love you more than anyone else in the world and want to spend the rest of my life with you. I don't have a ring but we can go get whatever you want. I just want to be with you forever. Please say yes."

***

The first thing Amber did when she left Caleb's apartment was head straight to Port Authority. As in the past, Bruce would have the money dropped off for her about an hour before the job so she rushed as quickly as she could to retrieve it. She pulled herself together in the cab and yelled at the driver when he asked her where to.

"Just drive, asshole!" she commanded. At the next block he threatened to throw her out of the cab if she didn't give him any direction. Her makeup had lost its appeal and her clothes were in disarray. Her worn duffel bag was bursting at the seams, due to all the extra clothes she had purchased over the last few weeks. With clothes, shoes, and purses falling everywhere, her first stop was to a vendor where she bought a piece of cheap luggage to contain her mess. Then sprinting through the station to get to the locker, she tripped and fell, her short skirt bunching up above her waist as she slid across the cold floor. A crowd of people stared at the spectacle. Then her heel broke under her. She sobbed while she pulled herself together and harshly condemned anyone who tried to help her. She hobbled to the lockers where her uncontrollable crying caught the attention of a police officer. Her hair was all over the place and her smeared mascara gave her raccoon eyes. She looked as if she were fleeing an abuser or was a hooker. The officer watched as she searched the empty locker in vain before he approached her.

"Miss? You okay?" the short officer asked, looking up to her. His sparse ashy brown hair molded itself to his forehead. His nametag that read Officer Starkey, also bore drops of this sweat.

"What? Oh yeah, I'm fine," she said. She attempted to smile and furiously wipe away her tears.

"You don't look so good. What were you looking for in there?" the officer said, his stubby finger pointing to the empty locker.

"What? Oh nothing. I was just leaving," she said, hobbling away.

"I'm going to need to ask you a few questions if you don't mind," he said, stepping in front of her. "Now, what were you looking for in there? You seem awfully distressed and if I search your bag and find anything suspicious I'm going to have to take you in."

"Take me in? What!"

"Miss, please step aside," Officer Starkey said. Amber noticed Bruce approaching with her loot. When they made eye contact, she slowly shook her head from side to side. The officer sensed she was communicating with someone and turned to look over his shoulder to see Bruce quickly walking away. The officer radioed into his mouthpiece Bruce's description for a fellow officer to apprehend him. Noticing another officer chasing him, Bruce broke out into a run, while the stocky officer stayed with Amber as she wailed.

"Freeze! Drop the bag, now!" the other officer demanded. Officer Randal, the young rookie, nervously drew his weapon and Bruce did as instructed.

"Who's that?" Officer Starkey demanded. "Is he your pimp?"

"I ... I don't know who that is, officer," she lied.

"You're lying to me," he said as he searched her bags finding upwards of $15,000 in cash. "What's this from? You owe it to him?"

"No...I..."

"You're coming with me." he said, as he dragged her off.

<u>19</u>

"What the hell, Amber? I'm going to kick your ass, I swear." Bruce said. They were both being dragged to the bowels of the Port Authority police station.

"I didn't ... "

"Fucking bitch. I should have known better," he spat at her.

"Enough you two. Now get in there," Officer Starkey said as he pushed them both inside two separate filthy holding areas. Amber was thrown in with women who looked like prostitutes who probably thought she was one too. Bruce was in a room with pimps, drug dealers, and petty thieves. After being held for three hours in deplorable conditions, they were brought in for questioning by the officers. They had rifled through her bags and they had not allowed her to change her shoes. The chair was cold against her bare skin beneath her short skirt.

After a round of vigorous questioning, the officers were satisfied after they called Bruce's agency and confirmed that yes, he was the head of a paparazzi agency. He disclosed the true nature of their relationship—that Amber was a paparazzi photographer for him and he was bringing her a payment for a job she'd done. She preferred being paid in cash because she often had to pay people off for access to celebrities and it was just easier this way. Amber continued saying she was upset because she'd just found out her boyfriend, Caleb Christopher, yes that Caleb Christopher, had shoved her when she tried to break up with him after finding out that he was cheating. All she wanted to do was go out to dinner in Tribeca tonight but he yelled at her and kept saying no. (At this bit of detail Bruce dropped his head in his hand.) He threw her things at her and shoved her down the stairs, which was how her shoe got broken, and told her to get out. He wouldn't let her get her camera, which she found odd because he often told her where to find her subjects and took half her money. She told Bruce to meet her there because she was so upset she was going to hop on a bus to go stay with her sister in Jersey.

She explained that she was so upset and didn't mean to cause any trouble. She just got scared when the officer approached her. Her apologizing went on forever. Bruce looked at her in amazement as she so naturally told this tale. The cops couldn't get past the fact that she was Caleb's girlfriend.

"You're telling me you're Caleb Christopher's girlfriend, and he shoved you and kept your camera and kicked you out of his house?" Officer Starkey asked.

"Yes, officer I am. Or at least I was," she sniffed.

"But that doesn't explain why you lied to us back there. You said you didn't know this guy."

"I was so upset and I didn't want to get him in trouble for no reason. I'm just a girl from Nebraska who left college to come out here to model. I started dating Caleb and nothing like this has ever happened to me before and I just panicked. I'm so sorry. I know it looked bad, but I just didn't want to get Bruce in trouble. It's not like anyone respects the paparazzi and I didn't want him in trouble because of me," she said, starting to cry again.

"Don't cry now. We're just trying to understand," Officer Randal said. He handed her a tissue. "And you're telling me that she works for you as a photographer?" he addressed Bruce.

"Yes sir she does. Modeling was going slow, so I hired her to make some extra money. I didn't mean to lose my temper back there, but sometimes I get overheated."

"Well you better watch that," the rookie said, looking dead into his eyes. Amber cried softly.

"I will, sir."

"Now Amber, you look like a model to me. You should be doing that, not hanging out with *this* guy. Nobody likes the paparazzi and I think you'd do good as a model. You're sure pretty enough," he said, as Officer Starkey nodded in agreement.

"You think so? Well thanks, that means a lot," she said, with a twinkle in her eye. "You mind?" she asked. She stood and reached for her bag across the table in front of her.

"No not at all."

Amber pulled out her pocket mirror and cleaned her face and applied her lip gloss. She held the men's attention.

"Actually, I am going to be in Caleb's new ad," she said. She snapped shut the compact as she sat and moved her hands slowly down her legs before removing her shoes.

"You don't say?" the officer said. By now they had relaxed their intimidating stature and simply watched her.

"Umm hmm. We shot it this morning and it's going to be hot," she said. She leaned over and arched her back with her legs slightly apart while retrieving a pair of shoes in her bag.

"Well, we don't want to keep you guys so you can go. Damn actors. Think they're so much better than everybody else. You want a ride back home, Amber? I think I need to have a talk with that Caleb Christopher," Officer Starkey said, as sweat poured down the sides of his head.

"Umm, that's okay. I'll be fine. I'll have Bruce drop me off."

"We have to follow up on all domestic issues, even with asshole celebrities. There's no time like the present."

"Well, okay. If you say so," she said. The officers handed over her bag along with Bruce's bag of money.

"Thanks Bruce and sorry about all this. I'll be heading to my sister's later so I'll call you when I get back," she said as she kissed him on the cheek. He smiled to the officers as he felt his insides boil in anger.

***

"Caleb, do you know what you're asking me?" Collette said, still stunned by his proposal.

"Yes, honey I do. I don't know what my problem has been. It's so obvious, Collette. You've been there all along right in front of me. My parents love the hell out of you, they ask about *you* every time I talk to them, and I love you. I don't want to be anywhere else but by your side," he said, still on his knee.

"We've never even dated though, Caleb. I mean, we've only, ya know, like once that night in Chicago," she cautiously stated. "I know I see you all the time now, but if we did this I would *really* see you all the time."

"I can't think of anyone else I'd rather be with all the time, C. I have made such dumb-ass mistakes and you have been the only thing I got right. I have known for a while now that I love you but have just been too chickenshit to do anything about it,"

"I—" she interrupted.

"Let me finish, honey. I know you're dating Spencer but can you honestly tell me that you love him? Honestly? Or were you planning to go to Rome because you want to go to Rome. Hell, Collette, I'll take you to Rome. We can go right now, except I'd have to ask you to get the plane because I don't know how you do that," he said smiling, shifting the weight on his knee.

"Oh, get up. You don't have to stay down there," she said, helping him up to her couch.

"Collette, I understand your reservations, but if you give me the chance I promise to make you the happiest woman in the world. I don't care if we've never officially 'dated' or whatever. I have known you for so long and love everything about you. From your beautiful hair, to your long legs, to your big heart, to the way you blush when you don't think you are, to, I don't know, everything about you, Collette! I know I haven't always acted like it, but you have made me a better person and I want to show you that I can be even better. I don't care about anything else. I only 100% want to be with you. Now and forever." Caleb kissed the tear that rolled down her cheek. "Please say yes. I love you so much."

"Oh my goodness, okay!" she said.

"Yes?!"

"Yes, Caleb yes. I love you too," she said, kissing and hugging him tightly. Everything was perfect.

<u>20</u>

Officer Starkey drove slowly and methodically through the busy streets while Amber sat in the backseat and changed her clothes. He tried in vain to keep his eyes on the road but found it difficult due to the manner by which she switched outfits. She did not try to conceal herself as she carefully unbuttoned her shirt, looking down seductively and tossing her hair back. She left her blouse open and didn't bother to scoot down as she retrieved another from her bag. Next she went so far as to remove her skirt and tossed it in the empty space next to her and proclaimed to herself, but loudly enough for him to hear, "Sure feels good to be out of that." When she wiggled into another skirt she leaned upwards in full view, her open shirt revealed her lace bra. "Whew!" she declared. "I've never done that in a back of a car before. Well maybe not a cop car," she laughed to herself.

"You be careful back there, alright," he said. She looked at him through his rearview mirror and he spied her bra. He caught himself and looked at her eyes in the mirror. She held his gaze while they sat at a red light.

"Oops!" she finally said looking down at her open chest at which point he looked away. She pulled the new blouse over her head and fluffed her hair out. After she licked her lips she asked him how she looked. She gave him one of her best coy smiles, as he peered at her in his mirror again.

"Nice. Real nice. That Caleb is, excuse me, was, a lucky bastard. He's gonna be sorry," he said shaking his head.

"Exactly," Amber concurred.

"Come on, I've got the keys," she said to the officer after they walked past the doorman Amber didn't recognize. They entered the elevator and arrived on the 11th floor as she fished for the keys in her bag. Standing behind her, the officer held her other bags and stared at her legs in a skirt that was shorter than the one she wore before. "Ah ha, found em!" she said, turning to him. She feigned shock when she saw his eyes fixated on her backside.

"Oh sorry..."

"Hmmm. Don't be, okay. You've been such a help to me tonight you know that," she said. He blushed and looked down at his feet. "Now let's go bust this bastard!"

"Alright!" he said, as she tried unsuccessfully to enter the key into the lock.

"I know this is the key. I don't know why it's not working." she jiggled the lock furiously.

"Lemme give it a try," the officer said, trying the lock himself. "You sure this is it? It's not even going in the hole."

"Move, let me try again," she shoved him out of the way. "What the fuck! Why isn't my fucking key working? I just used it a few hours ago." she said, banging on the door. "Caleb, open the door, it's me Amber. What the fuck!" she yelled. The other side of the door was silent.

"Excuse me, what's going on here?" the doorman approached from the elevator across the hall.

"I'll tell you what the fuck is going on. My key is not working. I'm Caleb's girlfriend, duh." she said.

"I'm sorry, ma'am, I'm going to have to ask you to leave. Caleb does not have a girlfriend. Please go now. Thank you officer for escorting her out," he said, calling the elevator.

"What? Who the fuck are you, asshole! Where's the other guy?" she said, as Officer Starkey pulled her by the arm.

"Okay, whatever ma'am. Just go please before you disturb the other residents. Officer," he said tipping his hat as the door opened.

"Come on, let's go Amber," the officer said. He was now dragging her, trying to contain her flailing limbs.

"Get your hands off of me, you fucking perv!" she said as they rode the elevator down.

"I see what's going on here, Amber. You probably met this guy in a bar and you stalked him till you found out where he lived and you come telling us this bogus story. Now, I know you didn't officially file a report and I only came over here to help you, but you can't do this to people. He seems like a nice guy and everything and you can't just show up and say you have the keys, which you clearly don't, and pretend he's your boyfriend," he said, escorting her out of the building.

"But he *is* my boyfriend! I'm not lying! That guy was new or something because I was just here earlier today. I don't know what's going on," she said, fuming.

"Look, Amber enough with the bullshit. You've wasted enough of my time and of taxpayer money. Get back in the car so I can take you to the bus station," he said as she angrily got in the back of the car. "People just like you come here with stars in their eyes every day. They meet some guy or some celebrity in a bar who they think can help them and they just latch on. See it all the time," he said, looking at her in his rearview mirror as he stopped at a pedestrian crossing.

"I know you think I'm lying, but I tell you I am not," she said.

"Amber, honey. Where'd you say you were from, Nebraska? Maybe it's time you go back there," he said. His words made tears spring from her eyes. "You're good. I'll give you that … had us all fooled."

"Well fuck you, asshole."

"Excuse me?" he said, looking at her as he violently pulled over.

"You heard me, I said fuck you."

"You know what? You're not worth the paperwork it would take to process you at the station. Get the fuck out of my car! Go call Bruce your pimp!" he said, pulling into an alley.

"I'm not a whore, asshole!"

"I don't have time for this shit. There are plenty of people out there who actually need my help."

"Yeah, make sure you act like a pervert around them too. I saw how you were looking at me at the bus station, in the car, and when I was trying to open Caleb's door. I should press charges against your ass!" she said, as he threw her bags on the concrete.

"You're fuckin' nuts, you know that? Maybe next time don't act like a fucking whore and I won't look at you like one. And if you pull a stunt like this again with us you won't get so lucky next time. I'll make sure the whole NYPD knows to book your ass and that you're nothing but a liar

and a trick. Have fun in Jersey at your sister's, you fuckin'
whack job." He sped away leaving her on the corner crying
with her things, as the doorman slipped a note under
Caleb's door.

Mr. Christopher,

The woman you left the photo of was here trying to
enter your unit. For some reason there was a police
officer with her and it appeared to me that she lured
him here under false pretenses of some sort and I
don't think he appreciated it very much. I did not
tell either of them that we changed your locks
earlier and that she was no longer allowed in the
building. As instructed, I simply told her that you
did not have a girlfriend at which point the officer
forcibly removed her from the property. Please let
me know if I can be of any additional service as I will
be filling in for Sherman during his vacation this
week.

Best wishes,

Dexter Carmichael, Doorman

<u>21</u>

Night turned into day as Caleb lay in Collette's bed the following morning. Feeling no need to leave the house to celebrate their engagement, they stayed in and ordered pizza which they ate with a bottle of Veuve Clicquot that Collette had in her fridge for the better part of the last year. They both turned their phones off and enjoyed each other's company uninterrupted, devouring each other ravenously throughout the night.

Jazz played softly in the background as the bright Saturday sun stirred Caleb from his sleep. He rolled over and softly smiled as he watched Collette sleep. Not wanting to disturb her, he crept out of bed and went to the kitchen where he returned with toast, jam, and orange juice. He sat with the breakfast tray in an old wicker chair next to her bed and waited for her to awake, which she did upon hearing the noisy chair creek.

"Good morning, sunshine," he said as she opened her eyes.

"Oh my, what do we have here?" she sat up and put on her tank top that had made its way under her pillow during the night.

"Just a little breakfast for my love," he said approaching her with the tray before sitting next to her on the messy bed. "I tried to be sneaky, but I guess the chair gave it away." The sun shone brightly upon him.

"Well this is very sweet," she said kissing him softly on the mouth.

"You deserve it, C. But I think the first order of business is going to the grocery store to get you some food. You had nothing in there."

"Yes, I could probably use a run to Fairway." She smiled.

"We'll take care of that right after we go get your ring. Whatever you want we'll go get," he said, kissing her deeply.

"Really? Anything?!" she asked, excitedly clapping her hands.

"Anything, you name it and it's yours."

"Actually, I already have what I really want," she said.

"You do? Do tell," he said, softly touching her cheek.

"Yes, Caleb I have you and that's all I've ever wanted. The ring is secondary," She placed her hand upon his.

"Have me you do, Collette. Always," he said, removing the tray from his lap as he climbed back into the warmth of her bed.

Threatening clouds had moved in by the time they awoke three hours later. At one o'clock on a Saturday, Collette didn't want to deal with the crowds to go ring shopping, so she promised they'd do it soon. Instead they went for a long lunch at Le Monde, where they were supposed to have had dinner, and enjoyed a bottle of Dom Perignon on the house. The restaurant manager brought them to a corner booth in the back of the dimly lit bistro, where they sat behind a drawn velvet curtain, giving them space to enjoy their meal. The waiter only checked on them twice during their two-hour lunch. They were so engaged with each other that the server did not want to bother them. After they finished their meal, Caleb graciously left a 50% tip on their $180 bill and they walked quickly back to Collette's place as the rain started to fall.

"Two bottles of champagne in two days. I could get used to this glamorous lifestyle of yours, Mr. Christopher," she said as they entered her apartment soaked.

"I hope you do, Ms. Smith, soon to be Mrs. Christopher," he said, kissing her against the wall.

"Mmmmm.....I like the sound of that," she whispered in his ear.

"Good, because I like it too," he said, pressing against her.

"But first, let's get you out of these wet clothes," she said. She began unbuttoning his shirt.

"I'd hate to get your place all wet." He tripped as she removed his pants. They ended up on the floor where they frolicked atop her Moroccan rug. They eagerly made love and collapsed in each other's arms. They fell asleep, both snoring loudly as the rain fell outside.

<u>22</u>

"But Victor, I don't think we should do it. He sounded really upset. Come on," Roberto said. They both lounged in bed watching the rain soak the plants on their veranda.

"I don't care how he sounded, Roberto. The contract's up in like three months anyway."

"But I would be the one doing the show, Victor, not you remember?"

"Obviously, you have forgotten that I am the one ultimately behind Caleb's line and that you do as I say. *You* do menswear, remember!" he said getting out of the bed. His bare chest bore evidence of his nonexistent workouts and his stomach jiggled in his outrage.

"Victor, I don't want to fight about this. I don't know why you made me apply for that show anyway. Caleb is a nice guy and I don't think we should do it," he said walking towards Victor.

"You're doing it because I can make a lot of money from it, that's why. I knew you'd get picked and you're already slated to win because I know one of the judges, so why don't you just shut it and do what I tell you."

"What do you mean I'm already going to win?"

"Oh, don't be so naïve," he said. He entered the large master bathroom and was about to close the door. "I called in a favor. Don't be so self-righteous. Now if you'll excuse me." He closed the door.

"No!"

"What did you say?" Victor angrily asked, emerging from the bathroom.

"I said no, I won't do it."

"Um, you'll do the show if I tell you to do the show, so get off your high horse and tell Caleb you'll expose him if he doesn't let you do it like I told you," he said, his hands on his hips.

"You can't make me do it, Victor, you can't. You didn't hear him on the phone. He was really upset and I think he will sue me."

"He's not going to sue you, Roberto, he doesn't have the balls to. Even if he does you don't have any money so what's he gonna get, some of your Gucci wannabe clothes or something?" he sneered. "Who wants that shit, for heaven sakes," he said to himself.

"Victor…"

"Listen, I'll get rid of you just like I got rid of Julien if you don't do this. You didn't have a problem with me creating his designs for him before so stop your damn complaining now."

"That was different, Victor. I wasn't doing a show then."

"Whatever, Roberto. Just zip it already and listen to me."

"I said, no Victor! I will not threaten him again."

"You'll do as I say." he said shoving him onto the bed.

"Victor, please. I don't want to ruin my career over this."

"You dumb fuck, I'm trying to give you a career. My intern has been giving me all those fabulous designs I give you for his line and I'm trying to do something for you here. Consider it a gift."

"What? You mean Jake has been doing the work not you?"

"Oh, for crying out loud Roberto. What're you five years old or something? Of course Jake has been doing it. Don't act so surprised," he said, turning away from him.

"I don't believe this," he said, shaking his head. "It all makes sense now. I see the way you look at him and you're always working with him late at night when you said you were working on Caleb's clothes."

"Yeah, so what? I'm fucking him, big deal. You just remember I made you in this town and if you want to keep your little career you'll do as I say!"

"Or else what?" Roberto demanded.

"Or else I'll tell my friend to have Jake win instead of you," he threatened.

"What? Jake is doing *Real Runway* too?"

"Yes, he's set up to be your main competitor," he said, slamming the bathroom door.

"He's competing with me on the show? I don't believe this is happening."

The bathroom door swung open where Victor saw Roberto crying on the bed, "Stop being such a baby. If you're not cut out for this business you can just go back to Bermuda or the Bahamas, or wherever the hell you're from. Jake is going to be huge and clearly has more talent than you and he's only 19. I'm trying to give you a chance to stand on your own before you move out."

"Move out? What are you talking about, Victor?"

"I was going to tell you later, but since you insist on behaving this way, I may as well tell you now."

"Tell me what Victor?" His voice cracked.

"I'm done financing your line. You've been here for more than four years now and when I looked at my finances I realized you don't sell enough to make it worth it for me anymore. I try to keep you in the press but it's just not working. Look, I really tried Roberto, I did, but you're out and Jake's in. Now I suggest you call Caleb and tell him you are doing the show, contract or no contract, or else you won't have a leg to stand on. You need to go see the producers for a meeting next week, it's all arranged. This is the only chance you've got to make something of yourself. Otherwise you're going to look like a big loser who just lost his financing out there looking for another benefactor like every-fucking-body else. Now, do you understand? I'm trying to give you something here! You go on that show and you'll win and you'll get a career. Jake'll give you a good run for your money and will place second. He's also set to win all the challenges – so you're not too surprised. You'll get a career and Jake'll get a lot of press, which of course, will be good for me, seeing as how he's my new boyfriend and all. With the prize money you will be able to pay me back for what I've spent on your line so far and for all those courses I paid for."

"But I thought you did that because you liked me and it was free," he whimpered.

"Free? You must be joking. Nothing's free in this town."

<u>23</u>

"Caleb, where are you? I've been trying you all day."
Katherine left a message on Caleb's phone. "The
photographer agreed to a reshoot for half the cost. I think
they felt bad for you. Let me know when you want to
reshoot and I can work with Collette on the casting end."

Both Caleb and Collette's phone had been turned off
for the better part of the past 24 hours as they blocked out
the world around them. When he finally checked his
messages he was pleased to receive Katherine's voicemail,
along with his agent's informing him that Trey Xu wanted
him for the lead in his new movie. That was one thing
Amber hadn't fucked up, he thought to himself as he
excitedly listened to the message.

Seeing as how it was now Saturday night, he had no
desire to go home and he and Collette continued playing
house. First they went for groceries, then Collette tidied up
the mess they had created while Caleb went to a corner
bakery and picked up fresh baked cookies for dessert. He
returned with a chocolate smudge on his lower lip, which

Collette promptly licked off when he walked through the door. While she put the groceries away Caleb called Julie and relieved her of her services as his publicist. She was shocked, but Caleb kept the conversation brief by telling her that a check was being FedExed to her, and that she would receive it on Monday. It would sustain her for a while until she found another job. Once he told her of the amount— $30,000—she didn't seem so distraught and simply said, "*Sweet!*" But then remembering that she was supposed to be humble and upset said, "*I mean uh, thank you. If that's what you really want, okay.*" She had been basically useless as his publicist and Caleb was happy that Collette could now relinquish the slack she'd picked up and hand it over to Katherine.

He was glad that this would allow her to have more free time that he wanted her to spend with him. He was so grateful that Collette had agreed to marry him that he still didn't believe it. He wanted to hurry and get the ring to make it official but with his busy schedule they would have to fit in the time to go shop for it. In the meantime he would enjoy continuing their night in the bubble they had created.

"C, your kitchen is so small. How do you do anything in here?" Caleb asked as he tried to maneuver his way around the small space looking in the cabinets and fridge for something to cook for dinner.

"Oh, I make do. I hardly use it anyway," she replied, handing him a six-pack of Diet Coke for him to put in the fridge.

"Well whenever you're ready for a bigger kitchen, you know my place is all yours," he said, winking at her as he placed the soda in the fridge.

"Really?"

"Of course, C. You could move in tomorrow if you wanted," he said, hanging the reusable bags on a hook on the side of her fridge.

"Hmm. I'll think about that, but in the short term I think I'll keep my place." She smiled at him.

"How come?"

"Well, we'll have the rest of our lives together and while I'm still working for you I am not sure that's the best idea. For either of us," she said. She poured herself a glass of Pellegrino.

"I hope you're not rethinking things." His eyes questioned.

"No honey of course not," she said touching his cheek. "I just don't want to rush into anything. I mean, I know we're engaged and everything, but until I find another job or something else to do I think I should stay here. That's all, okay?" She moved towards him.

"Alright. You had me nervous there for a second," he said hugging her.

"Nothing to be nervous about. Nothing at all."

As Collette was enjoying a dinner of roasted chicken, garlic potatoes, and sautéed spinach that Caleb cooked for her, Julien lay sulking in his cramped apartment. Being on the ground floor, he didn't have much of a view, thanks to the bars on the windows that looked out onto a back alley, and the noise was often unbearable. There was always a constant stream of sirens and both male and female prostitutes littered the alley, choosing his block to conduct their business. As he munched on his third fried egg roll and fourth Tanqueray martini, he increased the volume on his television to drown out the noise from outside. He grew more bitter about his situation. He loathed how Victor discarded him and yearned to hurt him greater that he had been hurt. It was high time he paid him and Roberto a visit but passed out on the couch before he could do so.

***

"So Katherine left me a message earlier," Caleb said to Collette over cookies after they finished their meal.

"Yeah, what'd she say?"

"She said the photographer will do a reshoot at half the cost."

"Oh my God, Caleb, that's awesome! I'll call her on Monday so we can start casting for it," she said. She started to clean away their plates.

"Don't worry about doing that. I had another idea," he said, removing the plates from her hand and sitting her in his lap.

"What's that?"

"I was thinking that you could be the model for the shoot. What do you think?"

"Me?"

"Yes, you. Of course you, C. You're beautiful and you would be great."

"Thanks, but I'm not a model, Caleb. If anything I'm a writer buried underneath here," she said, tapping her chest.

"Oh come on, you'd be great. Besides, now that we're engaged you said yourself that you'll have to find something else to do and being the spokeswoman for my brand could be a nice flexible job for you."

"Ah yes, there is that. I guess I will have to find another gig," she said, pecking him on the lips. "But are you sure? I mean, I've never really modeled before."

"I have every confidence that you would be awesome, C. I can't think of anyone else I'd rather have represent my brand."

"It's crazy, but I guess I could do it. It could be fun." she said hugging him.

"And if you like it I'll have Sean hook you up with an agent too so you can do more if you'd like."

"Let's not get ahead of ourselves. Let's see how this shoot goes first. But I am excited! Thank you so much, honey."

"Anything for you, C," he said, hugging her tightly.

After they'd cleaned up and finished off the cookies Collette finally checked her messages. Lou called twice wondering what she needed her mom for. Collette's mom left a concerned message because she hadn't heard from her all day, Spencer left a message just saying hi, enthusing about how he couldn't wait for Rome, and Katherine left a message wondering where Caleb was since she hadn't been able to reach him all day. She sent Lou a text:

Sorry I missed ur call and will call 2mrw.

We're engaged and I'm going 2 b the model 4 his line! Can't wait 2 tell u about it. Hope ur having fun! xoxo C

And then she wrote Spencer a short email:

Spencer,

Thanks for your message. Something's come up here and I am not going to be able to make it to Rome. We'll talk when you get back.

Collette

<u>24</u>

Sunday morning arrived moist, misty, and damp. Big puddles of water peppered the streets courtesy of last night's rain. Roberto walked glumly around these puddles on his way to a corner deli for his daily cup of coffee. At 7:15 a.m. he felt like the only resident in this large city. There was hardly any traffic and no one was on the streets. Surely, the rest of the city enjoyed their Saturday night more than he had, and was sleeping it off with no intention of waking up early to the dismal weather. He was haggard and tired as he had spent the better part of last night packing his belongings. Victor had given him two weeks to relocate but Roberto wanted it over with as soon as possible.

As he called his handful of friends, he realized that they were all Victor's friends and surely they would not open their doors to him. It would put them in an awful position and they would ask themselves, "What would Victor think?" It gave him a lesson in who his real friends were. Only one person he called offered her sofa sleeper to him. Her name was Sarah and they met at school and had maintained a friendship. She didn't follow through with a design career, but instead worked as a salesperson at Barneys and recently became a single mother. Her young son was only eight months old, so she warned that her space would be tight, but of course he was welcome. He was embarrassed to admit to her that he did not have a credit card for a hotel, or no real savings to move into his own place, because Victor had always handled the finances and kept his earnings, but she did not judge him for this; she simply told him that everything would be alright. He was to call to let her know when he would be arriving.

Feeling like he had no other choice, he told Victor that he would call Caleb again on Monday morning to tell him he was going to do *Real Runway.* He knew Caleb would be upset again but felt his hands were tied in the matter. His heart was heavy as he paid for his coffee and sat on a bench outside drinking it. It didn't matter that the bench was damp. Roberto felt nothing through his thin linen pants.

Julien awoke to the sounds of the weatherman cheerfully forecasting another day of rain. His body ached as he wondered to himself why he had slept on the couch and not in his bed. Looking around the room at the empty martini glass and open Tanqueray bottle he soon figured out why. A mammoth-sized cockroach nibbled on the remains of his dinner on the coffee table in front of him, and a mouse had made off with a discarded piece of chicken as it munched away in a corner. Julien wacked the cockroach with his shoe and tossed it across the room, aiming for the mouse. He missed the mouse by a mile and it continued its breakfast of sweet and sour chicken, indifferent to the threat. Julien instantly became sick and barely made it to the bathroom before throwing up into the sink. He cried like a baby as he wiped the thick, pink residue from the corners of his mouth. His fast-falling tears helped rinse out the sink as he scrubbed it with his verbena-scented Mrs. Meyers cleaning solution, nearly using the entire bottle.

He closed the door and turning on the shower, he let the steam fill the bathroom as he sat on the toilet seat, continuing to cry. The steam from the shower felt therapeutic as he let the hot moisture envelop him in the small bathroom for a half an hour. He breathed deeply and stood and began to stretch his tight muscles. He shed his moist clothes as he continued to stretch his body in the limited area that the space allowed. After stretching his calves, hamstrings, and quads, he began to reach up high, inhaling and exhaling deeply as he did so. He arched his back, which loosened up the muscles that had been dormant for so many years. He could smell the gin leaking from his pores, which seemed to drive him more in his stretches. He cried a few more tears as he ended his movements with his hands clasped together at his heart. He stayed this way for a solid five minutes as he wept softly to himself.

The fog was so thick that he could no longer see himself in the bathroom and he felt his way into the shower and allowed the hot liquid to beat down on his raw skin. Although it was painful, he had not felt this alive in years. He wailed loudly as the scalding water pounded on his back before facing the punitive stream head-on. His chest quickly turned red, but he stood still and took it. Soon his tears stopped and he breathed heavily as he added cold water to make the shower more bearable. He vigorously scrubbed his body and exfoliated every inch of his skin with preciseness careful not to miss a spot. He then moved to his head where he shampooed his hair so roughly he thought his scalp might bleed. He rinsed and repeated three times before squeezing out the last of a trial-sized bottle of Kiehl's conditioner that he had taken from work. While the conditioner worked its magic he slathered a hefty portion of Noxzema on his face and felt his pores tingle and open up. Long gone was the smell of Tanqueray, replaced now by a refreshing peppermint eucalyptus aroma.

After rinsing, he stood outside the shower and wiped off the mirror and simply stared at himself. It was as if he was really seeing himself for the first time. His red splotchy skin stared back at him and his hair lay flat at the base of his neck. He gathered this lock of hair in his hands, reached for a pair of scissors in a drawer and swiftly removed it. He tossed the hair in the trash without hardly a second glance. He turned sideways and admired the freeness of the back of his neck before returning to the front and gave himself a quick, all-around trim. He'd never cut his own hair in the past but found this exercise to be both exhilarating and liberating. Next, he took stock of his soft body. He had not seen the inside of a gym in at least three years and his limp muscles confirmed this. His round belly bore no hint of muscle and his triceps flapped when he lifted his arms. Although he knew that he had been complicit in his body's demise, he was still shocked to see how much his once strong, youthful muscles had atrophied.

He opened the door to a gush of cold air and to the loudness of the weatherman, reporting again on the day's dreadful rain. He turned off the television and turned on a soft jazz station on his clock radio. Disgusted by the state of his apartment, he scrubbed it clean for the next hour. His apartment needed a detox just as bad as his body. He poured out the remaining gin and emptied the other alcohol stored in his kitchen cabinets. Peach Schnapps,

Smirnoff Vodka, Bailey's Irish Cream, and Sherry—all gone. He couldn't even justify keeping the unopened bottle of Cavit Pinot Grigio he had in the fridge. It was like saying goodbye to an old friend, but he happily took this friend out to the trash in the alley. The loud clanging of the bottles against the dumpster startled the resident rats, sending them scurrying quickly from behind their home. He returned inside, dressed, and headed out the door. He wondered if Victor would be at his local deli getting his coffee at the ungodly hour of 7:00 a.m.

As Julien's cab sped uptown on the barren streets, his renewed vigor was matched by his loneliness. He had always found the city so magnificent and bewitching, but on this damp Sunday morning it just felt isolating. With no family or real friends to speak of in the area, Julien grew melancholy. He did not know what he was going to say to Victor, but he knew he had to get final closure on the issue in order for him to fully move on in a life that seemed to stall since the break-up with Victor. As the cab dropped him off on the corner of Madison and 60th, he saw a lone man sitting on a bench sadly drinking a cup of coffee. Seeing no one in the deli, he decided to wait on this bench while he contemplated what to say if Victor showed up. He and this stranger sat in silence for 15 minutes before the stranger made a call on his cell phone.

"Hi it's me. I can bring my things by later today if that's still okay," he said into the phone. Julien recognized this strange man's voice but sat still. "I know I can't believe this either. I can't believe Victor would do this." the man cried softly. "I mean, I did nothing to him."

Julien couldn't believe his ears. He'd come to make some kind of peace with Victor and was sitting next to Roberto. Those old feelings of anger crept up and he exploded.

"Roberto?" he said, startling him.
"Sorry?" He turned to look and his eyes grew wide in recognition. "Um, I need to call you back," he said into the phone before quickly hanging up. "JULIEN?" he asked as the remainder of his coffee tipped from his lap onto the ground.

210

"ROBERTO?" they both stared at each other in disbelief.

"What are you doing sitting here like a crazy person?"

"Well, I sure as hell didn't expect to see you," he said, rising from the bench. "Where is Victor, I need to talk to him." Julien steadied his hips with his hands.

"At home I guess. Or maybe with Jake. The hell if I know," he said with watery eyes.

"What are you talking about? Aren't you still his little boy toy?" he said confused.

"Not anymore, Julien. Are you happy now?" He stood up in a huff with tears streaming down his cheeks.

"What?"

"You heard me. I've been replaced by an intern apparently," he said as his eyes cast downward. "Look, Julien I'm sorry for everything that happened to you. I had no idea that Victor could be so cold. But I have to go." He started to walk away.

"Where are you going?"

"I don't know, okay? I just can't sit here and talk to you." he yelled.

"Goodness, Roberto I'm sorry. I had no idea. I don't mean you any more harm. I just ... I just wasn't expecting you. If you want you can tell me what happened," he said, taking his seat again on the bench as Roberto turned to look at him.

"I don't know Julien. It's not like you're my friend or anything."

"I know and I don't blame you for not trusting me, but I am serious when I say I don't mean you any harm and I'm sorry. I came here today hoping to see Victor to get some kind of closure. I'd been blaming him for the way my life turned out and for my not becoming the designer I wanted to be. I'm trying to move past it."

"Really?" he said, sitting back down.

"Yes really, Roberto. I am so sorry that I hurt you and I found out, just like you did, what an asshole Victor is. I had given him my life and had been with him for many years and was so angry when he dumped me for you. I was never angry at you, per se, but at him. He really is revolting."

"Oh my God Julien, yes, yes he is! He is trying to make me do the show *Real Runway* and he kicked me out of his house and is dating Jake the intern."

"I'm so sorry, Roberto."

"And he also wants me to threaten to expose Caleb if he doesn't let me do the show."

"What do you mean 'expose' him? Who is Caleb?" he asked, even though he knew the answer.

"Don't say anything, okay? It's supposed to be a secret," he pleaded.

"You've got my word."

"Christopher. Caleb Christopher the actor and 'designer,'" he said using quotation marks.

"What? Are you telling me you're designing his line?"

"Caleb asked me to do it and Victor went along with it and was designing it since I only make men's clothes. Anyway, now he is telling me that Jake was doing the work and not him and he is making me go on the show to win all this money to pay him back for the classes and for financing my line. I just don't know what to do," he said despondently.

"Are you kidding me? He's making you pay him back for all that stuff? What a jerk," he laughed.

"I know! I like Caleb and don't want to hurt him, but I don't have a choice. Victor already made me call him once and he was really upset. I don't want to do it again, but Victor is making me. I feel like I don't have a choice."

"Roberto, you have a choice in everything. Let's go inside somewhere before he comes around the corner or something and sees us together."

"Okay," he said. They both rose from the bench.

"So where are you staying tonight?"

"I don't know. I was talking to my friend earlier but I don't think she has any
extra room with her baby, but she was being nice."

"Do you not have any savings?"

"Only a little. Victor kept all my money I earned. He said since I wasn't paying rent that I owed him for everything."

"Unbelievable. He keeps all your money and is now making you go on this show so he can take more of your money?"

"I guess so. It's sad, I know," he said. His eyes misted again.

"Come on, let's go somewhere and talk. The rain is coming," he said looking towards the ominous sky.

<u>25</u>

"What?! What do you mean you're engaged, C? To Spencer or Caleb?" Lou asked eagerly through the phone. In her kitchen, Collette was comfortable in a robe adorned with cherry blossoms. She was making tea while Caleb was in the shower. It was only 9 a.m., but they had woken up early with the goal of looking for a ring before the crowds grew too big.

"To Caleb, crazy! What are you doing calling me so early? Where's Pedro? Shouldn't you guys still be asleep or something?"

"He's lying right here asleep. I got up to pee and got your text and just had to call. I can't believe you're engaged! That's so awesome, C!"

"Thank you. I'm really excited. We're going ring shopping today," she said, smiling.

"Oh my goodness! I'm so happy for you. You deserve it, Collette. What about Spencer?"

"I sent him an email telling him I wasn't going to Rome and would talk to him when he got back."

"And how did he take that?"

"He wrote back asking if everything was okay and said he could come back at the end of the week if I needed him. It was sweet, but I just don't love him, Lou. I just don't."

"That was pretty obvious."

"Yeah, I know, but I guess I needed to realize it all in my own time," she said, removing two cups from the cabinet.

"Soooo, how did he propose? Was it totally romantic?"

"It was a little weird actually. After I left the shoot on Friday I came home deciding that I was going to go to Rome. I was just going to take it easy with Spencer and have a relaxing time. I'd met this great woman who worked in a diner and I blabbed to her about my story and she helped me realize that life was too short to be in a mess like this at my age. So I was going to just tell Caleb that I had decided to go to Rome for a few days. I mean, I liked, okay, loved him, but there was too much drama with Amber everywhere and I didn't want to deal with it anymore and needed to get away."

"Can't forget about Amber."

"No, I couldn't. Anyway, on my way home from the diner I thought that he had obviously made a choice to be with her and not me and I would have to be okay with that. So, as I was waiting for him to show up so we could go to dinner and talk, he ran up the stairs saying how it was over with them and that he'd kicked her out and wanted to be with me. I just looked at him like he was crazy. He then dropped on one knee and asked me to marry him. It was crazy but so sweet."

"Oh my God. I go away for one lousy weekend and all this happens. Go on."

"There isn't much more to tell. I made sure he knew what he was really asking me and he said he'd loved me for a while and wanted to be with me. I suddenly just felt like what I had always wanted was right in front of me, so I said yes. I didn't think about anything else," she said, turning off the kettle and pouring the scalding water into cups.

"That's so romantic, C! It sounds just like a movie."

"You're funny! Yes it was romantic and we have been in my apartment ever since," she said blowing on the hot liquid.

"Really...making up for lost time are you now?" Lou asked.

"You could say that." She laughed.

"Well it's about damn time. What the hell was his ass waiting for? I mean, *hello*?"

"I don't know but everything feels right, right now. Oh, before I forget to ask you I need to talk to your mom about something," she said as she added agave to her tea and took a sip.

"Sure. What's up?"

"Caleb is in a bit of trouble."

"How?"

"Remember how I told you that Roberto Carnellos was doing his line?"

"Yes."

"I guess he wants to do *Real Runway* and is threatening to expose Caleb if he doesn't let him out of his contract."

"That sucks. Why does he need to talk to my mom?'

"Because some guy named Julien called and left him a scary message saying he was going to expose him and that he knew his line was a fraud and he wants to find out who Julien is and thought your mom might be able to help."

"Boy, he's in a pickle."

"Tell me about it. He also threatened to expose Roberto, so we think he's in the fashion business too if that helps."

"It does. I'll talk to my mom later and see what I can find out," she said as Collette heard the shower water stop in her bathroom.

"Great. Thanks, Lou. Listen, I think Caleb's out of the shower. I have to go. I'll have my phone on today if you can call me after you talk to your mom."

"I'll give you a ring soon. Have fun shopping for your ring! Do you know what you want?"

"Honestly, I don't know anything about rings, so I have no idea. I'll just pick the first thing I like. I don't want to spend too much time on it or put too much into it. I may just get a gold band or something."

"C, no! You have to get a big beautiful diamond."

"Well, we'll see. I'll talk to you later." Caleb entered the kitchen wearing nothing but a towel. "Good news," she said, addressing him.

"Yeah? What?" he said, kissing her cheek.

"Lou is going to talk to her mom for you and call me back later."

"Thank you so much, C. You're the best," he said, kissing her on the lips.

"You're welcome. I just hope she can really help so you can get out of this mess."

"Me too. No sense dwelling on the past, but I should not have gotten myself into this in the first place."

"Nope, probably not. You know, you could always retire the line before they expose you."

"What do you mean?" he said sitting at the table to drink his tea.

"Well, you said Roberto's contract is up soon anyway right?"

"Right."

"So why don't you just beat them at their own game? Maybe think about releasing a statement admitting that you had help with the line and are retiring because you're only going to focus on your acting career."

"Just admit it? For no reason?"

"For every reason, Caleb. If this guy is serious about doing this show and exposing you, then that's a greater firestorm than the one you're in right now. In your statement you won't actually say who helped you with it, only that you did receive assistance and realized the fashion business wasn't for you and you want to get back to your acting now. You could even say something like how you are glad Trey Xu is giving you a chance with his new movie and is allowing you to develop your craft, and since that is where your real passion lies, you don't want to risk this professional growth in any way. Trey would love that. Just beat them to the punch. Take the air out of the balloon before they even have a chance to blow it up."

"This sounds like it might work, C."

"I've been thinking about it and I think it will. If you release this statement people won't even care that you are admitting to having 'help' with the line. Everyone knows that celebs have people do everything for them anyway so it won't be a shock," she said. Caleb cast his eyes downward. "I'm sorry, honey but they do. By you coming clean first, you diffuse their story before they get a chance to do anything. Then if they expose you by calling you a fraud or something, they will look stupid and pathetic because no one will care. Everyone will be like, 'Duh, he already admitted that!' They won't have anything, get it?"

"But what about the reshoot?"

"We can still do it, but fast. I'll talk to Katherine about all this so we can move on it. We can time it for your release to coincide with the ad coming out. If they can turn around the ad quickly and get it in *Harper's, Glamour, Vogue,* or other publications soon it will guarantee the dress will be a best seller since it will be your last one. It's bound to create all kinds of buzz. You're already hot, but you'll be on fire."

"How do you come up with this stuff, C? Seriously it's brilliant."

"It's nothing, just think about it. The next time Roberto calls just string him along for awhile so he doesn't do anything in order to give us time to reshoot the ad and get it to press. Just threaten him back with a lawsuit for breach of contract or something. That should shut him up for a little while at least."

"I love it, C." he said jumping up from his chair to hug her.

"I'm glad. I really think it's your best option. I get the feeling your heart's really not into designing anyway? Am I right?"

"Yeah you're right. It has turned out to be a lot more than I wanted to take on and I do want to get back to focusing only on acting. You're always right, C. How did I get so lucky?"

"Oh now, stop. I'm just doing my job," she said. She placed her empty mug in the sink.

"Well if that will be my last ad, then you will go down in history too as the model."

"I guess I will. Even better!" she joked.

"Now enough of this work talk, why don't you go get dressed so we can get your ring," he said, softly kissing her left hand.

"I think I can do that," she said. He pressed himself against her.

"But I'd like to do something else first," he said as he untied her bathrobe and removed his towel.

"What's that?"

"I can't wait to show you," he said as he kissed her deeply. He used every available surface to make love to her in the small kitchen.

<u>26</u>

Fifty-seventh Street had been an even bigger hub of activity than usual over the past few days. Joan Rider was in town with her kids and had taken them shopping to Burberry before retreating back to her hotel at the Trump Hotel at Columbus Circle. Her dropping into these stores on Saturday afternoon had caused quite a stir and was a magnet for paparazzi. Because they were watching her every move, the paparazzi was staked out at various locations in the area. There was rumor that she wanted to go to Tiffany's before she left town, so Bruce made sure he had a guy outside the store in case she showed up. The photographer was so preoccupied with looking for Joan and her kids that he nearly missed Caleb enter the store with an unidentifiable woman. The guy had no idea who the woman was but they seemed really into each other. It was just after noon and Caleb and his friend were only the second people to enter the store so far. The photographer took up residence behind a light pole about ten feet from the door and waited for them to emerge from the store. He was surprised that they were back out within ten minutes with a little blue bag. The girl was so happy and Caleb held her hand tightly and stopped to kiss her frequently as they walked down Fifth Avenue. The photographer snapped about 30 shots in the one minute that they were in his view before jumping in a taxi. There was still no sign of Joan and kids but he had certainly gotten a money shot. He immediately called Bruce to tell him.

"Hey, it's me."

"Yeah, did they show?" Bruce brusquely responded.

"Not yet, but you'll never believe who I got."

"Better be good."

"Oh, it is. I got Caleb Christopher with someone who looked like his girlfriend. They went into Tiffany's and came out really fast with a bag and were all giddy." At this news Bruce perked up.

"Did she have red hair and long legs?" he screamed into the phone.

"No, some black girl. Real cute. They looked happy together."

"A black girl? You don't say. Alright, upload that to me right now so we can get it online. I've got the perfect caption for this one," Bruce said.

"You got it."

"And stay out there a bit longer in case Rider and all those kids show up. Apparently she hasn't left the hotel yet. The concierge said they're still there and I know he ain't lying cuz he needs the money too much."

"Alright, I'll be here till you tell me otherwise."

Within thirty minutes three photos of Caleb and Collette canoodling outside Tiffany's were available for the world to see. It was the caption that angered Amber as she viewed the photos, courtesy of her "Caleb Christopher" Google Alert, on her new iPhone: *CALEB CHRISTOPHER DUMPS AMBER SKYE FOR BEAUTIFUL MYSTERY WOMAN. LOOKS LIKE THIS ONE IS MARRIAGE MATERIAL. SORRY AMBER! LOOKS LIKE HER BAD BEHAVIOR COST HER THIS ONE!*

She screamed inside the crowded Starbucks where up until a moment ago she had been enjoying a cup of coffee and a bear claw on a dismal Sunday afternoon. Her howl drew the attention of everyone in the shop as she yelled, "What the hell are you looking at?" before storming out the door.

***

"That's fabulous Collette! You're doing wonderfully!" the photographer said to Collette swaying in the breeze.

"You're really sure I'm moving ok? I'm not used to heels this high or being all dressed up like this."

"Yes, you're doing great. And so much easier to work with," Joe said, snapping away at which point the crew collectively echoed his sentiments. Collette tried not to smile or laugh too hard at this and focused on the task at hand. She wore a body-hugging sleeveless silk ivory dress, with a simple scoop neck and lace trim that landed mid-thigh. This, paired with four-inch champagne colored platform pumps, made Caleb look at her in a new light. Her face was highlighted with gold accented makeup and her

229

skin also glimmered due to sparkly lotion she wore. She was a vision unlike anything Caleb had ever seen and he couldn't help but think she looked like a very fashionable bride. He beamed with pride and joy.

"Well, thank you," she said, continuing to move naturally to the disco beats, her music of choice for the shoot.

***

Collette had phoned Katherine first thing Monday morning to tell her that they were engaged. In case rumors started to circulate, Collette felt she should know as soon as possible. She urged Katherine to keep it quiet and not comment on it to anyone in the press. She also told her she would be the new model for the reshoot. Katherine congratulated her effusively on both counts. After Collette filled her in on the Roberto situation and the release she would have to issue, Katherine came up with the idea of an outdoor shoot to make it more exciting than a typical studio shoot, especially if this was going to be the last one. Joe had an opening on Thursday and had a connection at the W Hotel in Hoboken where they could use the roof and have a great backdrop of the city. It was also significantly cheaper than finding a rooftop at the last minute in the city. It was a beautiful spring day and Collette twirled to the music and played with her large fro. She was a natural and was enjoying herself. She was sad when the shoot came to an end but was happy that she had been a part of it. After the makeup artist helped her remove the fake eyelashes and some of the heavy makeup, she changed into jeans and a tank top and they all headed to the bar for a celebratory drink.

"Sorry for the delay but my mom was traveling and was only finally able to figure out who Julien is," Lou said to Collette when she returned her call after the shoot.

"Yeah, who is he?" she asked. She sat in a corner booth of the sleek hotel lobby while Caleb mingled with the photographer and crew and thanked them for a great shoot and for their accommodating him.

"You'll never believe this."

"What? Tell me!"

"Julien is Roberto Carnello's boyfriend—Victor's ex-boyfriend," she said satisfactorily as she dropped the bomb and listened to Collette's sharp inhale.

"No way!"

"Yes, can you believe it? It sounds like a lovers' quarrel or something funky to me."

"Oh my goodness. Sounds like this guy was jilted or something based on that message he left Caleb."

"Has he called back?"

"No, no one has."

"Good."

"How did your mom find this out?"

"Wasn't that hard actually. She knew Roberto was dating Victor because they were always photographed together, so she called a friend of hers who organized that Who's Who of Fashion party—"

"The party where we met Roberto and Victor," she interrupted.

"Yes, that one. Anyway, her friend told her that there had been a scuffle outside after the party and there was a picture the next day on *Page Six* of the three of them."

"Oh my God I remember that picture! I had meant to show it to Caleb, but he was busy the next day and I forgot and misplaced it somewhere," Collette said putting the pieces together.

"Crazy, right?"

"Was your mom able to get the photo?"

"Check your email, I already sent it to you, Ms. Supermodel," she joked.

"Ha ha! Shut up! Oh my God I have to hang up so I can check my email and tell Caleb and Katherine. Please thank your mom for me! I love you guys."

"We love you too. Call me later."

"Will do."

Collette ordered a vodka tonic from the passing waiter and checked her email on her BlackBerry and saw Julien's deer-in-headlights reaction with Roberto and Victor looking on. He looked greasy and dirty. His face was hidden by his long, dirty hair—only his right eye was visible. He looked sweaty and his hair stuck to the side of his face and some was in his mouth. She almost felt bad for someone being photographed in such a state. Her drink arrived and she grabbed it and practically ran to the other side of the room to find Caleb.

Julien had felt so bad for Roberto that he got him a room at the W for a majorly reduced rate; it was practically free at $65 a night. He didn't have room in his tiny place and it didn't sound like his friend could put him up either. Roberto felt indebted to him for helping him in this way, but Julien reminded him that business was down because of the recession and half the rooms in the hotel were empty anyway, which made him feel better. At Julien's urging, Roberto left Victor a message on Monday morning telling him that he had called Caleb. He didn't leave any details, only that he would be in touch soon. The *Real Runway* meeting was set for Saturday and he would have to come up with something by then.

Just as Collette was nearing Caleb in the bar, her mom called. She hadn't gotten around to returning April's phone calls over the past few days and thought it best to step outside the hotel and answer. In her quest for privacy surrounding her engagement, she hadn't told her mom yet because she didn't think she could keep the secret. Everyone in her hometown would know within a few hours and her mother would instantly be pressuring her for all the wedding planning details. Collette had still been trying to process the whole thing herself and wanted, for once, to keep something close to her heart until she felt like disclosing the information.

"Hi Ma," she said taking a seat on a bench outside the hotel on the desolate street.

"What do you mean, 'Hi Ma?' How come you haven't called me back? I've been worried sick."

"I'm sorry about that, but no need to worry I'm fine. I've just been busy."

"Busy? Chile', you ain't *that* busy you can't call your mama back."

"You're right. Look, can I call you back in a bit? I am right in the middle of something."

"Can you call me back? Girl, I don't have time to sit around and wait for you to call me back. I'm on my way to bible study. You tell Caleb he can wait a few minutes, we need to talk *now*."

"What's going on? Is something wrong?" she asked.

"Don't get all dramatic, nothing is wrong."

"What are you talking about? Why do we need to talk right now?

"Your daddy wants for us to go on a family vacation to spend some time together."

"Why?"

"Because we will be moving to Denver in a few months because he accepted a teaching position at the University of Colorado's medical school."

"Denver? That's so random."

"Don't I know it. He's always loved skiing so that will be good for him, but I don't know what I am going to do out there. I hope I can find a good church."

"When did all this happen? I can't believe you're leaving Chicago."

"It was kind of fast. One of his colleagues took a job there a few years ago and your daddy went out to visit him a few times and really liked it, so when his friend told him about an opening he put in a word for him."

"Wow. I'm totally speechless. Do you like it out there? It seems so far."

"As long as your daddy is there I'm sure I will like it too. It will be a change for sure, but I'll adjust. We've been here so long that we're actually looking forward to something different. He'll have more normal hours again teaching than he does here working in a hospital, so I'm looking forward to seeing him more."

"Wow. What are you going to do with the house?

"Just rent it for a while. We're going to try it for a year or two and see how we feel. We can always come back, Collette."

"Yeah, I guess you can."

"Besides, Denver is not that far from Chicago so we better see you out there."

"You will don't worry. So where does he want to go on vacation?

"Here, ask him yourself. Hampton! Collette's on the line. Yeah, finally, I know..." she yelled to her husband, who ran to the phone.

"Baby girl! How's my baby?" he said, a bit winded.

"Daddy, how are you? I can't believe you're moving to Colorado."

"Well you know, sometimes life gives you an opportunity for change and you have to take it. It will be nice." He deeply sighed.

"I'm surprised, but I'm happy if you are happy."

"So, are we going on vacation or what?

"Where were you thinking?"

"How about Paris and London? We could do three days in each city and your mom can show us her old Parisian stomping grounds," he said.

"That sounds good to me. It would be nice to be there and not be working. Let me run it by Caleb, I have to see what's on his schedule."

"Okay, but let me know soon. I want to book our tickets by this weekend."

"Okay I'll get back to you soon, I promise."

"Hampton, give me the phone!" April screamed in the background.

"Uh oh, here comes your mom again. Love you."

"Love you too Dad— "

"Collette are you and Caleb engaged?!" she interrupted.

"Engaged? What?" she heard her dad surprisingly echo.

"Uh, yeah. I've been meaning to tell you about that. How'd you find out?"

"How did I find out? Cheryl's niece from church just sent me an email with a link to TNV or something."

"TMZ."

"Whatever. It's showing some pictures of him with you coming out of Tiffany's. When were you going to tell me about this?"

"I was going to tell you soon, I really was. It's been so crazy here that I haven't had time to tell you. We hadn't really told anyone anyway because we're trying to keep it quiet."

"Collette, who did you think I was going to tell?"

"Seriously?"

"Yes, Collette. Seriously!"

"Everybody, Mom. We just weren't ready to talk about it yet."

"But why not?"

"Because we didn't want it to get leaked to the press. You know how these things are."

"Maybe, but I can't believe my own baby didn't tell me that she was getting married."

"Oh, I'm sorry, Ma. Just don't tell anyone ok. Except for daddy, okay?"

"Okay," she sniffled. "Oh, I can't believe my little girl is getting married!" she exclaimed excitedly.

"I know I can't believe it either."

"Well, you must have broken up with Spencer."

"Not really yet."

"Collette! That poor boy. What are you waiting on?"

"He's been out of town working and I can't just do it over email or something. I told him I would talk to him when he gets back."

"Just be nice about it, okay?"

"I will."

"What about the ring? Girl, how big is it and when are you going to send me a picture?"

"We haven't gotten it yet."

"You haven't gotten it yet? What in the hell were you doing at Tiffany's?"

"I went with him to pick up a gift for his mom. He missed her birthday and needed to get her something really nice. We were supposed to go get the ring but everywhere was so crowded that we didn't want to deal with it."

"Why did they write that you were engaged?"

"I don't know, Ma. Because those people have nothing else to do than write stuff like that. I didn't even see any photographers there. That's how sneaky they are."

"They must have gotten that from somewhere, Collette."

"Ma, I don't know. I'm sure they saw us coming out with a Tiffany's bag acting all lovey dovey and they just assumed. The press makes up stuff all the time. I don't know why you're so surprised. We never pay attention to any of it," she said, smiling at a few hotel guests passing by.

"So, if I hadn't received this link and asked you about it, you wouldn't have told me you were engaged?"

"I didn't say that. I swear I was going to tell you soon."

"Alright, Collette. You just don't get too big for your britches out there. Don't forget about us little people at home the next time you have some big news."

"Can we move on, please?"

"Umm hmm. So when is the wedding and where's it gonna be?" she asked.

"We don't know yet. First I need to find a new job before I do anything. Speaking of which, here's some big news for you—"

"You're pregnant with that boy's baby!"

"No! Are you crazy, Ma? I'm not pregnant but I am going to be in Caleb's next print ad for his line. We just had the shoot today."

"Oh my goodness that's great! He's payin' you extra, ain't he?"

"Ma! Of course he is. And very well, I might add."

"That's my girl!"

"Yes, I'm going to save it all so I have something to live on when I quit."

"Girl, you are marrying Caleb Christopher. Let him support you for a while."

"Ma, I don't want him to support me. Besides, we haven't set a date and I still have my place. So until we walk down the aisle or until I move I will continue to support myself."

"I guess you're right. Look honey, I have to go. Your daddy has to get to the hospital soon and we need to eat dinner."

"Okay, I'll call you soon about the trip. Love you."

"Love you too."

By the time Collette got off the phone and re-entered the bar, Caleb and crew were in full party mode, doing shots and dancing to the thumping music. She noticed one girl in particular who was speaking to him more closely than she would have liked. They seemed to be enjoying each other's company. The girl was whispering in his ear making him laugh hysterically and began an awkward seductive dance in front of him, which Caleb also found amusing. Collette couldn't believe the photographer, who was standing nearby, could be so complicit in Caleb's interaction with this girl. Men really do all stick together, Collette thought disgustedly to herself. After the girl stopped dancing and regained her composure, he began looking around the room for Collette. Spotting the angry look on her face across the room, he pushed past the girl and made his way towards her.

"C, where you been?" he said over the loud music.

"I was on the phone. Look, I'm tired and I'm going home now," she said walking past him.

"Come on, babe. Don't be like that. We were all just having a little fun," he said, taking her arm.

"Please, Caleb. I know what I saw," she said, releasing herself from his grip.

"What you saw was a girl talking to me, that's it."

"Oh that's it? I have to go."

"Come on, sweetie, look. You know I love you. Please don't go. We're just getting started."

"Yeah, you looked like you were just getting started. Now if you don't mind," she said. She tried to walk away again.

"Honey, it's not what it looked like."

"Well, why don't you tell me what it's like then because I'd really like to know!"

"She's Joe's girlfriend and was at the shoot when Amber was there. She was imitating the way Amber was moving in front of the camera after you left and was telling me all the raunchy things she overheard her saying to him."

"What?"

"Yes, that's exactly who she is. Her name is Laura and she's quite nice and I'd love for you to meet her. She's actually a wedding planner."

"Oh."

"Collette, if this is going to work you are going to have to trust me. I'm around women all the time. It's doesn't mean that I am not thinking of you or am going to act on it or anything. You're the only person I want to be with. I love you, C. You know that."

"I'm sorry, Caleb. I, I— ," she said blushing.

"It's fine. Just know that I love you and wouldn't do that to you. Now will you come back and join the party? They were all talking about what a good model you were and the photographer wants to use you for more stuff."

"He does?"

"Yes, of course. I guess you've found your next gig."

"I suppose I could at least talk to him about it," she said, hugging him tightly.

"And by the way."

"Yeah?"

"You're blushing again," he teased her.

"See what you do to me?"

Julien had been in Roberto's room discussing their plan over the last few hours. Having worked as the morning concierge, Julien's afternoon and evening had been devoted to fine tuning their strategy. Their next order of business was to head to the lobby bar to have a quick bite before going into the city. They knew they should sit down and speak to Caleb in person and they needed to talk about just how they were going to do that. Upon entering the bar, Julien asked the bartender about the large party that was in back and who was hosting it, for he hadn't seen a special booking on the schedule. He was shocked to learn that he had just missed *the* Caleb Christopher. Apparently he had a photo shoot on the roof and had a little impromptu party. The bartender explained that the girl he was with was really cute and they left with the photographer and his own girlfriend. He heard somebody say they were going to dinner somewhere in the city. Real nice folks. Big tippers too.

Instead of going out to dinner, they instead went to Joe and Laura's large West Village loft and ordered Thai and had a few beers. Joe showed Collette some tear sheets of images he wanted to try with her—they weren't that exciting compared to Caleb's shoot, but she would be well-paid and it would be relatively painless. His agency had been harping on him to increase his body of work to include more black models and Collette fit the bill.

"You're perfect for it, Collette, and I'm glad you can model for me," he said. He put away the images in his desk drawer.

"Thank you, Joe. I'm sure it will be fun and I'm looking forward to it."

She still wasn't totally comfortable with idea of being a model, but knew she could use the extra money for when she quit her job. She'd been thinking more and more about signing up for a writing class or two and the extra money would come in handy.

"Look guys, we have something to tell you. I mean if you're going to be shooting Collette and spending time with us, you may as well know."

"Well don't keep us hanging! What? What?" Laura begged as Joe and Collette joined them on the couch.

"We're engaged."

"Who's engaged?" Laura asked, confused.

"Me and Caleb," Collette said as she sat next to Caleb on the couch and took his hand.

"You're kidding! Oh my God! Congratulations!" They took turns hugging them.

"Thank you!" Caleb said.

"Do you need a planner? Laura is the best," Joe said.

"Stop, honey. But seriously if you guys do, I'd love to work with you," she said warmly.

"Thanks, but we haven't talked about anything yet but I'll be sure to let you know if I need your help."

"Let's see the ring," Laura said grabbing Collette's hand. "Where is it?"

"Actually, we don't have one yet, but I'm working on it." Laura found it difficult to hide her dismay.

"Oh, okay. I know a guy if you're looking for a deal. Not that you need a 'deal' or anything."

"It's okay Laura," Collette reassured her. "Things have just been so busy that we haven't had time to go get one yet, but we will."

"Alright, Laura let's let it go. How about a celebratory drink, eh?" Joe said, heading to the kitchen. "I don't have any champagne, but I do have a nice bottle of Chardonnay."

"Works for us," Caleb said. He joined him in the kitchen to carry the glasses.

"It really is okay," Collette whispered to Laura on the couch. "I'm not a big 'ring' type of person anyway."

***

The next day Caleb and Katherine flew to LA for a press junket to promote his film *Midnight Moon*. The Wanda episode was scheduled to air later in the week to coincide with the rest of the press. While in LA, he had dinner with Trey to discuss upcoming principal photography that was starting soon, and he also met with his lawyer, Richard, about the Roberto nonsense.

Although Roberto had not called Caleb back, Caleb didn't want this headache any longer. Richard decided the best thing to do would be to issue a lawsuit citing breach of contract if he chose to follow through with taping *Real Runway*. Most times, the threat of a lawsuit was all it took to make an issue like this go away, he reassured Caleb. Because Katherine had no luck locating Roberto when she contacted Victor, the problem would be finding him to serve him, Caleb worried. Richard assured him that they would find him and not to worry. He already had his photo from *Page Six* that Katherine sent over. His team was on it.

The junket was the next day starting at 8 a.m. at the Beverly Hills Hotel. The lobby was overcrowded with journalists from all over the world and Caleb wondered if Spencer would be there. This would not be the right venue to have a talk with him about Collette, but fortunately for him, Katherine told Caleb he would be doing his press from London, as his shooting schedule was too tight on his new project for him to travel to Los Angeles. Caleb was grateful for that.

"So, Mr. Christopher," a buxom journalist started.

"Please, call me Caleb." He sat uncomfortably under the hot lights. Although he knew doing press was vital for the success of the film, he had always found it annoying.

"Caleb." She smiled. "Did you enjoy working on *Midnight Moon*?"

"Yes, it was fine and the cast and crew were great. A real pleasure."

"What about your character? Tell us about him," she asked, with all the seriousness she could muster.

"Um, well, let's see. My character has to deal with his feelings for his best friend's girl. He basically has to figure out if he likes her for her, or if he likes her simply because his best friend has her," he said, shifting in his chair.

"I see. Now, what about you? Ever been involved in anything like that yourself?" she asked, suddenly changing course.

"I don't want to talk about my personal life, I'd rather just stick to the film if you don't mind."

"Hmmmm.... something tells me that's a yes, Caleb!" she joked. He blankly looked at her with no response for a full minute.

"Can we get back to the film please?" he asked.

"In a sec. First tell us if you're seeing anyone special these days."

"Excuse me?"

"I'm sure all your fans out there would like to know if you are seeing anyone," she said.

"Who I am seeing is private. Now if you don't mind," he tried again.

"You're a tough one to crack Caleb Christopher!" she said, slapping her thigh.

"What's your name again?"

"Sheila."

"Okay, Sheila. Here's a scoop for you," he said, addressing the camera. "I am stepping down from my Caleb Christopher clothing line. I would like to thank everyone who supported it, but I am going to focus solely on my acting career because designing was not for me. I don't know anything about fashion, and had someone designing it and doing all the work, which I probably should not have done, ethically speaking, but I did and it was wrong. So now, in realizing this, I am putting it all behind me and am going to devote my time and efforts 100% to becoming a better actor. I would also like to take this opportunity to thank Trey Xu for casting me as the lead in his new film. I am excited for this chance to grow as an actor and I did not want any distractions preventing me from being the best actor I could be. Thank you again for supporting my line, but in good faith and trust I just could not continue it," he said with a great sense of relief.

Sheila sat there stunned and was unable to ask any follow-up questions because Caleb calmly removed the microphone from his lapel and walked off the set. She was left stumbling for words.

"Caleb, what was that? I didn't think you were going to announce it until the end of the day," Katherine asked, following him outside.

"She wanted a scoop so I gave her one. I hate doing that shit anyway," he said, stepping on to the beautifully manicured front lawn.

"Where are you going? There are still other journalists to meet," she said, as he gave the valet his ticket for his car.

"I'll be back, Katherine, don't worry. Just tell them I needed a break."

"Alright. Are you okay? I mean how do you feel?" she asked. He always had a soft spot for Katherine's maternal side.

"I'm fine, thank you. Honestly, I didn't think I was going to say that either, but something about her just irritated the hell out of me and it was obvious she wasn't interested in talking about my film, so I just thought 'fuck it' and went with the flow," he said. He gave the valet a $20 bill. "Katherine, don't worry I will be back in an hour."

"Okay, Caleb. Let me know if you need anything."

"I'll be fine, thanks," he said, as he got into his car and sped down the long driveway, disappearing into the streets.

"Hi, I'm here to see Sean Donovan," Caleb said to the young receptionist in the lobby of his agent's office.

"OMG, it's really you. Caleb Christopher. In the flesh. I just started and you're the first star I've seen," the pretty girl said.

"I'm sure you'll like working here. Is Sean in?

"Oh, yes. Sorry. I'll just call him now. Please have a seat," she said. Caleb sat on the chocolate brown leather couch in the expansive lobby. The agency represented the hottest actors and directors and it looked like the agents' fees went directly into expensively furnishing the office. After a seven-minute wait during which time he restlessly flipped through *The Hollywood Reporter* and *Variety*, Sean's model-like assistant retrieved him from the lobby.

"Sorry to have kept you waiting, Mr. Christopher, but Sean was finishing up a conference call," she said.

"No worries at all. I'm sorry to just drop in like this especially on a Saturday, but I was in the neighborhood. I'm just glad you guys are in today," he said. They walked up the contemporary staircase, her Manolos echoing in the large space.

"Are you kidding? It's 24/7 here. Can I get you something to drink?" she asked, as she showed him to Sean's office.

"Maybe just some water."

"Of course. I'll be right back." She smiled as she walked in her tight skirt down the hall.

"Now that is some ass! Dude, what are you doing here? Sean asked, greeting his star client.

"I was just in the neighborhood and wanted to drop by."

"What's up dude? You excited about Trey's film? You are going to kick ass, man."

"Yeah I am," he said. The assistant handed him a sleek VOS water bottle and glass. "Thank you," he said.

"My pleasure." She winked as she left the large room that overlooked Wilshire Boulevard.

"I think she likes you. My buddy's already been there, but if you're interested I could send her over later."

"What, are you a pimp now? Jesus, man."

"Alright man, calm down. Just looking out for you like before, that's all."

"Okay, thanks, I guess. But things are different now. That's what I came by to tell you."

"Who'd you get pregnant? Not that Amber girl you were hittin'?"

"God no, please Sean. Give me some credit," he said laughing. He shivered at the thought of Amber. "I came by to tell you two things. Number one, I'm engaged, and number two, I quit the fashion line." He took a big gulp of water.

"What the hell are you talking about?" He rose from behind his desk, the bright sun backlighting him.

"What do you mean what I am talking about? I said I'm engaged and I quit the line."

"Alright, Caleb," he said, calming himself down. He sat on the edge of his desk, his face flushed to a bright shade of crimson. "Who are you engaged to and why the fuck did you quit the line? You know how long it took to find that guy?"

"Just calm down, okay. I know what I'm doing. I quit the line because the guy was threatening to do a show and—"

"He can't do that, that's breach of contract!"

"Didn't seem to matter to him. I just really didn't want to deal with it anymore man, it's a pain in the ass. I'd rather focus on my acting anyway.

"Your *acting*?" He snickered.

"What's wrong with my acting?"

"If all you like are romantic comedies, nothing. But dude, I was trying to help you out! And you just up and quit?"

"Sean, look. I appreciate everything you did, I really do. It obviously made us some money," he said, looking around the room. "But honestly, it was wearing me down and I just couldn't do it anymore. And contrary to what you might think, I am interested in more than romantic comedies and I don't want to fuck up Trey's movie with this design shit. I don't need any distractions right now."

"Jesus, Caleb you're killing me," he said. Sean returned to his desk chair. "I'm gonna need some oxygen or something."

"You're like 40 years old, Sean. Who's acting now, for crying out loud," he said. They both laughed.

"I guess so. Tell me who this piece of ass is you're marrying. Do you know what this is going to do for your image as an available bachelor? I mean, how am I supposed to sell that?"

"Please don't refer to Collette that way."

"Collette? Your assistant? You sly dog. I would have hit it too if I could have," he said, tossing a Nerf basketball into its basket.

"Look, don't be an asshole, alright? I just thought you should know but we're keeping it secret, okay? So don't go blabbing to anyone."

"Alright, whatever you want. I just never figured you two together."

"It just kind of happened, but it's all good."

"Alright, come here," he said, hugging his client.

"Listen, the least I can do is throw you a bachelor party tonight."

"Did you not just hear me? I don't want it getting out. We are trying to keep it quiet."

"Just something small. I insist. Just us and a few guys from the office. We'll do something at my house around nine, okay?"

"Just a dinner or something. But no strippers. Collette would kill me."

"Hey, what she don't know won't hurt her, right?"

"Sean—"

"Alright, alright, no strippers," he assured him. "Janice," he yelled to his assistant.

"Yes, Sean." She appeared at the door with a headset on.

"Get the crew together from here and order dinner and drinks for my house tonight at 9. We're throwing Caleb a little party."

"Oh, what's the occasion?" she asked Caleb while picking up his empty water bottle and glass.

"Don't you worry about that, Janice. Just take care of it," he said closing the door behind her.

"You have to be so rude, man?"

"*I'm* rude? She's the one who turned this down," he said, forming a circle with his hands around his crotch thrusting like a 12-year-old boy.

"Gee, I can't imagine why. Alright I have to go. I'll see you tonight."

"Alright dude. Don't be late," he said. Caleb walked out of the office and back down to the lobby.

"Janice?" Sean asked, after Caleb left.

"Yes?" she asked reappearing in the doorway.

"Make sure you order up those girls like you did for James's bachelor party last week.

"Oh, he's engaged, that's wonderful," she said.

"Yeah, we'll see for how long though."

27

"Collette, baby, I did it!" Caleb said on his lunch break from the junket in a penthouse suite. He ate a club sandwich and absently watched a talk show. Reluctantly, he returned to the hotel to complete his obligations, although he had no other big scoops to the chagrin of the subsequent reporters.

"Did what?" Collette replied from her living room where she had been cleaning out her drawer. She came across Spencer's postcard along with admission packets from the University of Colorado, NYU, and Columbia University. Knowing that she would be stepping down as Caleb's assistant sometime soon, she wanted to start getting serious about her writing.

"I quit the line. I gave my little speech during the first interview I had today."

"No way!" she said, falling onto the couch.

"Yes, babe, and it felt great. I wish you could have been there. I think I scared Katherine a bit, but oh well."

"Oh, that's awesome honey. I'm so proud of you."

"I couldn't have done it without you. You must know that."

"Well, it was you who did it."

"Listen, can I call you later? I have to finish my lunch and head back downstairs."

"Sure. What are you up to later? I think I'm having dinner with Lou."

"Sean's having a dinner or something for me at his place later."

"Or something, huh? You watch out for that one. He's trouble."

"Yeah, I know. I already told him no to the strippers."

"I'm just kidding. You go have fun and I'll call you later."

* * *

"Roberto Carnellos?" A friendly man wearing a denim jacket approached Roberto outside of the Columbus Avenue office of *Real Runway*.

"Yes?"

"You've been served. Have a good day," the man said quickly vanishing into the crowded streets.

"Served? What is this?" He panicked as he ripped open the letter. The words "breach of contract" and "cease and desist" sprang from the page and made him nauseous.

"Let me see this," Julien said, taking it from his sweaty hand. "Oh dear. He's suing you if you go through with this. I don't believe it."

"See I told you! Victor thought I was lying, but I knew Caleb was upset. What am I going to do?"

"Let's just go in and do like we planned. Let's just talk to the guy and tell him you can't do the show."

Julien let Roberto lean on him as they entered the producer's office of *Real Runway*. The producer watched the nightly entertainment news while going over some paperwork.

"Hello, Arnie. This is my friend Julien," Roberto said nervously to the short, bald man, who had something stuck between his teeth and sauce stained his shirt.

"Pleased to meet you Julien. Take a seat." He gestured to the chairs in front of his desk. On the screen Sheila, an entertainment reporter, was enthusiastically telling the audience to come right back because she had the inside scoop on Caleb Christopher. Roberto and Julien both looked at each other before staring at the television set.

"What's wrong with you guys? You both look like you've seen a ghost."

"Uh. Well, I came to talk to you about doing the show," Roberto began.

"Yeah, it should be a good one. You and Jake should really bring in the ratings we are looking for."

"Well, you see, about that. I don't think I can do it."

"What do you mean you can't do it? Does Victor know you're here? The show starts taping in two days for chrissakes. What kind of stunt is this?"

"I'm sorry sir but—"

"Don't sorry me, you fucking prick! I can't replace you now, it's too late!"

"The thing is, Arnie, if I may—" Julien interrupted.

"Who are you again?"

"Julien, Roberto's friend. I'm just here for support. Here's the thing: Victor is making him do this and he doesn't want to and—"

"I don't give a shit about that," he angrily replied. "You have any idea how hard it is to cast a show like this?"

"Sir, I can't even imagine, but please listen—"

"And now, back to my interview with Caleb Christopher," Sheila was saying on the TV screen which stopped Julien mid-sentence as they all looked on.

"… … .I don't know anything about fashion, and had someone designing it and doing all the work, which I probably should not have done, ethically speaking, but I did and it was wrong. So now, in realizing this, I am putting it all behind me and am going to 100% devote my time and efforts to becoming a better actor. I would also like to take this opportunity to thank Trey Xu for casting me as the lead in his new film… … ." Caleb continued as Roberto and Julien's jaws dropped to the floor.

"Why the hell are we watching this for? Who gives a shit about Caleb Christopher?"

"SSSHHHHH!" Roberto silenced him.

"… … *I am excited for this chance to grow as an actor and I did not want any distractions preventing me from being the best actor I could be. Thank you again for supporting my line, but in good faith and trust I just could not continue it,*" Caleb finished before walking off the screen.

"Look, I'm starting to get real mad here. Now why are you coming to me with this?" Arnie said to Roberto whose eyes were welling up.

"This whole thing is horrible! I can't do it and now I am going to be sued!"

"What the hell are you talking about? You guys better start making some sense. I don't have time for this bullshit."

"Arnie, we're sorry for all of this, but basically Roberto was designing Caleb Christopher's line, or at least he thought Victor was until he told him Jake was doing it."

"What? Jake? What?"

"Yes, Jake. He's trying to force Roberto to do this show so he can take all his money even though he never let him keep his own earnings anyway. Victor told him to tell Caleb he was going to expose him if he didn't let him out of his contract. Now thanks to the program we all know that Caleb just quit the line. Right before we came in Roberto got served by Caleb's lawyers."

"Holy shit. Let me see that," Arnie said as Roberto handed the papers over. He turned off the television so he could concentrate. "Jesus. Victor never said nothing like this to me. He didn't mention none of this crap. I don't want to deal with all this."

"You especially won't want to deal with it if we are forced to take this to the press," he said, handing over a manila envelope to Arnie. "It's a copy. I have the original at home." Arnie looked inside the envelope.

"Where'd you get this? You piece of shit!" Arnie said. The green matter dislodged itself from his teeth and landed on the wall across the room.

"I was with Victor before Roberto and sometimes he had me secretly videotape him when he felt like being with other people. He said it was like his own little porn library. That's just a still photo I made from the camera but I have the DVD and other still photos at home. You see, that piece of shit Victor kicked me out of his house and replaced me with Roberto— "

"And now you're just a bitter queen? Is that it?"

"No, that is not it. Please just listen."

"This is bullshit!" Arnie said, ripping up the photo of him performing fellatio on Victor, and tossing it into the trash.

"As I was saying, I was angry at Victor and Roberto for so long that I let it eat away at me and it almost ruined me. By chance, I ran into Roberto the other day and he told me what happened and I was so disgusted by what Victor had done and was trying to do, that I knew I could help him."

"So you want out of the show, fine. Just get out!" he said, angrily rising to his feet.

"Not so fast. Obviously you were willing to go along with what Victor wanted and now Roberto has nothing. Hopefully, we can get Caleb's lawyers to drop the suit once we tell them everything, and *show* them everything if we have to," he said raising his brows at Arnie, prompting him to return to his seat. "Roberto has no money, no career, and now that he won't be winning your show, at least against Jake, he has nothing in his immediate future."

"What the fuck do you want me to do about it?"

"We want you to get on the phone and tell Victor that there has been a change of plans. Instead of Roberto being on the show and Jake winning, both Roberto and I will be contestants and Jake is off. Roberto will win first place and I will come in second."

"What? You can't just come in here and tell me to do that. Are you outta your mind?"

"It's a copy, remember," he said nodding toward the wastebasket. "I'm sure Sheila would love another scoop.

TAKE II

<u>28</u>

"Sean, I'm on my way to your place. Do you need me to pick anything up?" Caleb asked as he drove up Sunset Boulevard on a beautiful LA night.

"Don't be silly. You don't need to bring anything. I'll see you soon," replied Sean from his 500 square-foot granite kitchen. His 9,000 square-foot home was nestled on a side street off Beverly Drive in Coldwater Canyon. There was nothing subtle about the place. Fenced in behind a large iron gate and ten-foot high bushes, it was the ultimate bachelor pad. The white marble floors made the space uninviting and cold, and the gaudy Grecian statues both inside and outside the house made it seem outdated and past its prime. A long, dramatic staircase led to the master bedroom upstairs where at the push of a button a large theater screen would emerge from the floor. There were flat screen televisions in his large walk-in closet and also in the bathroom, lest he miss a moment of dialogue from walking across the room into another area. After hanging up from Caleb, he barked orders at his staff that the guest of honor would be arriving any minute. He demanded them to get out but not before they retrieved the other guests and strippers from downstairs—where they had been playing pool and partying for the last hour.

***

Enjoying a quiet moment before her dinner out with Lou, Collette enjoyed a cup of tea while reviewing the writing brochures. She logged onto the website of the University of Colorado at Boulder and fantasized about the nice change of pace it would be for a while. To be able to rent a cute apartment in the foothills of Boulder and focus on her writing was something that she had been dreaming about for a few years now. It would be an added benefit that her parents would be nearby in Denver so she could see them more. But knowing that was just what it was—a fantasy—she looked more closely at the programs in New York. She would have to start the application process soon if she was serious about getting in. Registering for the GRE and getting recommendation letters from former professors would be a pain, but she would have to do it. At the moment, those issues could wait; she needed to get ready for dinner and first had to think about her photo shoot tomorrow with Joe. She hoped it wouldn't take too long because she needed to meet Trey Xu's assistant in the afternoon to get the final shooting schedule from him. She'd suggested he just email it to her, but the assistant thought it would be nice to meet since they would be working together soon for the next ten weeks. And then of course she needed to begin packing for her upcoming trip with her parents. She was flying out on Caleb's third day of shooting and she hoped he'd be alright for a few days without her.

"I'm downstairs," Lou said from the buzzer.

"Okay, be right down." Collette quickly ran into the bedroom and changed her jeans and shirt, threw on some hoop hearings, and put on a bit of lip gloss. She was ready for a much needed night on the town with her best friend.

"So, when are you going to get the ring?" Lou asked.

"Oh, we'll get to it," she said flagging a cab for them.

"Don't sound so excited Collette."

"Don't get me wrong, it's not that. It's just that we're trying to keep it quiet and will more than likely do something really small. If I start wearing around this big 'thing' right now it will do nothing but draw attention." They hopped in to a taxi. "Great Jones and Lafayette Street, please," she said to the cabbie.

"I guess I can understand that. Are you excited though?"

"Yeah, I am. I'm looking forward to being married to him but not necessarily all the stuff it takes to plan it. I haven't asked him yet, but seriously, I just want to go to the courthouse or something."

"Well there's something to be said for a small, simple wedding."

"I think so. Working for Caleb can be such a production sometimes. Not him himself, but everything around him, know what I mean? And I just want for the wedding to be as far away from that as possible."

"Got it. So you looking forward to your trip with your parents? Is that going to be fun at all?"

"My mom is a riot, so yes, it will be alright. It will be nice to get away."

"You better hope you don't run into Spencer. You are going to London after all, but I guess that would give you an opportunity to break up with him," Lou joked.

"Ha ha. Very funny. London's a big town, so I'm not worried. Besides I am sure he will be in Rome by the time we get there anyway."

***

The party started as soon as Caleb walked in the door. Sean greeted him with a welcome shot of Patron a Corona, and a line of coke, the last of which Caleb politely declined. He watched as Sean and his friends passed around a mirror with the white powder.

"Come on buddy, make yourself at home. Yee haw!" he said, directing him into a living room that resembled a nightclub with table service. There was a full bar and scantily clad women carrying serving trays and taking everyone's order.

"Sean, I told you I didn't want any strippers here."

"They're not strippers, man. Haven't you ever heard of exotic dancers? Mali, come over here a sec," he said to an incredibly thin brunette with almond-shaped eyes and hot pink lipstick.

"Yes, what would you like?" she purred to him.

"Tell our guest here that you're not a stripper."

"Oh no, I'm dancer. I never take it all off like strippers do—unless you want me to ..." she said, as she toyed with the top button on her see-through white shirt tied underneath her breasts. She wore a red lace bra that showcased her large nipples.

"See, what'd I tell you," Sean said addressing Caleb. "Now why don't you go fetch us a coupla martinis," he said, slapping her on her bikini-bottomed behind.

"Okay, be right back!" she said scampering off.

"Sean, what is this?" Caleb asked. He pointed out the other four women who where each cozied up with the remaining four guys. The music was thumping and one of the girls hopped on a table and rolled around like a dog in heat.

"Caleb. Dude, just relax. Just a few guys letting off some steam," he said. Caleb watched as one of the guys did a line of coke off a girl's stomach. "They're harmless alright?" he said looking into his eyes. "Okay buddy?"

"Alright Sean, but I have to take off after dinner.

"Will you just relax? It's your bachelor party. What are you worried about anyway? You know us all. We're all friends here, you know that."

"Yeah...."

"Yeah, then just enjoy your own party. You're not married yet. Just have some fun."

"Sean!"

"I didn't mean it like that; I just want you to enjoy yourself. You've had a long day. You can go upstairs and call Collette any time you feel like you need to. But seeing as how she is 3,000 miles away I just say have some fun! Woo! Let's go crazy! You go girl!" he said walking away from Caleb, leaving him with Mali and his drink as he joined the table dancer in her writhing.

"Don't worry. I don't bite," Mali said. She looked up at him with wide eyes. "Unless you want me to, that is." She giggled.

"Mali, get over here and show this girl how to move." Sean beckoned to her. The other guys took liberties and swatted her behind as she joined Sean and the other girl on the table. "That's what I'm talking about!" Sean said as he got up and gently pushed together the heads of the two girls as he watched their lips lock in a passionate kiss.

"Caleb! What are you doing over there? Get over here." one of the other guys called. Caleb slowly walked over and was met with cheers of Sean and the others. One of the guys took a long swig directly from a tequila bottle and passed it around amongst them. Caleb took a smaller swig and passed it on to Sean, who, instead of drinking from it, gave it to one of the girls and had her drink it before using his tongue to lick the moisture from her lips.

"Holy shit, you guys are nuts," Caleb said, relaxing a bit.

"Here babe, see if Michael wants some," Sean said to Pamela, a petite blond with extra large boobs.

"Hey, you thirsty?" she asked as she sauntered up to Michael while drinking from the bottle. He wasted no time lurching his tongue down her throat in search of the harsh liquid.

"Who needs a lime?" Brandi asked before placing the fruit between her breasts held by the underwire of her bra, as Sean and Michael fought for it. This tussle landed them on the floor with her giggling beneath them as they both pawed at her for it.

"Here let me help." Pamela leaped onto the floor and offered to help. "Step back boys," she said as she pushed them out of the way and untied Brandi's shirt. Her florescent pink bra bore holes where her nipples were. She squirted the limejuice on each of her exposed nipples and licked each one. "There, the lime is ready for you now," she said, getting up to go to the bar to make more drinks.

Caleb could not believe that this was all happening. It was impossible for him to look away especially having done another tequila shot followed by a martini that suddenly appeared in his hand. He was much more relaxed than he was 30 minutes ago, when he arrived. Walking into the kitchen, he looked for signs of dinner and only saw a small plate of finger food left out with a bag of tortilla chips.

"Hey, I thought you said we'd be eating dinner, Sean," Caleb said when he walked back into the room. The music was louder and someone had dimmed the lights and drawn the shades.

"Dude! Seriously? Who the fuck needs dinner when you got all this?" he asked. The other guys cheered as they each fondled a girl. The girls didn't seem to mind—they just giggled and tossed their heads back occasionally.

"Oh come on, Caleb, we're just having some fun," Mali said, taking him by the hand. "We can order some takeout if you want. Later…" she said, toying with him. "Here have another drink."

"Alright, but then I have to get going." He took a seat in a large, comfortable chair. Mali knelt down and removed his shoes and began rubbing his feet. "Ahhh, that feels good," he said, as he closed his eyes.

"See, we just want to make you feel good. It's your party so just relax," she said as she moved her hand up his pant leg, startling him.

"Whoa there, Mali."

"I'm sorry Caleb. Was I bad? You can punish me." She stood in front of him and bent over and to pick up a near-empty vodka bottle. She dumped the rest down her throat.

"Easy, girl," he said, allowing himself a smile.

"Here, I saved some for you." She gave him the last swallow of the Ketel One.

"Looks like somebody's relaxing now," Michael said from across the room. He was now shirtless and Pamela stood in front of him dancing.

"This is fucking nuts. Sean, I guess you do know how to throw a party," Caleb said ignoring his growling stomach. He had not eaten since his club sandwich at lunch, causing the alcohol to go down faster and smoother than he would have anticipated. Mali was again there with another martini, which he tossed down in two gulps.

"Shit, I'm hungry. Mali, dear, would you mind bringing something to eat in here?" Caleb asked.

"My pleasure. Whatever. You. Want," she said, touching his chin with each slurred word. She returned with the plate of eggrolls that were on the counter.

"Thank you so very much," he slurred back, smiling widely. Caleb inhaled the six small cold eggrolls in five minutes and drank another beer to wash them down.

"Hey watch this buddy." Sean said to Caleb. "Brandi, hit that button."

"You got it, babe." She pushed a small button on the wall. A disco ball emerged from the ceiling and a pole emerged from the floor.

"Dude, no fucking way!" Caleb said. The other guys sang their approval.

"Yay!" the girls enthused. They all started swirling around the pole as the guys hooted and cheered them on. The upbeat throbbing club music was very loud and the room had gone nearly pitch black, save for the strobe lights from the disco ball. Caleb could have sworn he saw at least one of the guys with his hands in his pants, but he couldn't be sure. Casey, one of the shyer guys, poured tequila over Brandi's now exposed breast and Ryan, also generally shy, gently pushed Mali's head into her breast to lick it off, which she seemed to do with delight. While Mali was enjoying Brandi's breast, Candy, the fourth girl, placed a chair directly in front of Todd, the fourth guy, and stood on it and shook her ass directly into his face. A moment later, Sean pulled up another chair in front of the pole and directed Caleb to sit there.

"Dude, this is awesome," Michael said, as Caleb sat down. Mali placed another drink in his hand which he downed swiftly as the four women circled him and removed their bras.

"Isn't this fun, Caleb?" Brandi cooed as she ran her fingers through his hair.

"Uh huh." It was all he could muster.

Mali placed one of his hands on her breast and leaned over and whispered, "The real thing and all yours whenever you want em."

***

Collette could not believe how crowded the Great Jones Café was, but since it was one of her favorite spots in the city, she and Lou decided to endure the wait. In the meantime, they found a tiny spot behind the bar in which to stand. They couldn't see anything.

"Excuse you, asshole!" Collette heard a familiar voice say.

"Sorry, ma'am, I didn't mean—" said a man.

"Ma'am? Do I look like a 'ma'am' to you? You fucking jerk." the girl said in a voice Collette recognized as Amber.

"I was just trying to get my drink, I said I was sorry. No need to be such a bitch."

"Oh, *I'm* being a bitch? You can just kiss my ass!" Amber said.

"What's going on here?" a female bartender asked.

"This doofus almost knocked me down, that's what's going on." Amber snapped at the tattooed, multi-pierced bartender.

"Well, this is Josh, one of our regulars and I'm sure he didn't mean it, so just cool it will you," she said, turning to fix a drink for another customer.

"You'd just better watch it. I'm Caleb Christopher's *girlfriend* and I will have your little dick on a stick if you aren't careful," she threatened the man.

"Yo, Robbie," the bartender yelled to the host at the door.

"Yo?" the muscular black man yelled back.

"Get this fucking skinny ass bitch outta here before I jump over this bar and beat the shit out of her myself," the bartender said.

"Hey, come on now, get your hands off me!" Amber yelled to Robbie.

"You heard her. Get your ass outta here. And don't come back either," he said, pushing her out the door.

"But I'm waiting for my friends to join me ... "

"Well you ain't comin' back up in here, so step!"

Collette and Lou just stared at each other in disbelief before bursting into laughter. The bartender turned up the already loud hip-hop music to celebrate Amber's departure from the bar.

"What the fuck was that?" Lou asked Collette.

"I don't know, but obviously she doesn't know she's not dating Caleb anymore and that he's mine," she said waving her ringless hand in Lou's face, before realizing she was not wearing a ring, which sent them both into a fit of laughter. They eventually were seated and an hour later finished up their jalapeño cornbread and seafood jambalaya—specialties of the house.

"You ladies want another round?" the waiter asked.

"Nah, we're all set, thanks." Collette replied.

The seven drinks they had between them were enough. They stumbled out of the bar laughing and, not paying attention to who was around them.

"Watch it, will you?" A cold voice said to Lou as she nearly tripped over the woman.

"Amber?" Collette said looking up.

"It's you! You're the bitch who ruined my life!"

"What?" Lou asked.

"Don't mind her, Lou. She's just jealous because Caleb kicked her sorry ass out of his house. Let's go," Collette said as she locked her arm in Lou's and started walking away. Just then she was violently pulled back by the hair.

"Ouch!" Collette said, as she fell backwards onto to the ground.

"Get off her, you crazy bitch!" Lou said. "Help! Help! Somebody help!" Lou yelled as Robbie was walking outside for a smoke. He pulled Amber off Collette who had gotten away unscathed, save for a small scratch on her forearm. "Are you ok?" Lou knelt down by Collette.

"Yeah, I'm ok. What the fuck is wrong with you? Are you fucking crazy? Collette asked as she approached Amber.

"Go ahead knock her ass out. Ain't nobody gotta know," Robbie said as he held a squirming Amber tightly.

"Thanks, man, but she ain't worth it. Her skanky whore ass is jealous because *I* am Caleb Christopher's woman. He threw her trick ass out his house and she's still bitter," Collette said directly into Amber's twitching face.

"Awww shit. She told your ass!" Robbie laughed.

"Come C, let's go. We got better things to do," Lou said, reaching for her friend.

"Yeah you better go. His ass is mine. And don't you forget it," Amber said, as Robbie kneed her in the back of her leg, causing it to buckle.

"Ouch! Asshole."

"Say somethin' else. I dare you," Robbie said.

"Taxi!" Lou screamed for a cab. They all seemed to be taken but she was determined to get one.

"I said, go BITCH. Your ass is mine if I see you again." Amber said. At this Robbie kneed her so hard she fell face first onto the ground.

"I got you," Robbie said to Collette. "Don't even worry about this."

"No, I got *this*," Collette said. She walked over to Amber and kicked her in the stomach and spit on her.

"Heeey, Ms. Thang handled her business! I ain't mad at cha," Robbie said pleased.

"You fucking bitch," Amber murmured from the ground.

"What did you say? Don't make me finish what she started," he said, as he waved to Collette and Lou as they got into a cab.

"Nothing."

"That's what I thought," he said before reentering the restaurant. Amber was left hugging the cold cement.

"Where to, ladies?" the cabbie said.

"Gansevoort and Greenwich please," Lou said, directing the driver to her apartment. "C, are you ok?" She held Collette who cried in her arms. "Oh honey, don't cry, it's okay."

"No, it's not Lou. Is this what I am going to be marrying? He never did tell me exactly what he said to her, so maybe they didn't really break up."

"Oh now, don't say that. You know he did break up with her, Collette. She's just crazy. That's all. We'll call him when we get home if it will make you feel better," she said.

"But seriously, Lou, if he broke up with her why hasn't she gone away? I don't want to be dealing with this."

"And you won't be, honey. Trust me, she's just a bad apple that couldn't take a hint and leave. You know Caleb loves you, so I wouldn't even worry about it."

"Maybe you're right."

"I know I'm right, C. He loves you and that's all that matters."

"He just needs to take care of his business before we get married or go any further. I don't need this, ya know?"

"I know," she said handing her a Kleenex. "It's up on the left there," Lou directed the cabbie. "Come on. Let's go get a glass of wine and then to my place call him." She paid the driver.

"Okay."

"But you got her good though. I was very impressed!" she said, making Collette smile. "Come on. Try to forget about her."

***

In the darkness all Caleb saw was Michael grinding on top of one of the girls—he couldn't tell which one—and Sean passed out in the corner. Two of the other girls tickled

293

each other to the delight of Todd and Ryan, who were now in their underwear. Another girl was completely naked and giving Casey a lap dance. Caleb could barely see and stumbled out of the room to find a bathroom. The entire house was dark, save for a television that was on upstairs. Not knowing where any of the lights were, Caleb climbed up the stairs, leaning heavily against the wall until he was joined by Mali halfway up.

"Oh, I got it," he said, holding on to the wall for dear life. "Just trying to get to a bathroom."

"Let me help you." She laughed and was hardly able to walk.

"Let me help you both." Another girl appeared at the top of the stairs. The gorgeous blond with perfect features transpired out of thin air. "Give me your hand. I've been waiting for you," she said to Caleb. She pulled him up the remaining stairs before going back for Mali.

"What?" Caleb asked as the blond undressed him.

"Just relax honey. This is where the real party is," Becca the blond said.

"What are you?"

"Here honey, drink this. It's good for you," Becca said, handing him a clear liquid in a wine glass. "Don't worry, it's just Ketel One. Don't have any mixers up here though." Caleb drank and melted into the bed. "See, doesn't that feel better?"

"I need to piss," he said getting up.

"I think you're gonna need some help," Becca offered, as Mali undressed and made herself comfortable on top of the bed.

"Almost there," Becca said guiding him to the toilet where she held his cock from behind as he urinated. "Umm that's better, huh," she said, giving it a little squeeze.

"Uh huh," he mumbled as he felt his BlackBerry vibrate in his pants. "I gotta answer this." He reached for his phone as Becca took it out of his hands. In the darkness of the bathroom she accidentally pressed the answer button when she went to place it on the counter. Collette's voice was drowned out by the jazz Mali had put on while they were in the bathroom.

"It might be Col—" he started, as Becca led him back to the bed, laid him down, and pulled off his pants, quickly taking him in her mouth as he groaned loudly with pleasure. Mali then placed herself directly on his face and thrust herself atop his willing tongue as he held her ass. A few minutes later she and Becca lost themselves in each other giving him a performance that had always fulfilled their clients' fantasies. Each time he came closer to closing his eyes and passing out, one of them would lean over and stimulate him again. When they were finished, the girls tucked themselves into the bed on each side of Caleb. Soon, they all fell peacefully asleep.

<u>29</u>

"Collette! So great to finally meet you," said Nelson, Trey's assistant. He greeted her in front of the Whole Foods at Columbus Circle. At 9:30 a.m., it had been difficult for her to wake up on a Sunday after a restless night of sleep, but she knew Nelson had to catch a noon flight out of LaGuardia and had limited time to meet.

"Nelson, thanks for coming up here. I know you're staying downtown," she said over the traffic noise at the busy intersection.

"It's no bother. Here's a copy of the final script that Caleb wanted and, are you okay?" he asked as he looked into her red eyes. "My cousin had pink eye once, and it was no fun. Is that what you have?"

"Thanks, but I'm okay. I'm not sick," she said through a tight smile.

"Well, what's wrong then? Sit," he said, pulling out a chair for her at one of the café tables.

"Oh, it's nothing. I just didn't get enough sleep last night. Should have gone to bed," she said with forced effort.

"When will I learn?" She put the documents in her bag, avoiding eye contact.

"Oh, honey. I know this is not about sleep now is it? I know we just met, but we're going to be working together for a few months, so we might as well get to know each other," Nelson said, softly touching her hand.

"Nelson, I really appreciate it, but I'm fine. Really," she said.

"If you say so. But if you're still looking this way when I get back to town in a few days, then promise me you'll let me take you out to cheer you up. I know a great pastry shop in Alphabet City and I've been wanting to check out some of the boy bars in Chelsea," he said.

"It's a deal." She stood to go. "Have a safe flight and I'll see you on Tuesday," she said as she shook his hand.

"A handshake? Girl, you better give me a hug!" he said, embracing her tightly. "Honey, you're not okay, are you?" Collette felt her body release with tears.

"I'm sorry, look I have to go," she said. She put on her dark Ray Bans. "I'll see you soon."

"Okay, Collette. Go home and get some rest. Take care." Nelson kissed her on the cheek and watched her disappear down the escalator to the subway.

***

Sunday morning brought a headache unlike anything Caleb had felt in a very long time. His memory of last night was spotty, at best, but when he awoke at 7 a.m. to use the bathroom, he was surprised to find himself naked with two women next to him. A soft jazz station played on the radio and his underwear was sopping up a puddle of vodka on the nightstand. After throwing up in the bathroom toilet, he found his cell phone on the counter displaying ten missed calls and four text messages, all from Collette. He didn't know if he could explain his way out of this one. His body was covered in sweat as he quickly dressed. He left his underwear in the vodka puddle. That was the least of his worries.

"Caleb," Janice said. Two maids were quietly cleaning up the living room and kitchen. Janice was there to supervise.

"Janice! What are you doing here?" Caleb asked. He tucked in his shirt as he came down the stairs.

"I'm sorry to bother you, Caleb. I'm just here to clean up the mess and pay the bills," she said, indicating the cleaning crew and four envelopes bursting with cash with the names Pamela, Brandi, Becca, Mali, and Candy written on them.

"Oh. Where's Sean?"

"Probably still drunk somewhere. I just do what I'm told," she said.

"He makes you come to his house this early on a Sunday to do this?"

"Like I told you in the office, it's 24/7. Look, I know you have to go so I won't keep you. Do you need anything?"

"Just a new agent," he said, unable to believe the state he was in.

"Don't worry about anything okay? I am not going to say anything," she said. She raised her eyebrows and glanced toward upstairs. "Sean has these parties all the time so please don't worry."

"Please don't worry? I may have fucked someone last night and cheated on my fiancé but I was too blasted to really remember and you tell me not to worry?" he asked, moving closer to her.

"I, I…"

"All because Sean ordered these fucking whores when I told him not to. Do you realize what I have done! Christ, even if I didn't fuck them I sure as hell did something."

"I'm so sorry, Caleb," she said, looking at her feet. "He just said to get the girls again and I really need this job."

"You got the girls? He told you to order them after I explicitly told him not to?" he yelled.

"Shhhh, you're going to wake them up," she said.

"You think I give a fuck if I wake up these assholes?" he yelled louder, causing the maids to turn around and look.

"No."

"SEAN! SEAN! WAKE THE FUCK UP!" He ran through the house looking for him.

"Miss Janice?" one of the maids approached her.

"Not now, Lupe. Please."

"But Miss Janice …."

"SEAN!" Caleb yelled searching through the house. The house was silent save for the maids downstairs.

"Not now!" Janice raised her voice at the maid.

"But Mr. Sean is sleeping in there," she said pointing to the living room where they had been cleaning. "He is on the couch."

"Oh, thank you. I'm sorry Lupe."

"It's okay Miss Janice," Lupe said, returning to her methodical cleaning.

"Caleb, he's in there," Janice said pointing to the living room. Caleb's face was bright red as he lifted Sean by his collar and shook him violently.

"Hey, what the—" Sean mumbled and rubbed his crusty eyes. Caleb steadied himself and punched him with all his might.

"You're fired, your fucking asshole," Caleb spewed in his face.

"Wha—" Sean said, as he held his face.

"You heard me. I can't believe I trusted you. I told you I didn't want any fucking strippers, Sean! And you do this?" he said.

"I just wanted you to have some fun," he said.

"Your idea of fun has probably cost me the woman I love. After all these years this is what you do to me after everything I've done for you, huh? I'm finally happy and you do this."

"Come on, man. She's just a *broad,* man. Are you even serious about even marrying her? You told me you didn't get her a ring yet. You didn't do anything I wouldn't have done. You were just having some fun at your bachelor party."

"You do not refer to her that way," he yelled. "Her name is Collette and I love her and because of you I may have lost her."

"There wasn't a gun to your head Caleb, so just get over yourself. You got laid last night, big fucking deal. You should be thanking me."

"Thanking you?" Caleb asked incredulously.

"Nobody was forcing you to do anything. Besides, it looked like you were enjoying yourself, if you ask me," he said.

"I didn't ask you. Goodbye, Sean," he said, walking out of the room.

"Caleb, come on."

"I'm sorry," Janice said. He swiftly walked past her as he held his stomach, trying to contain his sickness.

"Whatever. Why don't you go tend to your pimp boss. You're no better than him," he said, slamming the door behind him. He threw up again on the front lawn and called Collette, but got her voicemail.

"C, I'm sorry I didn't answer when you called last night. I was at Sean's and fell asleep. Will you please call me? I'm sure you're upset with me and I don't blame you. Please call me. I love you," he said, as his voice cracked through every word.

30

"Collette, honey, please calm down. You don't know what happened. Just call him back," Lou said, as she tried to console her friend over brunch at a noisy café.

"I know what I heard, Lou," she replied. Her eyes were swollen red.

"No, what you think you heard was a grumble or something and some jazz music," she said, as Collette looked at her dubiously.

"I heard moaning and some girl's voice. That's what I heard."

"I know it looks bad, but—"

"Looks bad? He was at that sleazebag Sean's house, Lou! I don't trust that guy as far as I can throw him. There's no telling what was going on in there," she said, pushing aside the remainder of her eggs Benedict.

"You know Caleb wouldn't do anything like that to you, C. Don't you?"

"Well, how do you explain me hearing that through his phone?"

"I don't know, maybe someone else at the house had his phone?" she offered.

"What?"

"I don't know. I just know that Caleb loves you and you shouldn't jump to any conclusions until you talk to him. Isn't he coming back tonight any way?"

"Umm hmm."

"Just talk to him then. I promise you everything will be okay. In the meantime, why don't you call him back before his plane leaves?"

"I kinda don't feel like talking to him right now."

"Fair enough. Just make sure you talk to him tonight."

***

Caleb thought his head was going to burst on the way to the airport. LA being what it was, the sun shone brightly through the window of his car, irritating his headache even more. The 405 was jammed as usual and he felt grateful that the driver drove him in silence. Just as he was dozing off for a nap, his phone vibrated. He quickly answered the blocked number hoping that it was Collette.

"Hullo," he answered.

"Hi, Caleb. How are you? Are you going to make your flight?" Katherine asked from her home office in Pacific Palisades that overlooked the ocean.

"Oh, hi Katherine. I'm alright. On my way to the airport right now."

"So, I received an email from your lawyers about Robert Carnellos."

"Oh God, what did it say?"

"Actually, it wasn't so bad. Roberto left him a voicemail yesterday—get this—saying that even though Victor was the one who was *supposedly* doing your line, it was actually Victor's intern who had been doing it. Roberto was going to do the show and could you please drop the suit since it technically wasn't him or Victor anyway."

"What?"

"I know. It gets better. He also said he was bullied into threatening you by Victor and that he had proof that one of the producers was working with Victor behind the scenes with his scheme."

"What scheme?"

"The guy was going to guarantee that Roberto would win so Victor could keep all his prize money. In addition to that he arranged to have the intern come in second, but win all the challenges."

"Are you serious?"

"Afraid so. Sounds like a soap opera."

"Yeah, we can drop it. I don't want to be tangled up in all this shit. It's getting out of control and the last thing I want is for the press to get wind of it."

"That's the last thing you want or need. I'll call and take care of it."

"Thanks, Katherine. I really appreciate it."

"You're welcome. So it turns out it was good that you quit the line when you did. I can't tell you how many emails and calls I've received praising your honesty."

"Really?" he perked up.

"Yes. Seems like no one was really surprised—I'm sorry, but they weren't—and were glad to hear an honest answer from someone for once. I doubt Roberto would get any sympathy from the public if he *did* try to rat on you after your admission."

"Well, let's hope he keeps his mouth shut."

"It was a bold move doing it on TV like at the junket, but it looks like it worked in your favor. You owe Collette big time for that one."

"If only I could get her to call me back."

"What?"

"Nothing. I'll call you tomorrow and thanks for everything the past few days."

"Any time. Have a safe trip."

"Oh, you should know that I fired Sean this morning."

"What? Why?"

"It's not really important, but I should have done it a long time ago. If I had, I wouldn't have gotten into this Roberto mess."

"I'm sorry to hear that, but you'll find a better rep more suited for you."

"Yes, I know. I'm going to talk to the guys over at Coastal Talent. I hear they treat their talent really well."

"Good idea. If you need anything let me know."

***

Caleb's plane had a long delay and Collette was already asleep when he arrived back at her house. He made the driver pass by her place first, but at 2 a.m., he didn't want to wake her up to explain something he wasn't entirely sure of yet. Monday was a new day and he decided to get a good night sleep instead.

<u>31</u>

"And in case you missed it on Saturday, Caleb Christopher publicly stepped down from his clothing line. The actor and designer admitted that he had not been designing it fully himself as previously thought," the perky morning TV host said. Amber watched the television with disdain. "Although he admitted not being the creative force behind it, the public's reaction has been largely positive. Take a look," she said as the footage started.

"At least he admitted it and didn't lie about it!" a teenage boy exclaimed to the reporter. He wore a pink Mohawk and wore skinny black jeans, while slurping a soda.

"I didn't even know he was a designer. I can't keep up," an overweight baby boomer from Texas said in the middle of Times Square.

"Yeah, whateva. Who cares. I didn't buy his stuff anyway. It was wack!" a twenty-something girl with bloodshot eyes said, dismissing the camera as she walked down the street.

"Do I seriously care that a spoiled celebrity admitted to something he said he had been doing? No. Do I care about the economy and the war in Iraq? Yes. Don't you guys have more important things to report on?" a professional woman on Wall Street asked.

"Looks like that Caleb Christopher got off easy on *that* one," the TV host said before throwing the segment over to the weatherman.

Amber panicked and wondered aloud if her ad would still be coming out. She picked up the phone to call Caleb but was greeted by an automated message saying that the number was no longer in service. In her angst she threw the bowl of cereal she had been eating into the sink filled with dishes her parents demanded she wash. She couldn't help but burst into a rage of tears.

"Amber, what's wrong?" her mom asked entering the kitchen. Wearing pink slippers and a long cotton nightgown, Amber was disgusted by the sight of her low-hanging breasts and wide hips.

"Nothing, I'm fine," she said, wiping her eyes on the sleeve of her fleece robe.

"You sure don't look fine." Her mother approached her with open arms, hoping to comfort her.

"Mom, I said I'm fine," she said, rejecting the embrace.

"Doesn't look that way to me. You sure nothing's wrong?"

"Just stop it, okay? I said I was fine." Amber turned off the television and started to walk out of the kitchen.

"Now you wait a second, Amber. Ever since you got back from New York you've done nothing but pout and have a sour attitude about everything. Now it's bad enough you went out there without telling anyone, but I will not allow you to come back and live in our house behaving this way."

"You just don't get it. Just leave me alone."

"You get your fanny over here and sit down. Now, Amber!" her mom yelled. She grabbed her arm and yanked her into a chair, into which she reluctantly sat.

"I don't know what the hell you were doing out there with that Caleb because you sure as hell never called or returned our messages. I only knew you were alive when I saw you in those magazines, looking like some kind of prostitute or something, hanging all over him like that."

"Mom!"

"Don't you 'Mom' me, Amber. Your father and I have put up with your mess all your life, and there's been plenty of it. We could never figure out why you turned out the way you did. Always chasing some guy who didn't want you. We still can't work out why you didn't turn out to be more like—"

"Like Ashley? Yeah, you've already said that before. A lot."

"Yes, like your sister. *She* didn't cut school. *She* didn't get pregnant. *She* went to college. *She* settled down and got married. *She*—"

"JESUS CHRIST MOM, I KNOW I'M NOT ASHLEY!" she screamed jumping from her chair. Sorry to be such a huge disappointment to you guys!" Her mother gave her a hard slap across her face. "You bitch." she said, as she held the side of her reddened face.

"Amber I—"

"What? You're *sorry*, Mom? Is this the way you treat your own kid?"

"I didn't mean to hit you, but you better watch your mouth, young lady. We haven't asked you for one penny in rent. What we ask is that you respect our rules. But you do nothing but sulk around here all day eating everything and not paying one bill while walking around here dressed like a whore."

"Fuck you!" Amber yelled pushing past her. "You won't have to worry about me any more if that's the way you want it." She ran up the stairs and slammed the door.

"Amber! You get back here. Don't make me call your father home from work!"

"Oh yeah! Go ahead and call him! Maybe he'll pay attention to me now because he sure as hell never did before!" she yelled from her bedroom upstairs.

***

When Caleb received the text from Collette that she was on her way over, he quickly cleaned up his apartment and sent the concierge to the corner for the best bouquet of flowers around. He took the world's fastest shower and spritzed himself with his pine and citrus-scented cologne. He hadn't worn it in a while and had to fish it out of a drawer. His hair was still damp when she knocked, and he nervously opened it with flowers in hand. She looked tired and her hair, usually in a large Afro, was pulled back in a tight bun. She was also more conservatively dressed in a simple pair of jeans and sailor striped t-shirt with navy Chuck Taylors. Her clean freckled face bore no makeup.

"Thank you. They're beautiful," she said.

"I missed you." He hugged her rigid frame.

"Caleb, we need to talk."

"Okay," he said, taking her cold hand in his. They both sat on the couch, quiet, while she waited for him to speak.

"Well?"

"Collette, I'm sorry I didn't call you back the other night. I ended up sleeping there."

"Well, that much I figured."

"Honey, I had a lot to drink that night. You know how Sean is, and—"

"Yes, I do know how he is, which is why I am not a fan," she interjected.

"Listen, I don't want to lie to you, C," he said, feeling the clamminess of her hand.

"Then don't. I know what I heard, Caleb, and it didn't sound like you were sleeping."

"The thing is, Sean had all these strippers at what was supposed to be a low-key dinner, and things just got out of hand." She snatched her hand away from his and grabbed her face to catch her tears.

"Are you telling me that you fucked some stripper?" she asked, unable to look at him.

"No, honey, that's not what I am saying at all," he said lifting her chin and looking into her eyes.

"Well, what are you saying, then Caleb? Huh?"

"I, I don't know. These girls kept giving us drinks and before I knew it I was hammered and eventually passed out."

"What do you mean you 'eventually' passed out?"

"This is hard for me too, Collette."

"Oh really? Is this confessional of yours really that hard for you, Caleb? Why don't you just 'act' your way out of it then," she said defiantly folding her arms tightly.

"I'm just trying to say it's not so cut and dry. I had a lot to drink and I eventually passed out. Everyone was doing coke too, which I did NOT touch, but—"

"But what?"

"But I was so drunk that I'm sure I hooked up with one of the girls."

"You don't know if you slept with someone or not?"

"No, I mean, I'm pretty sure I didn't because there wasn't a condom anywhere." He was almost positive that she was going to punch him. He almost wanted her to. But then he looked into her eyes and knew she didn't have the energy to even lift up her arm.

"Great. You fucked a stripper without a condom. Are you crazy?"

"I mean, I remember just getting a blow job," he said softly.

"What did you say?"

"I said I think I just got a blow job. I'm sorry Collette." He fell back on the couch, covering his face.

"You're *sorry*? Is that supposed to make it better? Your getting a blow job from some dirty stripper?" she said, as she choked through tears. She could barely breathe.

"No, it's not and I am so sorry, C. I remember when you called but I was so out of it I couldn't answer the phone. I found it in the bathroom the next morning and saw that you had called."

"What the hell, Caleb! You go out of town for a few days and you cheat on me like this? I should have known I couldn't trust you. I've seen the way you were with other girls," she said, standing.

"It was Sean's fault. I told him I didn't want any strippers there or anything like that and he said it was only going to be a dinner. I swear, Collette."

"You can't make decisions for yourself, Caleb? I don't care what the fuck Sean did or didn't do. No one told you to drink like that or do anything. You should have known you couldn't have trusted him."

"I know now, which is why I fired him," he said, standing next to her.

"Well good for you for coming to your little senses after cheating on me and blaming it on him," she said, turning to leave.

"C, I'm sorry. Can't we talk more about this?'

"I think you've done enough talking for the both of us. It's over and I quit."

"What?"

"You heard me Caleb. It's over. Go find yourself another girlfriend, excuse me, 'fiancée', and a new assistant. I'm done."

"Collette, please don't go," he said grabbing her arm, which she promptly snatched away. "At least I told you. I didn't want to lie to you."

"Well go give yourself a goddamned gold medal for your honesty because I don't give a shit anymore," she said, not bothering to close the door behind her.

<u>32</u>

Caleb always hated the first day of shooting. The set was foreign, he didn't know the crew, and sometimes the director turned out to be a totally different person than in pre-production. Although he had publicly expressed his gratitude to Trey for casting him in this film, the director remained skeptical. He was a perfectionist and did not allow for any ad-libbing from his actors and everything had to be exactly as written. His directorial style had so far been proven successful and he had claimed a string of box office hits. Trey tried to be understanding when Caleb stumbled through take after take, forgetting the simplest of lines or missing his marks repeatedly. Trey knew he was under stress but had no plans to coddle his star; he had enough to worry about. Nelson did his best to make Caleb comfortable, which was especially challenging after Caleb nearly chewed his head off when he asked of Collette's whereabouts.

After an excruciating thirteen-hour day Caleb went home, had a few glasses of wine, and fell asleep in his clothes. His call time was 5 a.m. the next morning but didn't wake up till 7 a.m., having forgotten to set his alarm. Fortunately for him there was an issue in the lighting department, which delayed shooting by 2 ½ hours, so he was spared a lecture by Trey. The second day was not much better than the first. No one said hello or tried to make nice and assumed he was the angry person he portrayed himself to be yesterday. Katherine arrived on set at lunch with a few resumes for Collette's replacement that he pushed away. He made it clear to her that he didn't want to talk about it right now. Instead he asked if Katherine could help pick up some of Collette's duties for a few days.

***

Collette had not gotten out of bed in two days. She cancelled the photo shoot she was supposed to have with Joe, claiming her flu-like symptoms came out of nowhere. Lou tried to coax her with pedicures and shopping sprees but her heavy heart kept her in bed. She listened to sad songs, crying all day and night. The only thing she had to look forward to was her upcoming trip to Europe. She did not want to go but her parents insisted when she told them she had broken up with Caleb. Her dad's heart ached at his little girl's weak voice and promised to give her the biggest and best hug she ever had in her life when they landed in New York for their flight to Paris.

***

Dear Caleb,

Words cannot express how sorry I am with the way things happened out here. I have, or rather, had been, working for Sean for two years doing everything he asked, not really thinking about how my actions affected other people. Granted, I wasn't always asked to book strippers for parties, but other requests were just as unethical from time to time.

Anyway, enclosed please find the underwear you left in the bedroom; I thought you would want them. I went upstairs after you left only to overhear Becca and Mali, co-conspiring to make money off them. They talked about contacting the press with some crazy story about how you slept with both of them. One would claim to be pregnant, and then miscarry so she wouldn't have to produce an actual child. After I'd taken the underwear from them and ordered them out, Sean's reaction was not as I thought it should have been. He was so angry at you for firing him that he tried to stop the girls from leaving and vowed to give them the proper press contacts, for a piece of the profits, of course. Not only did this instantly sicken me and change my opinion of him, it also made me see that everything I had been doing for him had just contributed to his inexcusable behavior. I quit on the spot.

Why am I telling you all this? Because I feel directly responsible for your pain. I am so very sorry and will do anything I can to help repair the damage. Incidentally, I have contacts at all the agencies in New York and will do anything on your behalf that you need to secure new representation. Please let me know if I can

help you in any way. I feel absolutely terrible and again
apologize profusely.
Warmly,
Janice Tucker

Caleb was stunned by what he'd just read. A production assistant had brought him this FedEx package along with his lunch on the third day of shooting. Not due back on the set for three hours, he sat in his large trailer on a side street in the West Village and read the note again. Screaming women shouted his name outside behind metal barriers. The alcohol wafted from the FedEx box and Caleb ran the events of the night through his head. He took comfort in knowing that he had not slept with them, but the thought of having lost Collette over his infantile behavior brought tears to his eyes. He could not remember the last time he had cried over anything, but the tears came so fast they surprised even him. He lay down on his bed and cried himself to sleep.

***

"Amber? What the hell are you doing calling me?" Bruce asked on the phone in his Times Square office. It was an unusually slow day in the usually bustling office.

"What do you mean, 'why am I calling you', honey? I'm calling to say hi," she said. She stood outside of a Duane Reade across the street from his office.

"*Honey?* Who do you think you're talking to? After that shit you pulled at Port Authority I should hang up on you right now," he said. He muted the volume on his large screen television turned to *Entertainment Tonight.*

"I know. I'm sorry about all that. Will you forgive me?" she said, twirling her hair.

"You got my money? You stole it, remember? Had me lookin' like a fool to those cops. You could have ruined my business, Amber."

"I said I was sorry, Bruce."

"And I said do you have my money? I'd like it back in small bills like I gave it to you in the first place," he said, absently looking out of his window onto Eighth Avenue.

"Well, I kinda don't have it," she said, looking up towards the sky.

"Is that you standing down there?" he asked. The red hair and long legs looked very familiar.

"What? Down where?" she asked, looking around.

"In front of the Duane Reade. Shit, that is you! What the fuck are you doing, Amber? I thought you were in Jersey with your pretend sister."

"Oh my God, is your office around here? I'd totally forgotten," she lied. "I thought it was on another block."

"You know damn good and well where it is. I don't have time for your shit, Amber. What happened to my money?"

"I kinda spent it all in Chicago when I went home."

"All of it?"

"Most of it. I needed some new clothes."

"I doubt that. You'd better find a way to get it back to me soon. You got one week." He slammed the phone down and returned to his desk. A moment later he looked again out the window and saw her pacing back and forth on the sidewalk. Her pink skirt was so short and heels so high she could have easily been mistaken for a prostitute. His phone rang again one minute later.

"What!" he barked into the phone.

"It's me again. Don't hang up."

"Amber, I'm busy. I don't want to hear from you again until you have my money. Now, I gotta go—"

"Wait! Bruce, that's what I'm calling about," she said, looking up towards his window.

"What, Amber. Make it fast," he looked at her again through the thick glass.

"I kinda need a place to stay and some money."

"You kinda need a place to stay and some money. This is some Class A bullshit, Amber. I don't know why the hell you're calling me."

"I'm planning to see Caleb again and well, I wanted to give you the scoop for a little extra cash."

"Haven't you done enough to this guy already?"

"He's in the city and I found a way to reach him again. You just have to trust me."

"Trust you? Yeah right," He laughed into the phone. "I'd trust a hungry pit bull with my newborn kid over you."

"Come on, Bruce. I've always delivered, haven't I? Uh, don't answer that. Just believe me, okay?"

"Maybe."

"Good! Now do you think I can stay with you?"

"Hell naw! You better sleep at the bus station or something."

"I really don't have anywhere else to go, Bruce."

"Not my problem."

"Not even if I, um, work off what I owe to you?" she asked, bending over to adjust her shoe, partially exposing her thong, much to the delight of the passing cabbies who honked and hooted loudly.

"Damn, girl. I'm trying to be done with you and leave that shit alone," he said, turning his back to the window.

"Come on, Bruce. You know it was always good and I could come up right now," she whispered into the phone. He turned back around, and his eyes met hers.

"Yeah, it was a'ight. Yes, it was."

"And it still is. Then I could go to your place you keep downtown and be available whenever for you."

"Damn, you sure as hell know how to push my buttons," he said, as she giggled. "Get your ass up here and you can start paying off your debt right now."

"And I can stay with you too?"

"Yeah, but I can't have you up in there too long in case my wife decides she wants to come to the city."

"I'll be right up."

Amber quickly called City Casting to confirm that, yes, she would be available to work as an extra on Caleb Christopher's movie. She didn't mind that at fifty bucks she was working basically for free, she just wanted to work in film, no matter what. After hanging up, she put her phone back in her bag, careful to make sure her wallet, which was bursting with $100 bills, was closed securely.

Thank goodness for Google Alerts, she thought as she crossed the busy street into Bruce's building, she had never heard of City Casting before but called them right up when she saw they were casting extras for his movie.

<u>33</u>

Collette,

I have surpassed my own level of stupidity this time. I understand what I did was wrong on multiple levels and I can't apologize enough for hurting you in this way. Worst of all, I fear I have lost you and I don't think I can deal with that. I don't blame you for not returning my phone calls or texts, I completely deserve your silence, but please know that I love you so much and I made a horrible mistake.

I know you're leaving today for your trip, but know that I will carry you in my heart while you're gone. I hope you have a wonderful time with your parents and I know that I miss you terribly and will do whatever is necessary to win you back. I love you more than you can ever know. Please call me when you return next week, or anytime at all. Anytime.

All my love - Caleb

Collette's Caleb

Lou read the note to Collette as she helped her finish packing for her trip. She would be meeting her parents at JFK in a few hours for their flight to Paris. Unfortunately, she was still feeling sluggish and blue. Collette had no response to the note or to the large bouquet of flowers that accompanied it when they were delivered earlier in the day. As Lou followed her around her apartment reading Caleb's words, Collette continued to gather her things and turned on a blues station on her iTunes.

"C, look at the flowers! Aren't they pretty!" Lou said as Collette sang along to the song's sad lyrics.

"C, come on, this music is dreadful. No wonder you're depressed. And let's get some fresh air in here," she said, as she opened a window, instantly bringing the life of the city into Collette's apartment. "Ahhh that's better," she said, inhaling the vibrant scents that permeated the space.

"It's how I feel, Lou. I was just cheated on in the worst possible way, remember?" she said moving through the apartment humming under her breath.

"Yes, honey I do know. But he made a mistake."

"Well, he should've thought about that before he decided to get a blow job from a stripper," Collette entered the bathroom to gather her toiletries. She glanced at herself in the mirror and grimaced when she saw the red puffy eyes that looked back at her.

"I'm not saying it was okay, but at least he was honest and he's apologized like a million times." she said, appearing in the bathroom doorway.

"His apology means nothing to me, Lou. He broke our trust."

"I know he did and you've been having yourself quite a pity party the last few days to remind yourself," she said gently.

"Whose side are you on here, Lou? Because if you're on his side then you can leave," she said as she pushed past her into the bedroom.

"I'm on your side, of course, but I think you need to just listen to him. I mean, he was at *Sean's* house for crying out loud and you know how he is. I don't think any man could have been good over there," she argued.

"You're just going to make excuses for him? Is that it?" she said, throwing her bag of toiletries on the bed.

"I'm not making any excuses, I just don't want you to lose a great guy because you were too stubborn to forgive him. He got wasted at his *bachelor* party and the girls took advantage of it. It's not like he went out stone sober and cheated on you in some planned, methodical way. People make mistakes, Collette, and let us down sometimes. None of us are perfect." She sat in the creaky wicker chair.

"I know, but he chea—"

"Yes, he cheated on you. Do you think you're the first person to be cheated on? Need I remind you of that party in college where you got drunk and hooked up with that guy from BU when you were dating Dan? Remember that?"

"Umm, vaguely," she said, her face reddening.

"Uh huh. You tried to apologize to him for days and he wouldn't listen to you and you were so torn up about it, Collette. All you wanted was to explain and for him to forgive you, but he didn't. You didn't even know that other guy, C. You were just having fun at a stupid frat party and had too much to drink and it got back to your boyfriend. You didn't even tell him, C. Dan had to find out in some roundabout way from someone else who was at the party. At least Caleb was honest with you."

"I remember, okay! Jeez, Lou. Are you trying to purposely make me feel like shit?"

"No, I'm not, but I'm just reminding you that you weren't always such a saint yourself and if you love Caleb as much as you say you do, you'll work this out with him. Sean is no angel and Caleb probably made the mistake of going over there, but I'm sure those girls just zeroed in on him because he's famous and completely exploited the situation. True, he should have been stronger and not have drank so much, but that is something that he will have to live with too. Honestly, it was probably the wake-up call he needed in terms of Sean."

"You think he needed to cheat on me to wake up?" she asked, wiping the tears from her eyes.

"Collette, you're not listening. Sean is a douche bag and everybody knows it. You've known it for years and I knew it from the second I met him last summer at Caleb's movie premiere in LA. I'm sure he set it all up and planted the trap for Caleb to walk into because he doesn't want to see him happy and in love. It's easier for him to market a young hot, single guy, than a married one. I'm sure he was doing his part to help his bottom line. "

"You think so?"

"Do I think so? Have you seen the guy? He's totally sleazy."

"That may be true, but Caleb didn't have to do what he did. He really hurt me, Lou," she said, flopping on the bed.

"I know he did and it wasn't right, but you're going to either forgive him and try to move on, or leave him for good, and I don't think you're ready to walk away from him. Personally, I think Caleb is a great guy and has a good heart. Sure, he's made some bonehead mistakes, we all have, but he's a different person around you. He seems to have changed from when you first met him till now. I just don't want to see it all thrown away over a stupid blow job that

I'm sure he was too wasted to even know what was happening, let alone enjoy."

"I don't know, Lou."

"Just try to see it from his side. You can think about it but just don't be so quick to judge. You know he loves you and he knows he has made the biggest mistake of his life," she said, wrapping her arms around Collette. "Now, let's finish getting you packed and get you to the airport."

"Okay."

"But first let's change this droopy music. It's starting to bring *me* down."

***

Collette tried to be strong, but as soon as she fell into her father's open arms at the airport she cried like a baby. Her parents told her that the time away would do her good and tried to console her, but in her distress she wondered what she was going to do with her life. After checking in for their Air France flight in the first class line—although they were flying coach—they were given passes to the airline's exclusive lounge and escorted to the head of the security line, thanks to Marcielle, their check-in agent. Collette had been friendly with her due to her constant and extensive travels on the airline.

The swank lounge was filled with distinguished men drinking from snifters while reading the *Financial Times,* women with rigid bob haircuts speaking multiple languages, and a handful of Burberry and Petit Bateau-clad children with their Nordic nannies. The lounge's private seating areas, free food, drinks, and entertainment afforded it a luxurious comfort lost on the average traveler. They nestled into a private booth and ordered a bottle of Louis Jadot Pouilly-Fuissé along with a baguette and an assortment of pungent cheeses.

"I just don't know what I'm going to do. I seriously thought I was going to be with Caleb forever," she said, as she sipped the chilled wine.

"Oh honey, you'll figure it out. You'll see things aren't so bad," her father tried to reassure her.

"Not so bad? Dad, I don't have a job or a fiancé anymore. I think that's pretty bad."

"I'm not saying it's not, but think about the big picture, Collette. Were you really going to get married anyway? He didn't even give you a ring," her father said as her mother delicately agreed.

"Well, he was going to get me one. We started looking."

"Yeah, I know, but what kind of man proposes to a woman without a ring? Maybe he just wasn't ready," her father said. He wrapped his arm around her shoulder.

"Oh, daddy!" Collette said, allowing herself to be held by him. "What am I going to do?"

"Collette, you come from a strong family. You will figure it out and we'll be here to help you. Every step of the way." Her mother handed her a Kleenex.

"Just think about what you want, honey. Are you still interested in writing?" her father asked, as a nanny chased a quick-footed three-year-old through the lounge.

"Yeah."

"Well, there's no time like the present. Not right at this moment, I mean, but when we get back. Figure out what you need to pursue and just do it!" her mom exclaimed.

"But what am I going to do about a job? I didn't give any notice or anything. I just quit."

"Baby girl, we can help you out for a bit if you need it until you find something else," her father said.

"I don't deserve you guys," Collette said, taking her parents' hands.

"We don't deserve *you*, Collette. We are your parents and we love you no matter what and will help you through this. You've always landed on your feet before and we know you will again," her mother said.

"Excuse me, Collette?" A tall, Air France employee interrupted.

"Hi, Marcielle," she said, standing to hug the woman. "Thank you again for the passes. It was very kind of you." Her parents stood to shake the woman's hand.

"It's no problem. I'm sorry to bother you, Collette, but if it's okay, can you please ask Caleb for an autographed photograph for my niece here in New York? She's turning 12 soon and just loves him."

"I would, but I don't work for Caleb anymore."

"Oh, I didn't know. I'm sorry. I hope everything is alright," Marcielle said carefully.

"It's fine. Give me her name and address and I will pass it on to his publicist and she will take care of it."

"If it's not too much trouble?"

"None at all. It's the least I can do," she said.

"Oh, thank you so much Collette! You have the best daughter in the world. You are very lucky," she said to April and Hampton. "I'll just go get the address."

***

Amber grew more frustrated as the day wore on. It was bad enough that she had to get up at 4:30 a.m. to be on set at 5:15, having to maneuver around Bruce's dark apartment because he wouldn't let her turn the lights on. For the past four hours, she had been relegated to the holding area with the rest of the extras. She complained to the production assistant, claiming there must be a mistake because she was sure she was to have a trailer or at the very least a separate space from the other extras. They were all classless loudmouth slobs who would do anything to be in a movie, she explained. She also tried to explain that she told City Casting that she was only supposed to be in scenes with Caleb Christopher and suggested that maybe they had not received the message. This protesting didn't help and she finally took a seat in the unglamorous gymnasium with everyone else. Here, she was careful not to engage in idle conversation, instead choosing to listen to her iPod with her Prada sunglasses on. A few people approached her to see if she wanted to play cards or Trivial Pursuit to pass the time, but she made it clear that she didn't want to play any dumb games or socialize with them in any way.

After waiting around for two more dreadful hours in the windowless gym, she was hopeful when she was finally sent to set for her big scene. She reapplied her new Dior lip gloss and quickly slathered herself with shimmering body lotion for that extra glow that would surely be noticed by the director. She was soon disappointed when the set assistant led her to the back of a large crowd of what seemed like a million other people. She wondered if her bright green mini skirt and sheer ivory tank top had something to do with her being placed in the back. City Casting had told her to wear sweat pants and a sweatshirt, but she would never be caught dead in those, even if the content of the scenes called for such an outfit. When told to rant loudly like an angry mob, she ignored this directive and pouted instead, reviled by the close quarters with the overly eager extras. The fact that Caleb was not even in this scene frustrated her even more. In fact, there was nobody in the scene, just a stupid shot of extras screaming like idiots. After an hour of this torture she was back in the holding area with a pathetic meal of cold pasta, ham slices, potato chips, and a Diet Coke.

"Excuse me!" she said, to the production assistant. She had to climb over an overweight woman who was on her fourth bag of Doritos.

"Yeah," he nonchalantly replied.

"I think I told you before that my name is Amber Skye and I was supposed to only be in Caleb Christopher's scenes."

"Well, that's not what I was told, so just have a seat." He turned turning away from her, talking in to his headset.

She tapped on his shoulder, "Look, maybe you just had the wrong sheet of paper or something, but if you look again you'll see my name is Amber Skye and I'm not supposed to be back here with *them*," she waved her wrist at the crowd of rowdy extras.

"Amber. I guarantee you this is where you're supposed to be. So please just take a seat. I'm sure we'll be calling you again in a bit," he said, as he returned to his headset.

"I didn't want to 'pull rank' with you or anything, but you leave me no choice," she said. She turned his shoulder towards her as he continued speaking in his headset.

"Hey, get your hands off me. I told you to sit down!"

"Look mister, I'm Amber Skye. That's A-M-B-E-R S-K-Y-E and I'm Caleb's GIRLFRIEND. Got it, moron? Now get me outta here! I told you I'm supposed to be working with him today."

"*Moron?* Who you calling a moron? If you're his girlfriend, what the hell are you doing here in extras holding? Now sit down," he said and turned away from her again to speak into his headset. "Yeah, we got a loose one here. Says she's Caleb's girlfriend. Get security and Caleb's assistant so we can let him know what's going on."

"Just check your sheet again, alright? I'm telling you there must be a mix-up. I'm Amber Skye!"

"Oh God, not you again." The officer from the Port Authority police station approached her.

"Officer Starkey? What are you doing here?"

"Go get your stuff, you're coming with me," the officer ordered while the rest of the extras looked on.

"What the fuck?" she replied.

"Hurry up! Go get your crap!" the officer barked. The production assistant laughed.

He didn't have to tell her again as she gathered her belongings and was escorted out of the building.

Humiliated, she thought of protesting once more, but thought better of it.

"Thought you should know that security just escorted an Amber Skye out of the building. She was in extras holding and was saying she was your girlfriend. They only told me because you don't have an assistant here," Nelson said to Caleb between takes.

"Jesus Christ. Thank you, Nelson."

"Anytime." He smiled at him as Caleb went to his trailer and sent an email from his laptop.

Janice,

Thank you for your package. I'm sorry the way things turned out for you as well, but perhaps you have made a wise decision in leaving Sean. If the offer is still open, I could use your assistance. I am in great need of an assistant and would like for you to come to New York to work with me at least for a few weeks until I work out a permanent solution since you live in LA. Obviously, I'll cover all your expenses and promise not to put you in any compromising situations like your previous employer. Let me know at your earliest

convenience. Katherine is cc'd so you can work out the
arrangements with her.

Caleb

"I can't keep up with all these media requests about your line, Caleb," Katherine said over breakfast the next morning in his trailer. *"People, US Weekly, Entertainment Tonight, the New York Times, LA Times,* the list goes on ..."

"Why on earth do they want to talk to me?" he asked as he stirred his coffee. He flipped through bills sent to him by his business manager that needed his sign-off.

"They want an exclusive as to why you came clean about quitting your line. In this world of entertainers doing everything and taking all the credit, they are blown away that you were so candid and honest."

"Not interested. Besides, I already gave an 'exclusive' to that dipshit at the junket. That's all I'm gonna say. It's over as far as I'm concerned," he said. He scrutinized an assessment for his co-op maintenance fee. "Seriously, am I being charged ten grand for a rooftop garden that I'm never going to use? Did we meet about this?" he mumbled to himself.

"I don't know, Caleb. I could ask Collette though. She would know," she replied as she sipped her tea.

"No, don't bother her with this. I seem to remember her showing me something about this a few months ago and I just blew it off. She told me to look at it carefully but I didn't. I guess this is what happens when you don't pay attention to your assistant, Katherine. You get screwed, that's what happens." He pushed aside the papers.

"Are you alright? You haven't been yourself lately."

"I've been better, I'll tell you that. It's a wonder I haven't been fired from this job yet because I can't focus, I have no idea how to do anything for myself, and this crazy bitch Amber keeps showing up everywhere. So no, I'm really not okay," he said. A production assistant knocked on his door to give him a ten-minute warning.

"Caleb, I've been in this business a long time and I have seen things that would shock even you. Things are grim now, but they'll get better. I'm here to help in any way I can," she said, trying to comfort him.

"Thank you, Katherine. Really. Thank you," he said.

"Don't mention it. Listen, I received an email from Janice Tucker last night. She's due to arrive tomorrow night and Nelson spoke to housing and has her hotel lined up. I'll be sure to get her up to speed when she arrives," she said as she gathered her things.

"You're an angel, Katherine," he said hugging her.

"One more thing. I spoke to the guys at Coastal Talent and their head guy in New York, Darien Jennings, is planning to meet you tonight after you wrap to discuss representation. He knows Sean and joked about what took you so long to fire him. When I told him that Janice was going to be working with you for a while, he confirmed that she was a good girl who worked for a jerk."

"Well, that's good to know."

"Yes, she seemed sweet. Alright, I have to get going. After you've gone through everything," she said, indicating the pile of bills, "let me know and I'll send a courier to pick them up."

"Thank you, Katherine. I'll be in touch later." Caleb watched as Katherine left the trailer. A security guard helped her navigate the crowds of fans on the street until she was safely in a cab.

Caleb brushed his teeth and wondered if he should email Collette again. He sent her an email last night to make sure she arrived in Paris safely but she hadn't written back. He didn't expect that she would be traveling with her laptop, but didn't want to call her. He tried his best to put it out of his mind and went to work.

***

"Bruce, come on. Be reasonable," Amber pleaded as he watched television while eating handfuls of Chex Mix. The room seemed to grow darker by the moment when the clock hit seven o'clock.

"Be reasonable my ass, Amber. I don't know why I listened to you again," he said crunching loudly. "Just go."

"You'll get the shot, Bruce. I swear."

"How, Amber? You got kicked off the damn movie, remember? Where is my shot of him kissing you? Huh? You just had to go down there and act a fool."

"It wasn't my fault, Bruce. I was supposed to be working in his scenes," she said sitting on the couch next to him.

"You were an extra making fifty bucks, Amber," he said. How the hell did you think you were going to get close enough to him where I would get my shot? Did you think I needed a shot of your dumb-ass crowd scene with all those people dressed in sweats? Do you think my guy appreciated hanging out down there all damn day waiting for your text that you and Caleb were shooting now, only for him to see you get thrown out later? Naw, Amber none of us needed that," he said turning back to the television.

"But, but—"

"Just get your ass outta here. I'm done messin' with you."

"You just have to trust me Bruce. I have another plan." Amber fished out a call sheet from her purse that she had managed to swipe while on the set.

"What the hell is that?"

"It's the call sheet for today."

"So?"

"Sooo...it says what time Caleb wraps today," she said, pleased with herself.

"Big fucking deal."

"Well according to this he wrapped about 10 minutes ago and I'm sure he's on his way home. Maybe we can meet him there."

"And how do you know that he doesn't have plans after work, Einstein?"

"I guess I don't, but in case he is home wouldn't you love to find out where he lives so you can get the perfect shot of me kissing him in front of his place? I'm sure your readers would like that."

"Fuck. You better be on the money this time, Amber. Let's go." Bruce grabbed his camera and they darted out the door. He did not know how she was going to pull this off, but she was just sneaky enough to prove him wrong.

***

Darien Jennings was a tall, classically handsome man, and also one of the leading talent agents in New York. While living in Los Angeles in his early twenties, he took an entry-level job in the legal department at Coastal Talent, and eventually became an agent. Known for his level-headiness and keeping his talents' needs first, he represented only the best of the best. Although it was rare, every once and awhile he'd take a chance on someone he believed in. Caleb fit into this category.

He was eager to meet with Caleb on set when he wrapped at 7 p.m. He thought it was a good idea that he quit working in fashion and was confident he could get him in front of the best directors. This Trey Xu action film was a good place to start - at least it wasn't another mindless romantic comedy. He knew with the right material he could work with the best directors. He sensed there was a serious actor under all that formulaic romantic comedy bullshit.

"Mr. Jennings, it's my pleasure," Caleb said, shaking the hand of this powerful agent waiting outside his trailer.

"Please, call me Darien. Pleased to meet you and thank you for seeing me here. I know you are busy," he said, following Caleb into his trailer.

"It's an honor. Can I get you a drink? I think I may have some beers in here," he said.

"Sure, why not." Caleb rummaged through the refrigerator and handed Darien a Blue Moon.

"Blue Moon? Where is this from?

"Denver, my hometown. My assis– I mean, former assistant, used to always find it and have it delivered. Katherine, my publicist, had it brought in."

"Yes, I heard you will be getting a new assistant soon."

"Yes, Janice Tucker. Sean's former assistant. Apparently, she got fed up too," he said.

"I could see how that could happen. Anyway, listen, if you are interested I'm sure we can get you set up fairly well at Coastal. We listen and respect our talent and try to only get the best work to be had."

"Yes, I know. I've heard nothing but great things about you guys. Obviously, I need better films than I have been getting."

"As bad as some of your movies have been, all that romcom stuff, your acting does shine through and I know you can do better with the right material," he said producing a docket of paperwork. "This is a copy of our contract and what we can do for you. This is your copy to look over. I already sent one to your lawyers as well."

"I appreciate the vote of confidence," he said, skimming through the small print. So far he liked what he saw—it included guidance in forming his own production company, private planes for press junkets, first refusal deal, $20 million a picture—the list went on.

"You don't have to tell me now, but let me know after the weekend. Take the time to decide if you want to be with the Coastal family. But do know that we only represent serious actors so there will be no more fashion design or other interests not directly related to the art of film," he warned.

"No need to worry about that. That's all in the past. I just have one more ad coming out next week because I had a supply of merchandise that didn't sell that I need to get rid of. It's a nominal amount so we're calling it a 'limited edition' collection, but it shouldn't interfere with anything on a major scale."

"One other thing. We represent serious actors and expect them to conduct their private lives in a professional and discreet manner."

"Okay…" Caleb replied perplexed.

"What I mean is our actors operate largely under the gossip radar. Sure, it's more difficult to handle in this day and age, but for the most part you won't see our talent in any compromising positions of any sort. They typically don't pop up on TMZ, Perez Hilton, or any of those places. We like to save that space for B-list talent and the reality stars of the world. Also know that we reserve the right to rescind the offer or dissolve our working relationship if we feel that your work is being overshadowed by your private life. It's all in the contract."

"Got it."

"Please don't take offense but I only bring this up because you have, how do we say, been 'out there' quite a bit lately. You're a young guy and that's expected, but you have been in the press a lot with various women in different situations. We are not trying to run your life, but we can't have the audience and critics distracted from your craft because of your public antics."

"No offense taken. It would be my intention to do everything possible to not only represent myself in the best light, but also Coastal," he said thinking of their talent roster. He knew they only represented A-list talent, most being Oscar winners. He felt honored to soon be represented by them.

"Please don't think you're the first person with whom we've had this discussion. We've added a few actors over the past few years whose primary body of work was romantic comedies and action adventures, and they endured the same press as you. But with our guidance we have been able to transition them to better bodies of work and better qualities of life," he said, reassuringly.

"Thank you for bringing it up. I appreciate your candor."

"Great! Now that that's out of the way, tell me what the hell happened up at Sean's?"

"You heard about that?" Caleb asked, a little worried, not knowing which part he heard.

"Hate to tell you this, but everybody heard about it. Sean and his team weren't so discreet after you canned him."

"Oh God."

"Well he said some pretty crazy stuff went on up there and I doubt any of it was really true, those guys have a rep for partying hard and embellishing the truth, to put it mildly. It sounded like a crazy time," he said, finishing the beer.

"Darien, you're going to need at least another beer to hear the half of this one."

Caleb spent the next hour telling Darien every sordid detail about what happened at Sean's place. Tired of hiding from the truth and not having the energy to lie, he came clean about everything. He wanted a fresh start with Darien and thought it best to answer his questions truthfully. He told him how Collette had warned him about Sean so long ago, about how Sean set him up with Roberto, and how Caleb's behavior had cost him his fiancé. He held nothing back as they went through a few beers and sent a production assistant out for a bottle of wine and take-out. Darien just took it all in and shook his head from time to time saying none of Sean's behavior surprised him—he'd heard variations on this before from other actors. In the spirit of full disclosure, he even went so far as to tell him about how Janice came to be his new assistant.

He was enjoying this catharsis so much that instead of going home, they headed out to a jazz club. For the first time in a while, Caleb felt like he had an agent he could trust.

While they were enjoying the best jazz the village had to offer, Amber was convincing an angry Bruce to give Caleb another hour to come home. Perhaps he wrapped later than she thought, but she was sure he would come home soon.

"We've been sitting out here for damn near three hours, Amber," he said from the park bench across the street from his loft.

"I know and I'm sorry. I'm sure he'll be back soon. Want me to get you another hot dog?" she asked, jumping up towards the vendor.

"Sit down."

"Okay." She sat at the opposite end of the bench. "Hey look!" she said, pointing across the street. She didn't recognize the guy who accompanied Caleb, but they sure looked like they were having a good time.

"Is that him? I can't tell from here."

"Yeah, let's go!"

Bruce readied his camera and they ran across the street unnoticed. The tall man had all Caleb's attention as they were shook hands and said their good nights. Before Caleb knew what was happening, Amber had knocked the tall man out of the way and threw herself onto him. Her skirt was so short that when she leapt into his arms and wrapped her legs around him, his hands had no choice but to hold her butt, clad in red lace, in his hands. She kissed him hard and fast, throwing him back against the door of his building as Bruce fired away. Caleb was finally able to push her off as the doorman came to his aid.

"Amber! What the hell are you doing?" Caleb asked. Her behavior sobered him up quickly.

"Did you get it, Bruce?" she yelled to Bruce who was snapping away.

"Got it, let's go!"

"What the fuck is going on here?" Caleb demanded.

"Nice seeing you again, Caleb." she said as they disappeared down the busy street.

34

Saturday morning Collette awoke feeling refreshed. After they landed in Paris, they checked into their quaint hotel on Boulevard Raspail, just steps away from the Bon Marche. They did a bit of shopping in this famous Parisian department store and strolled around the city before having a wonderfully cheap meal in the Latin Quarter, while April reminisced about the days when she would hang out in the neighborhood painting portraits of tourists. After late-night Nutella crepes and red wine, she collapsed into bed and slept more soundly than she had in a long time. Her father was right, this trip was exactly the tonic she needed. She was enjoying herself and had already planned a trip to see her parents at their soon-to-be home in Denver.

While watching the BBC news over coffee and a baguette with butter and jam, she retrieved her computer from her bag—glad that she had decided to bring it at the last minute. She logged into her Facebook account and updated her status as "*Collette enjoyed waking up in the city of lights this morning and is so happy to be out of New York!*" She rarely updated her status, to the chagrin of her friends who always thought she was off doing something fabulous as Caleb's assistant but this morning she was feeling especially open. She caught up on her friends' many photo albums and made a few comments here and there. After fruitlessly browsing the site for a while, she logged off and checked her email account. There was an email from Lou saying hello and wishing her a good trip, an email from the University of Colorado's writing department asking if she'd received their literature, a few spam emails, some work emails from a few people who didn't know she was no longer Caleb's assistant, (which she re-routed to Katherine), and an email from Caleb. Maybe she had been too hard on him after all. He did apologize a million times and after a good night's sleep she was thinking more clearly. She took a long shower to compose her thoughts and when she returned to her computer she turned off the television and browsed *Timeoutparis.com* to see if there was anything special going on in the city. After making a few notes, she went to *People.com*, her guilty pleasure from time to time. She always thought it was entertaining to see what was being said about celebrities even though she knew it was mostly false.

It was a good thing she was sitting down because what popped up on the screen knocked the wind out of her. In the incriminating photo was clearly Caleb's hands holding up the back-side of a girl in red lace underwear as he kissed her. The girl's hands were running through his hair furiously as they made out in front of his building. *"GOOD-BYE MYSTERY WOMAN HELLO AMBER SKYE! CALEB CHRISTOPHER REUNITES WITH MODEL/ACTRESS AMBER SKYE IN PASSIONATE EMBRACE IN FRONT OF HIS HOME. AMBER SPEAKS TO PEOPLE EXCLUSIVELY!"* She read the article.

"Caleb and I were meant to be together and we've been seeing each other a long time. He just couldn't get enough of me when we were apart ... He tells me he loves me all the time and he is just so romantic! He told me he wants to be only with me and not with Collette, his assistant, who came between us before. I'm even going to be in his next ad!"

Collette couldn't breathe and collapsed onto the bed in tears. Her mom knocked on the door to see if she was ready and when she saw her daughter, she rushed to hold her, not paying mind to the damaging photo alongside the image of Collette and Caleb happily exiting Tiffany's only a few weeks prior.

Collette could not get out of bed all day. Ignoring housekeeping when they entered her room to clean, the maids apologized for their interruption when they saw her lying in bed with a wad of tissues next to her and quickly left. Although it was still late morning and she was well rested, she took a sleeping pill and fell back into a deep slumber. Her parents stayed close by in their room in case she needed anything, but for the most part left her alone. When she finally woke up starving six hours later, she called her parents' room to make plans for an early dinner in the hotel restaurant.

"What did you guys do today?" she asked sipping a Coca-Cola Light. Wearing the shirt she had slept in and a pair of cotton pants, her disheveled appearance was a contrast from the other stylish patrons of the hotel.

"Oh honey, we didn't do anything. We were too concerned about you to leave the hotel," her mother replied.

"Yes, we were right next door to you all day, sweetheart," her dad said as he took her hand, chilled from the soda.

"I'm sorry to have ruined your trip. I feel bad you didn't go do anything."

"If you're not alright, we're not alright. Doesn't matter if we are here or at home, Collette," April said, nearly choking up.

"Ma, don't cry. Oh, I feel so bad," she said. She held her mom's hand.

"We just hate to see you going through this, Collette. As your parents we feel every ounce of your pain." Her father handed his wife a handkerchief.

"Well no matter how I am feeling tomorrow I want you to get out and enjoy the city before we head to London. I'll be fine. I promise," she said, attempting a smile.

"We'll worry about tomorrow, tomorrow. Right now, let's get you something to eat. You're looking too skinny over there," her father said.

"Alright, but then I want you guys to go out tonight and do something fun. Okay?"

"Alright, but only if you come with us," April said.

"No you go. I need to figure some things out. No sense in you guys wasting your trip."

After her parents headed out for a stroll along the Seine, Collette returned to her room, made a stiff drink from the mini bar, and went to work. She loved 70s pop, but opted for something different and turned on some disco tunes which made her feel better—temporarily at least. She checked her email and replied to Lou's concerned message about the image of Caleb and Amber. Lou just didn't know how on earth he could do this to her after everything they've been through and encouraged her to call as soon as she could. Collette replied that she was okay and would call soon. Next, she deleted the five emails from Caleb without reading them. With subject lines like "I'm sorry," "This isn't what it looks like," and "Please call me," she was sure they were filled with empty apologies and hollow words. She sent a quick email to Katherine with Marcielle's photo request and wished her well. This would be the last thing she would do on behalf of Caleb, and it felt good to clear the plate of her assistant responsibilities. Before she moved a few emails to her trash bin, she opened the email again from the University of Colorado and looked more closely at their admission requirements. After not having been in school for so long, she was terrified at the thought of having to take the GRE, and had already missed the deadline for fall admission.

After finishing her drink, she showered and climbed back into bed. It was only 8 o'clock and she was looking forward to devoting the rest of the night with her head buried in a suspense novel.

<u>35</u>

"Good morning Caleb, this came for you today," Janice said, entering his trailer on Monday morning. Having arrived in New York two nights ago for her new job she was nervous and still carried the weight of guilt and aimed to be the best assistant possible for Caleb. They had not gotten together yesterday like she had hoped because Caleb feared Amber would return with her photographer friend. He was not mentally equipped to deal with her again, and instead emailed Collette various times trying to explain the photograph—which Katherine informed him about the moment it hit the internet. Janice did not know what his expectations of her would be, and already feeling like she was skating on thin ice, she was going to try to be just as good as Collette, if not better.

"Humph. It's from Coastal," he said as he opened the couriered envelope. Darien didn't have to come out and say it, but it was obvious he was not pleased at Amber's little photo op three nights ago. Richard Erickson, his lawyer at Erickson, Whistle, & Rand, LLP, emailed him yesterday with his approval of the contract and encouraged him to sign and send it back to Coastal. It was a damn good deal, he'd written, and congratulated him effusively. The signed documents were ready to go and he planned to have Janice hand deliver them this afternoon, so he couldn't figure out what they could be sending him now. Perhaps it was a welcome note or invitation of some sort.

The words "rescind offer" and "best of luck" jumped off the page. He could feel himself turning numb. Janice's voice sounded a mile away as she nervously asked him if everything was okay. He read it again to assure his eyes weren't playing tricks on him.

> *Caleb,*
>
> *After further consideration, Coastal Talent has decided to rescind our offer of representation at this time. Due to recent events that have transpired, we do not think it is prudent to assume a high-risk client for fear of tarnishing the Coastal Talent Agency image. Perhaps your*

attorneys are better suited to continue handling
your affairs.

We wish you the best of luck with your career and
continued success.

Regards,

Darien Jennings

Coastal Talent

563 Avenue of the Stars

New York, NY 10025

Enclosure: People Magazine photograph
featuring Caleb Christopher CC'd: Richard
Erickson, Erickson, Whistle, and Rand, LLP

A copy of the photograph that cost him better
representation and a brighter acting career fell free from the
envelope. He collapsed on the floor.

"Security, I need your help!" Terrified, Janice called to
the security officer stationed outside Caleb's trailer. "One

minute he was fine and the next he was out," she said, as the guard rushed to Caleb's aid.

"I need the medic to Caleb's trailer. NOW!" he commanded into his walkie-talkie.

"Do you think he's going to be alright?" Janice asked. She picked up the letter and photograph and stuffed them into her bag without the guard noticing.

"I'm sure he's going to be okay, but the medic will be here in a minute."

In the two minutes that it took the medic to arrive to the trailer, they stared at an ashen-faced Caleb on the carpeted floor. The noise of the medic bursting through the door stirred him awake.

"Everybody step back please!" A large female medic with long dreadlocks knelt down next to him.

"I'm alright, thanks," Caleb said, as he used his arms to lift himself up. The security guard helped him to the couch.

"Let me just give you a once over," the medic said, as she retrieved her stethoscope from her bag.

"Really, I'm fine. Thank you for coming though," he said, refusing her treatment.

"Mr. Christopher, I just need to make sure you are okay. It'll just take a minute." She began to take his blood pressure, heartbeat, and checked his eyes with her flashlight. "Everything is normal. What happened?"

"I just got lightheaded. I didn't eat breakfast and had a really light dinner last night," he said. "But like I said, I am fine so if you don't mind…"

"Oh, yes of course," the security guard said, walking to the door. "I'll be right out here if you need anything." Janice thanked him for his help.

"Okay, Caleb. Your blood sugar is probably really low so try to eat something soon. A glass of juice would be a good idea right now," the medic advised.

"I'll get right on that," Janice said, walking out of the trailer in search of craft services.

"Thank you again. I promise to eat soon," he said as the medic left his trailer.

Caleb retrieved the letter protruding from Janice's bag and after reading it a third time, he ripped it to pieces, sat on the couch, and listened to his devoted fans scream his name outside as he waited for his orange juice.

***

Still concerned about their daughter, Collette's parents had not fully enjoyed their walk like Collette would have liked. She was only two chapters into her novel when she heard them enter their room next door. They had been gone less than thirty minutes and Collette had fallen asleep shortly after their return. Knowing that her parents didn't have the big night they deserved, she awoke early the next day and enjoyed the city with them. They took in all the major sites, including The Louvre, Notre Dame Cathedral, Musee d'Orsay, and Galeries Lafayette for shopping, and were exhausted when they arrived back at the hotel later that evening.

"Today was fun, huh," she said to her parents as they rode the tiny escalator to their floor.

"Yes, it was. London tomorrow!" her mother replied excitedly.

"Our train is at nine so we have to get an early start tomorrow," her father said. They exited the elevator and walked down the narrow hall.

"Alright. You guys get some rest. I know I'm tired," Collette said as she unlocked the door to her room.

"Sleep tight, baby girl. Love you," her father said. He tightly hugged her good night.

"I love you too," They all joined in a group hug. "I'll see you in the morning," Collette said as they parted ways for the night.

She took a shower and readied for bed. She stared at herself after brushing her teeth. The corners of her mouth slowly turned upward as she turned off the light in the bathroom before logging on to her computer.

***

Janice approached the trailer with trepidation when she arrived on set the next morning. With Caleb passing out on her first day on the job, she had no idea what today would bring. She still felt incredibly guilty for her role in everything and felt even worse that Coastal Talent had not worked out for him, though she took some solace in knowing that whatever caused that deal to fall apart had nothing to do with her. She entered the trailer to find Caleb reviewing his lines with Helene Murelle, his raven-haired voluptuous 19-year-old co-star. As a former model, this was her first film. She had only previously worked in television, guest starring in a few movie of the week period pieces, and the occasional commercial. Though she was eager to please and took her work very seriously, she was also a young girl who was excited to work with Caleb Christopher—and wouldn't mind if they had their own Hollywood ending.

Caleb was growing tired of practicing the same scene that they were not scheduled to shoot until much later in the day, but at the same time couldn't deny her requests to practice—he knew what it was like to be young and in need of a lot of rehearsal. She had arrived wearing a midriff top that revealed her cleavage and snug, low rider jeans, but this attention-grabbing outfit was lost on him. After an uncomfortable few minutes of small talk, they began practicing a scene where his character was trying, yet again, to get them out of a situation where his decisions had life or death consequences.

"But Blake, are you sure this will work?" Helene was breathlessly asking Caleb as Janice quietly entered the trailer. Helene minded the minor intrusion but remained focused on the scene. Janice quickly walked into the bedroom in the back of the trailer and closed the door. After a few moments Janice opened the door only an inch, allowing her to witness their practice by the mirror's reflection.

"For the last time, Carolyn you've got to trust me!" Caleb replied, exasperated.

"It's not that I don't trust you, it's just …." she said, bashfully turning her face away from him.

"What? Tell me, Carolyn. What is it?" he said slowly turning her head towards him as he looked into her violet eyes. "You've got to let me do this if we're going to get out of here alive." He kissed her passionately on the lips.

"Oh, I do. Yes, I do," she said, looking deeply into his eyes for an extended period before leaving the character. "I feel we should do it one more time. I'm not quite comfortable yet with it," she requested.

"I think you got it, Helene. I don't think we need to run through it again," Caleb said to his co-star who wanted to run through it for the fifth time.

"No, you don't think so?" she asked as he sat down and drank his coffee.

"No, it's fine." She closely sat next to him, a little too close.

"Okay. Well, maybe we can practice again later." She moved her leg to rest on his.

"Yeah, maybe," he said, standing up. "I've got some work to do with my assistant. Janice, let's get started," he said, a little louder as he cleaned off his table with the remains of that morning's breakfast of bacon and eggs.

"Oh, well just let me know if you want to get together again before we shoot," she tried again.

"Uh huh okay," he said. He continued to clean and gave Janice a stack of papers to review.

"I guess I'll see you later then," she said, standing in front of the door with her eyes fixated on him.

"Yep. Bye." He joined Janice on the couch and they began to chat.

"Alright then. I'll just be going," she said, leaving the trailer.

"Christ, that one is going to be a nightmare," he said to Janice after watching her walk a safe distance away.

"What do you mean?

"Did you see her? She comes in here dressed like *that* to rehearse? I feel bad for whoever she gets her claws into," he said, as Janice laughed and shook her head.

"She's just young. Maybe she won't grow up to be some kind of predator."

"Yeah right. Those girls will do anything to get what they want. Trust me. I know.

<u>36</u>

Collette and her parent's train pulled into Charring Cross station with force. The journey had been a fast three hours, and they were excited to head to their hotel in the bustling Piccadilly Circus neighborhood to drop off their things. Collette's mom had wanted to be in a location in the center of everything, and this was certainly it. It reminded Collette of Times Square with its massive crowds, shopping, noise levels, and diverse groups of people. Her mom seemed to be reveling in it all as they walked the crowded streets. After Paris, Collette was just glad to see her happy.

After deciding *not* to check her email—checking it in Paris had lead to disaster—she joined her parents in a walk around the city. She was enjoying the different experience of seeing the city by foot, Tube, and bus as opposed to being driven everywhere with Caleb. The city was bursting with personality and they stopped to have their photo taken in front of everything. After working up a hefty appetite, they stopped in a West End falafel shop for a quick bite and took a seat by a window of the restaurant and waited for their food. She laughed heartily at a story her father was telling, reliving his fresh experience of sitting opposite a stodgy Englishman on the bus who stared straight ahead and ignored the inquisitive child next to him for a good ten blocks. When she happened to glance out the window, she locked eyes with the person on the other side of the glass who was staring at her.

"Colette!" Spencer said as he entered the shop to greet her.

"Spencer, hi," she answered nervously, smiling. She stood to hug him and introduced him to her parents. He was as charming as he ever. "I can't believe I am running into you here."

"I was visiting a friend just down the block. You have an absolutely beautiful daughter, sir," he said to her father. "She is pure joy to be around," he addressed April before turning to Collette. "Love, this is such a fantastic surprise! I saw on your Facebook status that you were in Paris but I had no idea that you were coming to London! Why didn't you ring me?"

"I ... I ... I ... it was a last minute thing. We only decided to come this morning and I knew you were working." Her parents looked at each other.

"Fair enough," he said, smiling warmly. "Is Caleb here? Are you here working?" He looked around the room for his co-star.

"No, he's not here. I'm just here with my parents."

"A family holiday! How fantastic! Say, what are you doing tonight? I'd love to have you guys join my mum and sister for dinner," he said.

"That's very kind of you, Spencer, but I've already made dinner plans," Hampton lied.

"Do you mind me asking where you are going? Don't mean to pry, but my sister's a chef and I know all the good places and the ones to avoid."

"Umm, what was the name of that place, April? I forget," he said to his wife.

"Collette, where was it again?" April asked, passing the buck.

"Oh, some little place by the hotel. Chez something or other," Collette said, remembering the restaurant next to the hotel. She remembered commenting that she did not want to have dinner so closely to where they were staying, and especially at a French restaurant since they had just left France.

"Which hotel?" Spencer asked. "I'm really not stalking you, but some of these places can be quite dicey."

"Le Meridian Piccadilly," Collette said, instantly upset at herself at having disclosed their location.

"Chez Francis? With the blue door?" he asked.

"That sounds right," Collette said as her parents nodded their agreement like two marionettes.

"You're *kidding*! That is where we are dining tonight! Fantastic choice. It's one of the best French outfits in town," he said, eagerly grabbing her hand.

"Oh, what an awful coincidence," her mom said under her breath.

"What's that?" Spencer asked.

"Oh, I said what a lovely coincidence!"

"This is kismet, love!" he said turning to face Collette. "When you said you couldn't come to Rome I was devastated. My mum was so looking forward to meeting you, and now you are here. Really, Collette, I couldn't be happier to see you." He kissed her softly on the cheek. "Are you alright, love? Everything okay?"

"Oh, I'm just tired is all. Still adjusting to the jet lag," she said, gently removing her hands from his firm grasp.

"With all the traveling you do? I don't buy it one bit," he said. For a moment she didn't know if he was kidding until he burst out laughing. "I'm kidding, love! As much as I travel I still have a hard time with jet lag too." Her parents laughed uneasily. "Collette, love, I don't want to hold you up from visiting with your parents, and I've got to get going. I am so looking forward to seeing you all later. Really, I am." He hugged her tightly again.

"Wonderful to meet you, Spencer," Hampton said, shaking his hand.

"Both of you as well." He kissed April's cheek. "Oh, what time is your reservation?"

"Seven o'clock," Collette said, fibbing again.

"That's bloody early to have dinner in these parts! We'll just move our reservation up to meet you there. I'm so excited!" he said, before turning to walk out the door.

Collette could not believe that she had run into Spencer, especially on her first day in London. Not wanting to let her personal life ruin this first day like it had in Paris, she contacted the concierge at their hotel and secured a reservation for 7 o'clock. Her parents insisted that they did not have to go if it was going to upset her, but she assured them it was fine. They agreed that Spencer seemed like a great guy who genuinely cared for her and there was no harm in having dinner.

"Collette, love, I got the impression that something was wrong when you last emailed me," Spencer said to her outside the restaurant. He was right on time. Her parents went inside to have a drink while they waited for his mom and sister.

"How do you mean?" she asked, not wanting to explain her real reason for having blown him off. Never in a million years did she think she would have to explain herself in person. At that moment, she thought she would have still been Caleb's happy fiancée and she would break it to him the next time she saw him. She may have mastered being the bad guy as an assistant—having to constantly tell people that he wasn't coming to their charity event, or he wasn't interested in donating at this time, or no he didn't have time to read the script someone sent him after randomly meeting him on the street. She could turn away any one without blinking an eye, but she was no master at it in her personal life.

"Well, I'm not sure exactly but your tone didn't sound like your usual happy self."

"Oh," she said, her legs becoming wobbly.

"All you said is that you couldn't come to Rome and that we'd talk. Is there something you want to tell me?" he asked. He had a way of focusing on her as if no one else in the world existed.

"I was just overwhelmed. With work, with everything," she said, as her eyes remained on the street.

"Does everything include me?" he said lifting up her chin up with his slender finger.

"I guess it did. I just needed a break and thought it better to tell you when you came back than over email. I'm sorry."

"Is that how you still feel now? I'm not going to be back in New York for a few weeks still and that's more time away from me to give you the space you need. We could start over when I get back," he said.

"I think I just need to be friends right now. Honestly, I'm not even sure if I'm staying in New York. I don't think it's a good idea to commit myself if I'm not going to be around."

"Not staying in New York? What about Caleb? Aren't you still working with him?"

"Uh, no," she said, as her eyes found their way back to her spot on the ground.

"No? What happened?"

"It's a long story, Spencer and one that I'm not ready to share."

"Fair enough," he said. He noticed his mother and sister exiting a taxi. "We'll finish this later okay, love? My mum and sister are here."

A distinguished woman who reminded Collette of a model in a Brook's Brothers ad got out of the cab and glanced Collette over while Spencer paid the tab and hugged his sister. Her hair was a beautiful mass of silver and black thickness that rested on her shoulders. She was perfectly made up and her aqua eyes were accented under highly arched eyebrows. Her lips pursed as her eyes studied Collette from head to toe. Collette grew self-conscious about her Afro and the silver Birkenstock Birko-Flor sandals she wore. She also wasn't sure about the dress she had on—a red and white-striped tunic. She suddenly felt like she should have worn her black cocktail dress instead. Sensing her discomfort, Spencer quickly approached to introduce them.

"Mum, this is Collette," Spencer said. The woman's eyes were fixated on Collette, who was further unnerved when she paused for a long moment before speaking.

"It is absolutely my pleasure to meet you, Collette. Spencer has talked about you nonstop and now I see why. A vision. And please call me Jillian," his mother said, relieving Collette of any tension she may have felt.

"I told you, Mum." He winked at Collette. "Poppy, meet Collette," he said as his sister approached. Dressed the polar opposite of her conservative mother, Poppy wore a simple yellow cotton dress and Converse sneakers, her auburn hair hanging to the middle of her back and her skin so luminous it glowed sans makeup. She was warm and kind and gave Collette a big hug.

"So great to finally meet you, Collette. I've heard nothing but wonderful things about you from my brother, and he never talks about any of his girlfriends," she said. Poppy linked arms with Collette as they walked toward the restaurant.

"Really?" she said, glancing at Spencer.

"Yes, hardly anybody in all these years."

"Alright you two, break it up and let's get inside," Spencer said, opening the door for them as he bashfully smiled at Collette.

"Oh, and don't mind Mum, I can tell she likes you. She made my boyfriend uncomfortable too when she first met him and now she can't get enough of him," Poppy said, comforting her new friend.

This impromptu get-together was going much better than Collette would have expected. Poppy's sisterly warmth had put her at ease and they talked like old friends while enjoying a round of drinks at their private table. Being only 7 o'clock, the entire restaurant, illuminated by a sea of French vanilla candles, was solely theirs. It allowed them freedom to mingle to the backdrop of the soft playing blues music. After the second round of drinks Jillian lovingly began telling stories about Spencer's childhood, much to his chagrin. Before Collette could take too much pleasure in Spencer's discomfort, her parents joined the fun and contributed tales of her growing pains as well. To put a stop to their wild stories, Spencer ordered a bottle of vintage 1997 Château Latour Pauillac and raised his glass.

"Here's to running into my dear Collette and meeting her lovely parents. A most lovely surprise that I can only articulate as kismet. To kismet!" he said, focused on Collette as they clinked away. Collette was grateful for the dim lights of the restaurant because she was sure her cheeks were red. He kissed each one of them.

"So what's this about maybe leaving New York?" he said, pulling her aside to another table.

"Not sure yet, but I am seriously thinking about it," she said, carefully.

"Where would you go?"

"Oh, I don't know Spencer. I haven't given it much thought but I think I need a break from the city."

"I wouldn't be able to convince you to move here, would I?" he asked. He touched the top of her smooth hand.

"Honestly, that's one I hadn't thought of. But I think I am going to stay stateside," she affectionately replied.

"Well if you change your mind…"

"Thank you. I will keep that in mind."

"By the way, I love your parents. I can see where you get your wonderful spirit from," he said, looking deeply into her eyes.

"Thank you. I know they like you too. Your mom and sister are great."

"It's wonderful how they're all getting along," he said, as they took notice of the genial time they were having. "This is seriously one of the best nights of my life, Collette. Seriously. To have you and your parents meet Mum and Poppy is a feeling for me I can't explain," His eyes watered up, to Collette's surprise. "Sorry, love. Didn't mean to get all mushy on you."

"It's okay. Really, Spencer it's okay," she said, resting her hand on his.

"Will I get a chance to see you before you leave town?"

"Sure, I'd like that. But aren't you working?

"No, I'm taking a little holiday. I am using this time to prepare for Rome, which by the way, the offer is still on the table if you can join."

"Hmm. I am already here in Europe and I don't have a job anymore. Let me think about it," she said. She could tell this pleased him immensely.

"Poppy, Mum, Collette may join us in Rome!" He stood and excitedly announced it to the table.

"Oh please come, Collette! We would *love* to have you join us!" Poppy said.

"Oh, yes dear. I do hope you will join us," Jillian said.

"Well, thank you both. I will certainly think about it. Can I let you know in a day or two?"

"Of course," Spencer said. "No need to worry about a place to stay—we are bunking at my uncle's flat. The house is all ours and there's plenty of room. You are welcome too," he said, including April and Hampton.

"That is very kind of you, Spencer, but we will have to get back to Chicago, but thank you," Hampton said.

"Yes, we have to prepare for our move to Denver where Hampton has taken a job at the medical school there," his proud wife said.

"Will you be close to Aspen? We skied there a few years ago and it was simply magnificent," Jillian said.

"I think Aspen is about four hours drive from Denver, but Vail is much closer at just under two hours from the city," April said. "Hampton loves to ski so I am sure we will be there during the winter on the weekends."

"Fantastic!" Spencer said.

"Are you ready to place your order?" their waiter asked as he refilled the water on the table.

"Is Cherrise in the kitchen tonight?" asked Poppy.

"Yes she is, ma'am."

"Cherrise is an amazing chef. If you trust me I'd like to have her prepare something special," Poppy said to Collette and her parents.

"Of course. We're in your hands," Hampton said.

"Wonderful. Please ask her to prepare whatever she'd like for us. My name is Poppy."

"As you wish," said the waiter, scurrying off.

"Cherrise and I went to cooking school together and have worked in a few of the same restaurants. I always leave it to her to prepare my meals when I eat here, and she does the same when she is in my restaurant. It will be fabulous, you'll see."

"We completely trust you," Collette said.

"I promise you won't be disappointed." she said, as they laughed over good wine and shared stories like old friends for the rest of the night.

***

"You will NEVER guess who I ran into yesterday," Collette said to Lou from her hotel room after their three-hour satisfying and gluttonous meal of all things prepared with butter and cream. Her parents were enjoying a night cap in the hotel lobby but Collette couldn't think of anything else she wanted to do except fall into bed.

"Who?" Lou asked.

"SPENCER! Can you believe it?"

"No way!"

"Yes! We ran into him while we were having lunch and I can't tell you how shocked I was. I mean, I had just blown him off by email not that long ago and BAM! There he is!"

"What happened?" she asked walking down the street towards her apartment after picking up her dry cleaning.

"Well, I was totally nervous and everything, but he was his usual sweet self and he invited us to dinner with him and his mother, who I thought hated me at first, and his sister, who is a chef and so awesome, by the way."

"Really?"

"Yes. So anyway, I so did NOT want to go to dinner with them because I just didn't want to deal or anything, but he was so damn cute the way he was looking at me and my parents seemed to like him, so we just went."

"Oh my God, Collette! What happened?"

"Well, believe it or not I actually had a great time. Paris sucked ass because of that picture of Caleb with Amber."

"Asshole."

"So, I just tried to keep an open mind and just said 'fuck it', and went," she said, rolling around on the bed to get comfortable.

"That's my girl!"

"And guess what else Lou? I'm going to Rome," she said jumping from the bed as she excitedly twirled around the room.

"Rome? With your parents? I thought you were coming back soon?"

"No, with Spencer." She flopped down in a chair.

"Oh. My. God. No freaking way, C."

"He asked me again, even after I told him I only wanted to be friends and am moving to Colorado—"

"Umm, *Colorado*? Excuse me?"

"Oh, I was just about to get to that. I'm leaving the city, Lou. I seriously need a break."

"No, C! You can't! What am I gonna do? And why the hell are you going out there?" she asked. Lou tossed the dry cleaning on her bed.

"You'll be fine. Besides, you're never in the city anyway. You've been spending a lot more time in Miami lately with your mom."

"I guess so. But still, C. Leaving New York for Colorado? That's a big leap. What are you going to do there?"

"Well, my parents are moving there."

"What!" This is all too weird for me. Your parents are leaving Chicago to go to Colorado? What is going on here? Am I in an episode of the Twilight Zone or something?" she asked, sitting on her couch dumbfounded.

"My dad is going to be working at the University Of Colorado Medical School. He got a teaching post."

"That's great for him. I didn't know he was looking to leave the hospital."

"Neither did I, but apparently he had a friend who hooked him up. It'll be good for them because he likes to ski."

"Okay, so then are you moving with your parents?"

"Oh God no! They'll be in Denver and I've decided to go to Boulder."

"Boulder?"

"Yeah, it's about 30 minutes from Denver in the foothills of the Rockies and I'm going to enroll in CU's writing program."

"You can write here in New York, C."

"I know, but I'm hoping to find inspiration from the mountains and besides it's so naturally beautiful there with far less distractions than New York. I'm hoping to really be able to concentrate."

"Well, that's true. But, C, I'm going to miss you."

"You can always visit anytime you want. The next time you go to LA just stop in Denver on the way there or back."

"I guess it is sort of on the way out there. Wait, have you actually applied yet?"

"No, not officially. I sent away for a catalog a while ago before my mom and dad decided to move there. How random is that? But I never applied."

"So how do you know you are going to get in?"

"I guess I don't but I figured I could start with some basic open enrollment classes, they're so much cheaper than any school around here, and apply if I like the school and the town."

"When exactly did you decide all this?"

"Funny thing was when I saw that photo of Caleb and Amber I got so upset to the point where my parents didn't do any sightseeing that day," she said, reliving her somber day.

"Oh, C, I'm sorry."

"It's okay. The next day I just woke up and decided I had enough and I was not going to let him emotionally control me anymore. Know what I mean? And as luck would have it CU had sent me an email asking if I received their brochure and to call them with questions so I really took it as a sign. I mean, what are the chances of them sending me that email at the same time I saw that photo? So I thought the universe was trying to tell me something."

"Well, I guess I can see how you came to that."

"I mean, I never thought I would actually do it, but when we got home from dinner I registered for two classes starting the second summer session to give me time to get out there, find a place, and get acclimated."

"Wow. I can't believe it, C."

"Me neither."

"I've heard that town is crawling with hot guys."

"I'm sure it's full of ski bums, but I just want to go and be by myself for awhile."

"When are your parents going?"

"I think they will be there within a month of us getting back."

"Wow."

"Tell me about it. So I'm going to stay with them for a week or two until I find a place and just go do it. I've always wanted to write anyway and I just can't be around all the Caleb drama anymore. I mean Amber again? Seriously."

"Well, he never did get you a ring…"

"I know but to be fair, we were going to start looking for one. I guess it wasn't meant to be."

"Look at you, C. A new life and maybe a new man."

"Hey now, don't get ahead of yourself, Lou. I'm still only interested in being friends and only said yes because I have some free time on my hands."

"Umm hmm, whatever."

"What?"

"You can honestly tell me you don't feel anything romantic towards Spencer anymore? Be honest now. Remember who you're talking to," Lou said as she ransacked her closet and tossed items on the bed.

"Well, I don't know! I mean he's still cute, so maybe just a little."

"I think he has shown you what a real man is, fawning all over you like that. AND you got along with his mother? You are so in, C."

"You are funny, Lou. I'm just going to have some fun before I come home. I didn't tell him about Colorado but I suppose he'll find out soon enough."

"Alright, you. I have to get moving here. I'm on my way to the airport for Miami for a week or so."

"See?"

"Yeah, I know. Call me soon?"

"I will and have fun."

"Love you."

"Love you too. Bye."

Collette hung up the phone and posted an ad to Craigslist to sublease her place in New York. She then looked for apartments for rent in Boulder.

***

For the last few days Amber had been celebrating her latest financial windfall courtesy of her racy photographs with Caleb. Bruce had also been pleased that his time had not been wasted. He had even taken a few shots of some girl going in and out of Caleb's home and his trailer. Not knowing or caring who she was, he'd run with the photos of the brunette beauty with headlines such as "*CALEB CHRISTOPHER'S LATEST SQUEEZE ENTERS HIS HOME AND TRAILER. WHERE'S AMBER?*" This headline was followed by a forlorn looking Amber sitting in a park reading an issue of *The New Yorker*. The images were the brainchild of Amber—a way to keep the money flowing to her and a way to make her seem like the victim again. Bruce was fine with it and Amber eagerly continued to pay off her debt whenever Bruce was in the mood. She enjoyed playing house in his apartment when he was gone, rifling through his things, looking at photo albums of his wife and children, and eating all of his food.

Continuing to take liberties, she nestled herself in the back of his closet to rifle through a few seemingly benign shoeboxes. She came across a brilliant diamond Tiffany's tennis bracelet. Feeling like Christmas had come early for her this year, she twirled around wearing it in front of the mirror. She waved it in the face of a small teddy bear that sat smiling on the dresser. "Probably belonged to one of the dumb kids", she said aloud. After wearing it around the apartment for a few hours she grew to like the feel of it. Its weight around her wrist felt so natural, like she was born wearing it. She didn't think he would miss it since it was buried in his closet any way. She dropped it in her bag. If he found it missing she would say his housekeeper was probably to blame.

Her co-habitation with Bruce came to an end after a few days when he told her his wife was coming. No love lost, she quickly found a small apartment to rent. When the realtor asked if she had a job, she pulled out a thick wad of cash for the security deposit, realtor fee, and first month's rent. She was a high-paid model, she smugly replied, and if he didn't mind could she please just sign the lease and get on with it already because she had just arrived from Paris and was exhausted. After securing the keys to her new Lower East side 275 square-foot studio at the bargain price of $1800 a month, she dropped off her things and called the only person she knew in the city.

"Hey babe, guess what I did today?" she asked Bruce as she stood on the dirty parquet floor of her new digs.

"What?" he flatly responded.

"I got my own place. Wanna come celebrate?"

"Do you ever listen? I told you Linda is coming today."

"Oh the wife. Right."

"Yeah the wife. Remember that."

"Anyway, do you wanna come celebrate or what?" she asked.

"I got shit to do before she gets here. I need to have my spot cleaned after the mess you left it in."

"Yes! You should definitely call the maid to clean it up," she said, remembering her sparkly gift to herself.

"I gotta go. I'm busy, Amber."

"Well, what time is she getting here? You know you aren't that busy where you can't come get a piece of this," she teased.

"I am busy," he said, feeling himself grow excited at the idea.

"You sure?" she purred. "I can just handle it myself then."

"Shit. Where you at?"

"Right off Delancy by the bridge. But if you can't come, I'll just keep undressing myself here," she said, fully clothed.

"All the way down there? I don't have time to go that far."

"Maybe I can come to you at your office. I know how you like to take me over your desk in there," she said, making sure the tennis bracelet was not in her purse, but in her larger bag.

"You better get your ass up here now after talking all this shit. But hurry up because I don't have all day."

Amber hopped in a cab and headed uptown as Janice looked at another paparazzi photo of her online sitting in Caleb's trailer.

"Gosh, how do you handle this?" she asked Caleb. She showed him the photo of her leaving his home with a stack of scripts. He was on a break and Janice was going over some things that Katherine had brought to her attention.

"It's annoying as fuck, that's for sure."

"They don't even know who I am but keep calling me your *mystery brunette beauty*. I know they make up crap like this all the time, but I guess I have never been the subject of it."

"Hopefully they will go away and leave us alone. I'm as sick of it as you are."

"I'm sure Amber is behind this. Do you want me to try to do anything?"

"No, don't worry about it. It'll go away faster if I don't do or say anything. I don't want to add fuel to the fire."

"Makes sense. In the meantime, I'll just have to make sure I look decent when I come and go," she joked.

"Don't pay it a second thought," he said, looking through the papers. "Hand me a stack of headshots please." He froze when he came across Collette's email to Katherine with the request.

"What's wrong?"

"Nothing, I'm fine. Say, would you mind going to get me some lunch, please?"

"Sure, I was going to head to craft services anyway," she said, standing.

"If you don't mind, I'm not in the mood for crafty today. I think I want something lighter. Would you mind grabbing me some sushi from this place across town? It's on the Upper West Side. Randal knows where it is. Just ask him to take you up there and please get something for yourself," he said, handing her a $100 bill.

"What kind of sushi?"

"Whatever the lunch special is. Thanks."

"Okay, I'll be back as soon as possible," she said, as she walked out of the trailer.

"Take your time."

Collette had not responded to any of his emails since she had been gone and he had just been trying to concentrate on work until she returned. This note from Katherine was sure to deter him from that focus.

> *Katherine,*
>
> *I hope you are doing well. I wish I could say I was, but lately I'm not so sure about anything anymore and feel as though my life has been thrown into a tailspin. You may or may not have heard that me and Caleb are no longer together and that I am no longer his assistant. I'm sad that this is the case. Perhaps we just were not meant to be. I so wanted for our story to end up*

differently than this, but I guess some things are out of our control.

Nevertheless, I am enjoying vacationing with my parents in Europe at the moment. We are taking in Paris and London—what a different experience not being here with a celebrity! I actually have to pay for everything :)

In any case, Marcielle from Air France would like a photo for her niece if you could take care of it please. It should be sent to:

Grace Crillon

2390 W. 92nd Street, Unit 12

NYC 10010

Best regards to you Katherine, and do take care. It has been my pleasure working with you.

Love,

Collette

Caleb lay on the bed and stared at the ceiling as tears rolled from the corners of his eyes, moistening his pillowcase.

37

Bruce's wife Linda arrived to his apartment and was immediately impressed by its cleanliness. For once, the dishes were cleaned and put away, the bathroom looked like it had been scrubbed, and the linens were freshly washed on the bed. The place was filled with the scents of Pine Sol, Windex, and Tide. Wanting to surprise her husband when he arrived home in an hour, she quickly went to the store to pick up a few groceries and a bottle of White Zinfandel. She planned a special dinner to thank him for meticulously cleaning the house.

A meal of chicken thighs with saffron rice and red beans wafted towards Bruce as he walked through the door. He greeted his doe-eyed high school sweetheart and mother of his children, ages 11, 7, and 8 months. He pecked her on the cheek before excusing himself to take a quick shower. She enjoyed a glass of wine while she finished preparing the meal in the kitchen. Her silk robe skimmed her soft, fleshy body. She had been working hard to get herself back in shape after the birth of their youngest child and felt guilty about not exercising that day, as she stirred the beans atop the gas stove. Bruce left the shower, and still naked, pressed himself against her in the kitchen. He carried her to the bedroom and made love to her as if he hadn't in a long time. Sex between them had been sporadic since the birth of their newborn, and with his spending more time in the city for work, she found herself mostly home alone. Tonight was a treat because she couldn't get to the city often to see her husband and was looking forward to going out after dinner. After their lovemaking he was exhausted and hungry. She relaxed and turned on the television in the bedroom while he went to make their dinner plates, whistling as he did so.

Linda decided to check the batteries in the nanny cam to make sure they did not need replacing. It was rare that her kids were ever here in the care of a sitter, but just to make sure they were safe, she had purchased the cute teddy bear after all the horror stories she'd heard from other parents concerning their dilemmas with babysitters. She popped the SIM card into the television before she erased the contents of their last visit with the sitter. Initially nothing was amiss. When Bruce walked back into the room happy as a lark with two large helpings of food, Amber began to prance around on the TV screen. The images of Amber going down on her husband and her perfect naked body writhing on top of him left her speechless. She tried to scream but nothing came out. Bruce dropped the plates on the floor and looked on in horror as the time stamp showed that not only had Amber been in the house for multiple days, but on multiple occasions. Linda nearly hyperventilated as she watched Amber wave her tennis bracelet in the bear's face as she commented on how the bear must belong to one of the stupid kids before slipping it in her bag. Amber also incriminated herself as she took Linda's emergency cash stowed away between the mattresses. After Amber had the $2,640 in her hands, she laughed counting and recounting it before stuffing it into her wallet.

Bruce did not protest as Linda dressed, placed the SIM card in her purse, gathered her things, and left. She had forgiven him in the past for his rumored dalliances, but with concrete proof he didn't know what she was going to do, but was sure she would ask for a divorce. He cursed the bear for being the bear, and himself for forgetting to shut it off.

***

Collette said good-bye to her parents at the train station as they headed to Heathrow for their flight back home. She insisted that she knew what she was doing and promised to have a good time in Rome. She apologized again for ruining Paris, but assured them that London had really been great. Instead of seeing Spencer again after their dinner at Chez Francis, she'd opted to spend the remaining days with her parents, since she would be joining him in Rome anyway. She saw that they boarded the correct train and waited out front for Spencer to pick her up.

"Hi!" she said, receiving his light kiss on the lips as she greeted him in his tiny Smart Car.

"Hello, love," he said, glowing.

"Where are Jillian and Poppy?"

"They are meeting us at the airport later. We have about four hours until our flight, so I thought I would take you to my favorite spot for lunch."

"Great."

Collette was nervous and excited as Spencer sped through the streets to a destination unknown to her. He sang at the top of his lungs to tunes that played from his preset classic R&B station. Collette couldn't help but sing along and wondered to herself why she had never seen this side of him before. Twenty minutes later he whipped his small car into a teeny parking spot upon arriving at The Hummingbird Bakery.

"Cupcakes?" she asked, confused.

"I wanted to treat my sweet to a treat," he said, offering his hand. She quickly took it.

"Ohhhhh...."

"Besides, who says you can't have dessert first."

So taken in by the enchanting eatery, Collette enjoyed a red velvet cupcake and Spencer a vanilla one. The treats were so delicious that Spencer ordered a key lime pie with

the intention of bringing it to Rome to share with his mom
and sister, but instead they devoured the entire thing in one
sitting, laughing and enjoying each other's company. They
walked hand and hand through the fashionable
neighborhood and shared an order of fish and chips before
heading to his modest central London flat that overlooked
the Thames. The brick building partially covered in vine
with bay windows reminded Collette of the classic row
houses in Harlem. She was enamored by its charm. His
third floor unit was just as charismatic as his gingham sheets
were classic and crisp, and the few photographs on the walls
added to this simplicity. The bathroom was not fancy and
did not have a window. It exhibited signs of a bachelor—a
tube of toothpaste squeezed to its absolute limits with the
cap on the floor, sprinkles of his hair in the tub, generic
Tesco body wash, and a sink that could use a quick scrub.
But the living room with its mismatched furniture handed
down from his mother, and beautiful cherry wood dining
room table from his grandmother, was a welcome change to
Caleb's ultra modern taste. The view of the river was

partially blocked by a neighboring building but the windows allowed just enough light to make the space warm and inviting. At 800 square feet at best, it was simple, understated, and perfect.

"It's not much, but it's got a bed," he said.

"Oh, no Spencer. It's great. A real down-to-earth place with lots of character and charm."

"Is that a good thing or a bad thing?" he asked, not sure if he wanted the answer.

"It's a great thing." Her smile invited his embrace.

They lost themselves in a kiss Collette thought impossible for friends to share. At that moment, Collette didn't want to be friends with him at all.

38

My Dear Collette,

I hope you are enjoying your trip with your parents.
You certainly did deserve the break. I just came across
the photograph request for Marcielle and I will see to it
that Janice gets it in the mail to her niece right away.
FYI – Sean's former assistant Janice has been helping
me out. You are not replaceable but so far she's doing
ok.

I think you are coming back to New York in the next day
or so and I can only hope that you will call me when
you get back. I have been a mess since you left
and miss you more than you know. I am looking
forward to seeing you again and will do whatever you
need me to do to repair things between us.

Missing you.
Caleb

Caleb could only hope that Collette would respond to this email. His previous pleas to her had gone unanswered and he wanted to see her again more than anything. He knew that if he could speak to her in person that she would understand and everything would be okay. Amber seemed to keep popping up in paparazzi photos under salacious headlines, but he knew the public's interest in her would wane if he didn't engage her in the press. It disgusted him to know that he'd let someone like Amber ruin his relationship with Collette.

***

Spencer glowed as he and Collette arrived at the airport for their flight to Rome. Noticing their clasped hands as they entered the terminal, Poppy greeted Collette as if she were a long lost friend. Collette greeted her with the same enthusiasm and the two of them scampered off to the ladies room for a quick tinkle, leaving Spencer with their bags.

"Collette, it's so great to see you again! I loved your parents by the way," Poppy said, as they headed to the bathroom.

"Thank you! It's lovely to see you again too. Where's your mom anyway, isn't she coming?"

"Yes, she should be here any minute now. We had to come separately. Can we talk about how my brother is absolutely glowing out there, Collette? He looks really happy," she said, entering a stall.

"I'm glad he's happy. We sort of made up," she replied as her cheeks reddened.

"Made up? I didn't know you guys were apart?"

"Yeah, I needed a bit of space."

"Well, I'm glad you guys are back together. He never spoke like you were ever apart. Oh well! I guess I can't expect him to tell his sis everything, now can I?" she said, as Collette waited by the sinks.

"No, I guess not. He really is a great guy, Poppy. I mean, I think he was right—it was fate that we met up here again," she said.

"He's certainly got it bad for you. That much I do know."

"Yeah, he's made that pretty clear."

They left the bathroom to find Spencer and Jillian waiting for them. Jillian greeted Collette warmly and Spencer took her hand as they headed to the gate for their flight to Rome.

***

Bruce was so angry he didn't know what to do. He barked at his employees as they asked him the most benign questions. When he just couldn't take it anymore, he stormed out of the office and headed to a bar to decide what to do. His wife had not returned his calls and he knew this was the straw that broke the camel's back. After pounding a couple Heinekens and chasing them with two shots of Jim Beam at a Hell's Kitchen hole-in-the-wall, he felt it was time to teach Amber a lesson. He was going to rid himself of her once and for all.

***

"Good morning," Katherine said to Caleb in his trailer the next morning. He sent Janice on a slew of errands to keep her busy that morning so he could have time alone to speak to Katherine.

"How are you today, Katherine?" he asked. She sat at the table relieved to be away from the throngs of screaming fans.

"I'm alright. The question is how are you doing?"

"I've been better. Still no word from Collette but I'm trying not to let it bother me. I certainly haven't been able to give this film 100%, that's for sure," he said.

"Things will get better, Caleb."

"Yeah, thanks."

"Listen, your ad is coming out at the end of the week. We were able to get it in *Harper's*, *Vogue*, *Women's Wear Daily*, *Elle*, and *Vanity Fair*. It cost you a small fortune though," she said, showing him the photo of a resplendent Collette happily twirling about with the skyline behind her.

She looked so confident, as if she had the world at her fingertips.

"Wow. That is beautiful. She is beautiful," he said, mesmerized by the image of his former fiancé.

"Yes it is. She really knocked it out of the park. Stunning."

"Katherine, I don't know what to do to get her back. I'm dying here," he said.

"Caleb, I've never been too good at matters of the heart, but I do know that if you love her like you say you do then you will have to show her when she comes back. She's coming back tomorrow, right?"

"Yeah, I think so."

"Well, I would suggest you stop feeling sorry for yourself and do something," she said, lightly touching his arm. She was afraid he was upset with her because he was silent for an unusually long time before speaking.

"You know what? You're absolutely right. I fucked up and instead of crying over it I just need to fix it."

"That's the spirit. Go get what you want, Caleb. You're a fighter. Show her what you are really made of." Katherine felt her phone vibrate in her coat pocket. "Excuse me a second," she said, walking to the back of the trailer.

"Hello?"

"Is this Katherine Riley from Riley & Associates?"

"Yes. To whom am I speaking?"

"My name is Bruce from Celebs One, here in the city."

"The paparazzi agency? Why are you calling me and how did you get this number?" she asked, annoyed.

"I'm sorry to bother you ma'am, I called your office and your assistant transferred me to it so I don't actually have it. I'm calling because of Amber Skye and I would like to speak to Caleb Christopher. I understand he's your client?"

"Why are you calling because of her? And why do you need to speak to him?" she asked. Caleb busied himself on his computer oblivious of Katherine's call.

"Well, ma'am, like I said, I'm sorry to bother you and Mr. Christopher, but I have a proposal for him."

"Bruce, is it? Can you get to the point please?" Upon hearing Bruce's name, Caleb's ears perked up. He didn't personally know a Bruce but remembered Amber calling the photographer by this name when she ambushed him.

"Okay. It's a long story, but I know Amber has caused Caleb some, uh, how do I say it—troubles—and I have been the one behind the photos."

"Yes, your sleazy photos. I'm aware of them," she said as Caleb walked curiously towards her. He placed his ear next to the phone so he could hear the conversation.

"Yes. Basically, I would like apologize to Mr. Christopher for that."

"Apologize? That's a first," Katherine said. "What do you want Bruce?"

"I want to help Mr. Christopher get back at Amber."

"And why would you want to do that? What on earth could your prize subject have done to you?"

"She made me lose my wife. That is what the bitch has done," he said angrily.

"How'd she do that?" Caleb said, taking the phone away from Katherine.

"Mr. Christopher?"

"Yes, call me Caleb," he said, taking a seat on the couch.

"Nice to meet you, by phone, sir. Anyway, to be honest Amber and I sort of had a thing—"

"Really? You don't say." Caleb asked intrigued. "That girl really gets around."

"Uh, yeah. Anyway, it's a crazy story and I shouldn't have been fucking her in the first place, but I let her stay at my place, she took something that didn't belong to her, and long story short, Linda, that's my wife, left me."

"I'd say I am sorry, but you two have caused me a lot of stress and made me lose my fiancée. I don't think I can help you so—"

"Wait! Just hear me out. I know that what I did was wrong, and honestly I wouldn't even be caring about helping you get your girl back if she hadn't so royally fucked me over. I've got kids, man."

"I'm sorry that your kids will be affected by this, Bruce, but I don't know what you want from me. That girl is toxic and I don't want anything else to do with her. I just want the whole thing to go away."

"I know you do, and believe me I do too, but I've never come across a bitch like this before and the only way she is going to learn is by having the script flipped on her. Walkin' around thinking she's all that and her shit don't stank. I ain't no choirboy, but most other girls I've fucked around with have kept their mouths shut and didn't just help themselves to shit that didn't belong to them. But she's a whole different breed."

"Why should I help you? You're the fucking paparazzi!"

"Because she fucked us both over, that's why. If you help me, you won't have to worry about me or anyone else from my agency messing with you anymore. You have my word."

"You better not be bullshitting me, man. I'm tired of this shit. No more photos of me or my assistant or ANYBODY for that matter coming in or out of my house,

following me around, jumping out of the bushes. Anything.
I mean it. Just leave me the hell alone if I help you."

"You've got my word. For real."

"I hope I don't regret this. Tell me what you've got in
mind," he said.

39

They had only been in Rome for one day and Collette was having a great time. After they landed, a car drove them to a beautiful flat minutes away from the Spanish Steps in the heart of the city. The interior of the apartment was as antique as the exterior, but it was comfortable and had a good deal of light, even if it was noisy. The four of them enjoyed a three-hour meal at a local favorite of Spencer's uncle, where he signed autographs and posed with the owners. Collette, Poppy, and Jillian were serenaded beautifully in Italian by street performers as they sat on the patio.

After dinner they ventured through the ancient streets to walk off their large meal and three bottles of wine before returning home.

"Collette, I am so glad you're here," Spencer said. They were in the kitchen where Collette was making tea for herself and Poppy as Jillian slept soundly down the hall.

"Me too. Thank you for inviting me. I'm having a great time."

"I love you Collette!" he blurted. "Heavens, I'm sorry, love, I didn't mean to just say it like that, but I do."

"Wow, Spencer." She leaned heavily into the kitchen counter to support her weight.

"I didn't say it so that you would say it back, I just wanted you to know," he said, looking into her wide eyes.

"I have strong feelings for you Spencer, but I'm not sure I'm quite there yet."

"It's okay, love. I just wanted you to know how I felt. Always better to just say it, right?"

"Yes, it usually is."

"Alright then, I guess I'll leave you to your tea. Poppy loves this stuff and I don't want to keep you two from chatting or whatever you've got planned. Okay then," he said, turning to walk out of the kitchen.

"Spencer?"

"Yes, love?" He faced her full of optimism.

"Thank you."

"For what, love?"

"For being you."

"Umm. Okay." She pulled him close and kissed him gently.

"Just because I'm not 'there' yet, doesn't mean we can't still have a good time here, right?"

"Of course, love. We're going to have a great time, love. No worries at all," he said, kissing her on the forehead. "Whew!" He used the back of his hand to wipe the dollops of sweat that had formed on his brow. "I'll leave you and Poppy be and will see you first thing in the morning." The tea kettle began to whistle.

"Good night, Spencer."

Collette poured the tea in elegant cups and joined Poppy on the veranda where she could see Spencer switch off his light, leaving him in the dark.

40

"So you're sure this is what you want me to wear because it's butt ugly," Amber said to Victor in his studio for her fitting two days later.

"YES! Would you zip it already! Models aren't supposed to talk, or didn't your agency tell you that?" Victor asked.

"Hey mister, I have an *opinion* and I'm going to *voice* it. This dress is heinous. People will see me in this *thing* on the runway!" she said. She was referring to the simple silver metallic dress that hung to the floor. "And it's so *long*. How's anyone gonna see my legs?" She lifted up material to showcase her slender legs.

"Enough, Amber."

"And don't you have anything that actually matches my complexion? I'm a red head. I mean, *hello*, I don't look good in silver."

Even for Victor, this was enough. He grabbed her arm and yanked her from the apple box she was standing on. "Look, you. You shut your hole or you're out of here. I'm only doing this because you've been in the press lately and because of your relationship with Caleb, alright? That two-bit agency you're with played that up like you were hot shit or something, which you are NOT, so you just wear what I tell you to wear and keep your fucking mouth closed. Got it?"

"Got it," she said making a face behind his back as he walked away.

***

Bruce had convinced Caleb to go along with his plan. He knew that Amber had sassed her way into some minor modeling agency—she'd used her paparazzi photos as tear sheets and apparently convinced someone that she was the next big thing because she already had a celebrity boyfriend and could make lots of money. The agent wasn't too interested until she made it clear that she would do whatever, and she meant whatever, it took to get signed. He called her bluff and after performing fellatio on the paunchy middle-aged man she had herself a one-year contract with

Models-N-More, which she didn't bother to read. The small agency was a joke amongst the more reputable ones, Elite, Ford, Next, and IMG—primarily because the girls they represented couldn't get representation anywhere else. They didn't measure up in some way—too short, too heavy, or saddled with a negative attitude. It was also an open secret that the agent had no morals or ethics whatsoever and made full use of his casting couch.

Thinking she had done nothing wrong, Amber left Bruce numerous messages telling him about her big fashion show at some nondescript hotel in midtown. She knew this was going to be her big break and wanted him to be there to capture her New York modeling runway debut. She was sure the designer had booked only the top girls in the industry for the show and wanted Bruce to make sure he got a shot of her and the other supermodels after the show drinking Cristal, as she was sure they would be. Bruce didn't call her back, but only sent her a text that he would be there camera ready.

As her luck would have it, the show was happening on the same day that Caleb's ad came out that didn't feature her as she had hoped. It put her in the crabbiest of moods. From the window of the dressing room at the hotel she had the displeasure of seeing Collette's mug on a billboard across the street with the copy: *THANK YOU ALL FOR YOUR SUPPORT OF MY NOW RETIRED CLOTHING LINE. I COULDN'T HAVE DONE IT WITHOUT YOU AND MY LOVELY FIANCÉE, COLLETTE, FEATURED HERE. I LOVE YOU BOTH!* She didn't appreciate being upstaged by Collette of all people on her big day. It made her sick to her stomach and she didn't hide her anger or aggression with the other models, the crew, or with Victor himself. She snapped at the other models, none of whom were Lisel Wright or anything close. She especially didn't like it when the models tried to question the validity of her relationship Caleb, since she previously boasted about it at the fitting.

Bruce took his place with the other photographers at the end of the runway and snapped away and took pleasure as Amber stumbled over the fabric of her gown while wearing her best supermodel pout. As she turned and posed for the cameras, she involuntarily frowned as she caught a glimpse of Collette's billboard again. After she bumped into another model walking back from the end of the runway, she spent the rest of the twenty minutes backstage drinking champagne and smoking—ignoring the large 'No Smoking' sign. She just wanted the show to end. After Victor took his customary bow as the models filed down the runway at the finale, Bruce noticed that he was visibly upset as he walked off the stage and headed down the hall towards the men's room. The bright lights blinded Amber as she tried to seek out Bruce from the stage. She was annoyed that he was not there when she left.

Caleb sat in a back booth in a dirty coffee shop on Eighth Avenue around the corner from Amber's runway show waiting for Bruce. He was finishing his cup of coffee when Bruce located him.

"Well, how was it?" Caleb asked.

"She was so horrible, it was awesome!" Bruce said, as he high-fived Caleb. "I mean, she was stumbling around all over the place and kept frowning without knowing it. She looked terrible." He opened up his computer and prepared to upload the photos.

"Ok, let's see them," Caleb said as the images quickly appeared on his Power Book. Before his eyes were photos sure to bring her modeling career to a screeching halt. She clearly had a difficult time walking in something that wasn't a mini skirt or underwear, and her pout was laughable. "What's up with the lighting? It's terrible, man."

"All part of the plan, my friend. I was careful to shoot her only when the lights hit her at her worst, creating all these shadows you see and purposely played with the exposure to make it less flattering," he said, pleased with his handy work.

"Pure genius. I can't wait till she sees all of this. You sure she's gonna call and you got Victor's bit?"

"Yes and yes. She'll call cuz that's ALL she's been doin' lately. She's such a dumb ass, man. I swear I wanted to kill her after Linda left, but I think this is going to be much better."

"I hope you're right."

"Trust me, I am. She is the worst kind of press whore and will do anything to advance her 'career'. She kept begging me to come capture her big *debut* and shit, and I've only done what she asked," he said, laughing to himself. "She's the kind of person who won't take no for an answer and doesn't care who she steps all over to get what she wants. This will teach her ass a lesson once and for all and get her off both our backs."

"Hey, I'm all for it," he said, scooting out from the booth. "I've got to get going to fix my own mess. What time is this going to be up?"

"Give me about half an hour and check the wires. You'll be pleased."

"Alright."

"Oh, Joe, Laura, and Jesse were happy to help too. Thanks for getting them on board."

An hour later from her living room, agitated that Bruce had not returned her call or waited for her after the show, she eagerly read his text that came through.

Sorry I couldn't call. Your pictures are online everywhere. People, Style.com, US, E!, Entertainment Weekly, the papers. This is going to be IT for you! Congrats and good luck.

B

She nearly choked on a Tootsie Roll when she saw the atrocious, poorly lit, heavily shadowed photos on her computer screen. Bruce had released a photo of her squinting into the bright lights with a clenched jaw, another of her tripping on her dress nearly falling off the runway, one of her bumping into another girl, and one of her frowning. As if these images were not damaging enough, they were juxtaposed next to Collette's ad under the headline, *"CALEB CHRISTOPHER PUBLICLY DECLARES HIS*

LOVE FOR HIS FIANCÉE, COLLETTE SMITH, WHILE AMBER SKYE DISAPPOINTS AT HER RUNWAY DEBUT. LOOKS LIKE THE BETTER WOMAN AND MODEL HAS WON CALEB'S HEART. GAME OVER, AMBER!"

Angry tears sprang from her eyes as she hesitantly clicked on the YouTube clip titled: *"AMBER SKYE RUINS VICTOR'S SHOW".*

"That fucking Amber ruined my goddamed show!" Victor said. "She was absolutely the WORST model I have EVER worked with, and I've been around the block with these hungry bitches, and she had attitude up the ying yang. That low-rent agency she is with should drop her. I will NEVER book her again. NEVER! I mean, really, did you see her stumble all over the place? She wasn't even in high heels for chrissakes! She needs to get back on the first bus to Ohio, or wherever her corn-fed ass is from, because she's got no future in this business."

"Umm hmm," Jake said to the camera, from behind Victor.

"Umm hmm?! You're the one who booked her, asshole," he said. "What the hell were you thinking, Jake! Pack your bags because you're going to be on that same bus as her. Fucking amateurs." Victor said as he walked away from the camera.

Thinking it was over, she was about to shut her computer when the video abruptly cut to Joe the photographer and his girlfriend Laura, describing what a difficult model she had been to work with during her shoot. They also made sure to mention that she possessed no natural posing ability and made everyone uncomfortable with her repeated raunchy jokes and manner of speaking. Next up was Jesse, the production assistant. He also attested to her bad attitude, her bossy nature, and how he overheard her conversation to a paparazzi photographer. He was shocked to learn that not only was she selling Caleb's whereabouts, but was having a sexual relationship with this paparazzo as well.

As if these testimonials were not damaging enough, her unflattering images began to play over accelerated circus music as the video slowly faded to black.

<u>41</u>

"HOW COULD YOU DO THIS TO ME?" Amber yelled into the phone. She had called at least ten times in a row until Bruce finally decided to pick up.

"I only did what you asked, remember? You told me to shoot you at your *big debut* and that's what I did," he said. Bruce was in his office where he distractedly scanned his emails.

"You know what I mean, Bruce! You have ruined my career! You asshole!" She paced the dirty floor of her apartment.

"Whatever happens to you, you brought it on yourself. You'll think about that the next time you steal somebody's shit."

"What?"

"What my ass. You know what you did. You took Linda's bracelet and her money. Now don't call my ass again. If you do, you'll be sorry."

"How did you—"

"The goddamn *teddy bear* you dumb ass. It was a nanny cam that caught everything on tape," he said with disdain.

"That teddy bear had a camera in it?"

"Yes, it's a nanny cam, idiot! I have kids remember, but according to you they are just stupid and dumb, but you've got them beat there. Now don't call my ass again or else I'm sure your friend Officer Starkey would love to get his hands on it and your ass will really end up in jail this time."

"You wouldn't Bruce."

"Just try me. Better yet, just ask Linda. My *wife* who *left* me on account of you. Stay out of my life, Amber and DO NOT call me again," he warned. He slammed the phone shut.

***

Since Spencer's sudden and surprising declaration of love, he had eased off Collette a bit as to not frighten her, yet he feared the damage had been done. He noticed that she stayed in the company of Poppy and was hesitant to want to hold hands or be romantic in any way. He felt like a fool for exposing himself, and hoped that when he returned to New York they could see each other again and begin anew. He was hopeful as he joined his mother for an espresso at a café across the busy street from the apartment. Here they waited for Collette and Poppy to arrive so that they could enjoy an early breakfast before Collette's flight back to New York.

As Poppy dressed down the hall, Collette went online—the first time since arriving in Rome—to see if her flight was leaving on time. Pleasantly surprised that it was, she decided to check her email before heading out. A message from Lou with the subject *YOU'RE A STAR!* was too inviting not to check later, so she opened it up.

> *C – OMG! Your ad is amazing! I can't believe Caleb wrote that! You're back tonight, right? I'm in Miami till tomorrow and can't wait to see you and hear all about*
> *your trip. Call me xoxoxo*

With everything that had happened Collette had completely forgotten about the ad she had shot a few weeks ago. So much had changed since then. She Googled "Caleb Christopher ad" and a million hits popped up. She clicked on the first one to see a glamorous replica of herself blissfully happy on top of the W Hotel. The confident image she projected caused her a measure of sadness and Caleb's words made her weep. His thanking her publically and expressing his love for her, referring to her as his fiancé, overwhelmed Collette.

"Oh my God," Spencer said from behind her. She didn't notice that he had returned for his wallet. The outside noise had muffled his footsteps into the apartment.

"Spencer!"

"I don't know how I missed it. It makes perfect sense now. You've been dating Caleb this whole time."

"No, that's not true. Just let me explain," she pleaded.

"And you're *engaged*? Collette how could you?"

"We were, but we're not. It's complicated Spencer. Please," she said, walking towards him.

"Don't."

"Please, Spencer. Just listen. I didn't mean for this to happen. I was going to tell you. Honestly," she said, as tears rolled down her face.

"Don't you have a flight to catch?" he said as he calmly walked past Poppy who emerged from down the hall.

Trinette Faint

TAKE III

<u>42</u>

Caleb was growing more nervous about Collette's whereabouts by the day. After not returning when she was supposed to, he called her parents who assured him that she was fine, explaining that she just took a few extra days in Europe with a friend. They were cagey with the details and didn't tell him who this "friend" was. He felt rushed off the phone, but at least he knew she was okay. Still not knowing when she was going to return, he remained anxious. He had purchased the most elegant engagement ring that Cartier had to offer, and planned to make it official once and for all. He wanted to be at her place when she arrived to surprise her, but his demanding shooting schedule was difficult to plan around and he already felt he was on thin ice with Trey.

Trying to figure out when she was arriving home, he had Janice squeeze information from Lou and discovered that she was returning in three days and would more than likely be home by eight in the evening. Now that he had a timeline to work with, he put the rest of his plan in order.

Collette could hardly take in the beauty of Rome through her heavy tears as the driver took her to the airport. She cried as they sped through the ancient streets and knew that she would never again speak to Spencer. She had indeed hurt him deeply and felt awful for him finding out about her and Caleb in the way that he did, but perhaps she always knew it would happen this way. She had not yet found the courage to tell Spencer what was really going on and in the process her cowardice had produced this result. Lou had warned her to be careful, but she was just hoping to get out of Rome without having to go into any real details.

While waiting in the crowded terminal for her flight at the gate, she checked her email and responded to the many inquiries about renting her apartment. She asked three of the applicants to meet her at the apartment that night when she got home. She told those interested it would be available immediately. She replied to an email about a cozy house in Boulder that looked inviting. It was a small, two-bedroom with a deck that faced the foothills, and had a spacious kitchen. It was also on a cul-de-sac and the rent was half of what she was paying for her tiny place in the city. The renter had recently accepted a job out of the country and would need to rent her home right away.

She then opened a new email from Lou:

WARNING: Caleb's assistant contacted me for your return info. I lied and told her you would be back in three days – I thought you would need some private time before seeing him. Call me when you get home. Safe travels. xoxoxoxo L

A draining eleven hours later Collette arrived at her apartment where she was jolted back to reality. While in the cab on the way back from JFK, the driver eyed her suspiciously as they passed one of the billboards that featured her along the Hudson Highway. She met his curious eyes in the rearview mirror and smiled meekly. She hoped that by putting on her sunglasses he'd get the point that she wasn't up for a chat.

As she opened her apartment door, she was met with stale, pent-up air. The mood was somber in the tiny space, as if it had known that she had experienced a broken heart. She opened all the windows as wide as possible, the force of the noise and foul scents from the New York streets rushed into her apartment. She tried to relax on the couch for a half an hour, staring at the ceiling and breathing deeply. Finally she turned on the soundtrack to *Saturday Night Fever* on her iTunes. She loved disco and used the infectious beats to motivate her to unpack and clean the apartment. She only had two and a half hours before the prospective renters showed up and she still needed to call for movers to pick up her things in two days. She also had to go to the bank to wire a deposit to Abigail, her new Boulder landlord, and let her know exactly what time she would be arriving in Colorado to retrieve the keys.

The rental process had been incredibly simple. Abigail sent her a link provided by a credit agency for her to input her information, and it gave the landlord a decision instantly. During the time Collette was in flight, Abigail checked her references and spoke to her current landlord, who loved Collette and would hate to see her go, but didn't care so much as long as she found a renter to take over her lease. Collette had called Abigail from the cab, and she told her she would wire her a deposit by the end of the day, and thanked her profusely for allowing her to rent her beautiful home. It was just the tonic she needed. A fresh start usually does the trick, the woman affirmed.

"Lou, I just rented my place. The girl is only 24 but seems mature and is really nice," Collette said over the phone. She felt a mix of sadness and joy.

"Does she have a job?"

"She just graduated from NYU and is an assistant at some private equity firm, but her dad is going to be paying, so I don't really care. My landlord spoke to him so it's all set."

"Oh, I'm so sad. Do you really have to go so soon?"

"I really just need to get out of here. After the whole Spencer thing, which was absolutely nuts and totally my fault, I just can't be in this city with these billboards everywhere and ads all over the place."

"Yeah, I know. Must be hard being a supermodel and the object of so much affection," she chided.

"Ha ha, very funny. I doubt I'll stay out there forever, but for now it's looking pretty good. I really just want to move on from both Caleb and Spencer and find some peace, and I've heard great things about Boulder. You must come visit."

"Oh, I will."

"I'll be here all day tomorrow packing when you get back, so come by anytime."

"Okay. Oh, before I go, I have to know," Lou began with trepidation.

"What?"

"Did I do the right thing by throwing Caleb off by a few days?"

"Absolutely, Lou. I just am not in the space to see him or deal with him right now. It's best for both of us if I can just disappear."

"Alright, I was worried, but I figured you would need some down time before seeing him."

"You know me too well."

"I'll talk to you tomorrow. Good luck with all the packing."

"Won't be too bad because I'm giving a lot of it away to Goodwill. I don't need to drag all this stuff out there. I'm starting over in every sense of the word."

43

Collette spent the entirety of the next day packing and preparing for the movers who were scheduled to come at 7 a.m. the following morning. She partly felt like a coward for dashing out of town without saying goodbye to Caleb, but she really just wanted to move on with her life and start over. She knew Boulder's inviting vibe would help mend her broken heart and she was anxious to begin the writing courses at the university. Her parents would not be arriving for another few weeks, so she would have about three weeks to herself to continue her self-imposed exile in the mountains. Lou had stopped by and they shared a bottle of champagne and caught up on life and laughed into the wee hours of the morning. They said a tearful goodbye when Lou hopped in a cab at 3 a.m. She promised her best friend that she would come visit soon and wished her the best of luck.

Collette tossed and turned throughout the early morning and finally dozed off before the movers arrived late at 8 a.m. Goodwill came at 10, and were grateful for the 15 trash bags full of clothes, shoes, accessories, and other odds and ends. After that was over, Collette booked it to the airport for her 2 p.m. flight to Denver.

***

Caleb was starting to wear on Janice's nerves. For the past three days he had been so jumpy and hard to read. She thought it had something to do with Collette's return but she wasn't sure because he still had not disclosed a lot of information about himself. He always seemed to have her out on some wild goose chase for something all day, and when she returned to the set he would send her home early, even though she usually had many things to go over with him. Helene, his co-star, had not been back in his trailer for rehearsals, after Caleb made it clear to her— in front of everyone in line at lunch— that he was NOT interested. She curled up to him one day, cutting in front of the crew Caleb was talking with, to suggest that she join him at his home, or hers, for more rehearsals after wrapping. She was so embarrassed by his public denial that she barely spoke to him any more and even stopped talking to Janice. She thought Trey had been behaving oddly as well, and when Nelson told her it was because of Caleb's unfocused performance, she hesitated if she should tell him this bit of information. Keeping her boss's best interest in mind, she decided to mention it to him.

"Um, so I talked to Nelson today," Janice said. They were riding in an oversized black Chevy Tahoe SUV on their way home from set.

"Yeah," he said. She knew he wasn't paying attention to her when he was playing on his iPhone.

"He said that Trey didn't think you were giving it your all."

"Uh-huh," he said. He scrolled down the tiny screen before really absorbing what she said. "What?"

"We were just talking and he said Trey thought you weren't focused. I wasn't going to tell you, but I thought you should know," she said focusing on the bald spot on of the driver's head.

"And why did Nelson tell you this?" he asked, now at full attention.

"I don't know."

"You don't know *why* he would tell you that I'm not doing a good job?"

"No, Caleb I don't. Look, I'm sorry if I did anything wrong or overstepped my boundaries, I just thought you should know."

"Tell Nelson to have Trey talk to me directly next time," he said, looking out the window.

"Okay." They rode for the remaining 18 minutes in silence. Janice didn't think she had done anything wrong and didn't understand why Caleb had snapped at her. She only wanted to help. She liked Caleb and was trying to do a good job, but she felt as if Caleb wouldn't let her do most of the things Collette did, even though she was fully capable. She found that although she was his personal assistant, she worked more closely with Katherine in overseeing things rather than with her boss herself. If he was not going to trust her and really bring her into the fold, she questioned if it was worth it. She had only come to New York to help him because she felt guilty with what happened at Sean's, but she also knew that she could go back to LA and find another job with minimal effort. Arriving at her hotel, she said a pleasant good night and watched the car speed off.

Caleb instructed the driver to take him uptown for a quick stop before he dropped him at his home. Although it was very late at 3 a.m., the urge to drive by Collette's apartment was too strong to ignore. As they came around the corner of her block he saw who he thought was Lou pass him in a cab going the opposite direction. He discounted that it was her because he didn't get a good look. Besides, what would she have been doing at Collette's apartment so late anyway? He put it out of his mind and had the driver pull over as he looked up into her window for five minutes. He thought it was odd that her curtains were gone but thought that maybe she had sent them out to be cleaned before she left. After staring up at a dark window for a few minutes he instructed the driver to his home.

Collette's Caleb

Unable to find sleep, Collette went to the window and wistfully looked out onto the quiet streets and saw the back of a black Chevy Tahoe SUV cruise down the street through a succession of green lights.

<u>44</u>

Collette was awed and silenced by the beauty of the mountains as she landed at Denver International Airport. The past three days had been a whirlwind of finding a renter for her place, packing, and moving. Her decision was probably rushed, yes, but she felt it was the right one. She picked up her rental car and entered her new address on the GPS, 655 Juniper Ave, Boulder, CO. She navigated the wide I-70 freeway and took in the great expanses of land, with the numerous suburbs and strip malls on either side of her. Cruising down route 36 towards Boulder, she was blown away by the beauty of the foothills that sprang up from the distance when she whizzed through the small town of Broomfield, Colorado. The Rockies had been all around her, but now the foothills seemed close enough to touch. It was awe-inspiring and confirmed that she had made the right choice.

After meeting Abigail at the property, she removed her shoes and surveyed her new home. The photos online had not done it justice. It was far larger than the "small-two bedroom" it was advertised to be. Perhaps it was small to Abigail, whose hyper Miniature Pinscher, vied for Collette's attention the entire time. At 1200 square feet, it was more than twice the size of her apartment in New York for half the cost; a no-brainer for sure. Abigail left pleasantly surprised when Collette paid her rent three months in advance. Because her cost of living had just effectively been halved, she had more savings to play with. As she walked around her new home, the hardwood floors creaked sporadically under her feet as the late afternoon sun shone brightly in the spacious rustic kitchen that featured a separate dining area. The patio deck faced west, allowing her a view of the mountains' beauty every day. Collette opened the screen door and sat on the patio furniture Abigail left behind, and breathed in the fresh air and beauty that so many had come west to find.

She then entered her master bedroom, its closet featuring more space than the two closets in her New York place. The brightly painted yellow bathroom had a small window that also faced the mountains. Next, she went across the hall to the second bedroom that Abigail had used for an office/guest room. The hanging plants she'd left behind gave the room vitality, and the plush carpet felt welcoming under her bare feet. Collette took in the second bathroom down the hall next to the linen closet, before going into the large finished basement where she found a washer and dryer and an additional two closets for storage. Collette's furniture was due to arrive in two days, so she was grateful that Abigail had left the daybed in the guest room along with a small desk. She felt extremely blessed to be renting from such a generous woman, and felt happier and more at peace than she had in a long time. After unpacking the three large suitcases that accompanied her on the plane, she went to Target for odds and ends along with some groceries. She called her mom from the store's parking lot and commented on how everyone she came into contact with in the store seemed so chill and were all dressed so casually. She had never seen so many people in Birkenstocks, or in running attire. This would be the place to get fit, she said to her mom who was more anxious to arrive now that Collette was there.

After all her provisions were made, she walked to the Pearl Street Mall and enjoyed a delicious meal at an Italian eatery, Pasta Jay's, absorbing the sunshine as she ate on the patio. Absolutely stuffed, she strolled the pedestrian mall and watched the street performers as day turned to dusk before heading home for a restful night's sleep on the surprisingly comfortable daybed.

***

"Janice, I'm sorry for the other day in the car. I know you were just trying to help," Caleb said through the phone from his apartment. He was taking a much-needed break from reading a script. He was excited that Collette was coming home today from Europe and after thinking about his conversation with Janice yesterday, he thought he should apologize. It wasn't her fault that she wasn't Collette and that he didn't fully give her all her responsibilities yet, or that she didn't know what he was planning for Collette's anticipated return.

"It's okay, Caleb. I know you've been under a lot of stress lately," she said. She closed her computer at her desk. She had been checking out the job market back in Los Angeles and sending out a few resumes.

"I know I haven't given you much since you've been here, and have probably been getting on your nerves because I've been so anxious, but you should know that it has nothing to do with you."

"Well, that's good to know," she said, relieved.

"I know you're not going to say anything but, I'm planning to propose today to Collette when she returns later and I may need your help with pulling off the surprise."

"Anything, Caleb. Just let me know what you need me to do." she said.

"I'll get back to you in an hour with the plan, but first I'm going to need you to send Trey and Nelson each a gift certificate for two hundred dollars to Le Colonial on 57th with a note attached. I want it to say that I apologize for my lack of focus and poor behavior of the past few weeks and to please accept this as a token of my gratitude for having the opportunity to work with you. Something along those lines. Then arrange for a few of those party buses to take the crew around Manhattan for next Friday night after wrap because we're off next weekend. Make sure you send all the crew a note that says, 'thank you for your hard work so far'. Something simple like that. Start there and I'll get back to you soon about the plans for the proposal."

Janice hung up the phone elated that her boss not only apologized, but seemed to have a big heart as well. She banished any thoughts of moving back home. She knew that what happened at Sean's was a sign because its result had given her a great boss.

***

Rayleen, Collette's 24-year-old sub-letter, was so happy to finally be getting her own apartment. She had to share living space with three other girls in the NYU dorms for four years and since graduating a year ago, she'd been subletting a cramped apartment in Williamsburg with another girl. Her roommate's punk rock life style didn't agree with Rayleen's 9 to 5 schedule. Rayleen's father finally acquiesced and agreed to help her if she wanted to move. She found Collette's place while scanning Craigslist at work and pounced on it. It was cute, clean, and available *now*, which was most important on her list of criteria.

She and a friend unpacked her meager belongings from a small U-Haul truck, which didn't take very long. She had fallen asleep after returning the truck, when she heard the doorbell ring. Knowing that no one knew of her address and with it being past 10 p.m., she ignored the bell. The ringing happened again, and then she heard a rapid knock at the door.

***

Caleb had been sweating bullets all day. After speaking with Janice earlier, he charged her with the task of putting together a photo album with all the humorous outtakes from the W Hotel photo shoot she had done weeks earlier for his line. Katherine retrieved the extra shots from the photographer and Janice had to complete the album because he was running out of time and had other things to put into place. He also needed for her to make a 10:30 p.m. reservation at the French Bistro, Le Monde, where they had gone to celebrate their engagement, the first time around. He would pay whatever cost for the entire back of the restaurant to be reserved for the two of them. Janice needed to go there to place roses on the tables and make sure the area could be sealed off with a velvet curtain, like before. Caleb in the meantime showered, shaved, and thanked Janice profusely when she dropped off the beautifully assembled album. He looked very handsome as he nervously rode in a cab to her place with the ring and roses in hand. Arriving at her place, he saw the light was still on but her window treatments had been replaced by mini-blinds, which he thought was odd. When she didn't answer the bell he so eagerly rang, he waited until someone exited the building and darted up the stairs two at a time and knocked on the door.

"Hello?" Rayleen said from the other side of the door.

"Collette?"

"Sorry?"

"Collette please. Is she there? It's Caleb," he said, as sweat made its way down the sides of his face.

"Hang on a sec," She unlocked a series of deadbolts. Caleb double-checked the apartment number as he looked at this woman standing before him. "Hi, I'm Rayleen," she said, extending her hand.

"Hi, uh, where's Collette?"

"I'm afraid Collette doesn't live here anymore. She moved out the other day."

Caleb's eyes grew wide and he turned pale as the flowers fell from his moist hands. "Say, are you *Caleb Christopher*? The actor? Oh my God it is you!"

"Where'd she go?" he asked through a cracked voice. He felt tears form in the corners of his eyes.

"Not really sure. It was just fast is all I know. Say, are you alright?" she asked. He scanned the apartment that bore no traces of Collette.

"Thanks," was all he could muster as he turned and walked down the stairs.

"You forgot your flowers!" she called out as he struggled to make it outdoors before losing it. Once out of the building he stumbled down 84th Street until he found a bench and collapsed. He cried so hard that he did not care who saw him.

***

Collette woke up refreshed the next day, and strolled down to the Pearl Street Mall for an early breakfast. Today she planned to pay a visit to the University of Colorado's Registrar's Office. She could have easily printed out her schedule for *Intro to Fiction Writing* and *Character Development* courses online, but she wanted to see the large campus in person. The campus was stunningly picturesque. Young co-eds walked through the quad and played Frisbee with their dogs. Pretty girls yapped on their cell phones and tried to ignore the guys throwing said Frisbees, and the requisite nerds sat alone reading books. Collette registered for the courses and purchased her books, eager to begin the class in one week. After two more trips to Target and the purchase of a pair Birkenstocks, she dropped off her things, returned the rental car to the local Hertz. Feeling rejuvenated, she walked into the first bike store she saw on her way home and purchased a new set of wheels and rode home in the bright sunshine, basking in the elation that washed over her as she peddled to her new home.

***

Caleb sent Janice a text to cancel the reservation, but to leave the staff a 30% tip on top off the cost of what it was to secure the reservation. He then called Lou in a rage demanding where Collette was and why she had told her she would be home when she had obviously come and gone.

"Hey don't yell at me, Caleb! You're the one who couldn't get your shit together," Lou said to Caleb over the phone.

"What am I supposed to do, Lou? If you hadn't lied to me, this would not have happened!" he said. There were empty soda cans and beer bottles everywhere and piles of dirty laundry all over his floor.

"Caleb, I know you're pissed and I am going to pretend that you didn't call me like you did, but you and Collette broke up and she moved away. End of story."

"No, it's not the end of the story, Lou. I love her and you let her get away."

"Listen to yourself, Caleb. You're blaming me for something *you* let happen. Do you think it was easy for Collette to work around that pop tart Amber you had living with you? Or for her to get engaged without a ring? Honestly, Caleb. Grow up already!"

"I explained that Amber shit to her and I was going to get a ring, Lou. She didn't have to just leave and you could have said something," he said. He walked into the bathroom in search of Advil.

"It wasn't my place, Caleb. If Collette didn't feel comfortable telling you then how could I?"

"You could have said something! I looked like a fool up there tonight." he said stepping on a pile of dirty towels.

"You are so selfish Caleb! Collette just wants a life without the drama, okay? She only told me when she was in Rome that she was leaving."

"Rome? She was in Rome? Was she there with Spencer?" he asked, as his heart sank again.

"What?"

"You heard me. Was she in Rome with Spencer, Lou? Be straight with me."

"Yes."

"WHAT?"

"She didn't plan it. It just sort of happened," she said.

"What do you mean it just sort of happened?" he asked as the blood rushed to his face.

"They just ran into each other in London and she went to visit. You were broken up anyway, Caleb. What the hell was she supposed to do? All those pictures of Amber kept popping up and the one with her all over you in front of your house was enough to set anybody off."

"She was in Rome with Spencer—"

"If it's any consolation she never loved him, Caleb. You must know that, but she just couldn't wait around anymore for you to really get your crap together. She was tired of the bullshit and drama."

"Where is she?"

"I don't think I should tell you that, Caleb. I've said enough already. Just try to move on."

"Don't tell me to just *move on*, Lou. My life is a fucking mess right now. I just spent a grand at Le Monde tonight hoping for a private dinner with her. I bought a Cartier ring that's collecting dust and should be on her finger. I've had to shell out close to six grand for gifts for the director and crew just to save my ass from getting fired from this movie. I've been the worst actor ever and can't fucking remember my lines or do anything right because I'm so unfocused. I miss her so much. My apartment is a sty because I can't be bothered to clean up after my sorry self, so please don't just tell me to move on. I can't. I love Collette and need her in my life and I can't just put it all behind me."

"She's in Boulder."

"*Boulder, Colorado?*"

"Yeah. I'm as shocked as you are."

"What the hell is she doing there?"

"Waiting for you and pretending she's happy, I can only guess," she said, fearful that she had betrayed her friend.

"I love you, Lou. You're the best."

"I'm a shitty best friend who just told her friend's ex-fiancée where she is. *That's* what I am."

"Call it what you want but you're the best to me."

"Yeah, whatever. Now stop wasting time on the phone and get your ass out there and bring her home."

<u>45</u>

Janice thought Caleb had been in a remarkably good mood the past few days. It was strange considering Collette was no longer in town and he was not engaged again. Oh well. She tried not to give it too much thought and just plowed along with the large amounts of work Caleb finally gave her. Something had changed in him seemingly overnight. He brought her more up to speed on things and more involved in general. The day after the foiled re-engagement attempt, he called her early the next morning at 7 a.m., three hours before the car was due to take them to the set, and went over a list of things with her. First, she was to find a housekeeper that very day that could handle his mess. Amber had managed to scare away the previous housekeeper and he hadn't bothered to replace her. He was tired of living in his filth.

Next she was to communicate with his co-op board and cross check the next six monthly meetings against his calendar. He wanted to know more about his rooftop garden since he was paying heavily for it. He said he thought it could be therapeutic for him to get his hands in the dirt and help out instead of just writing a check. Then he wanted her to find him a private yoga and kickboxing instructor to help him with his focus and to get him in shape. The past few weeks, wallowing in his misery, he packed on a few extra pounds and his diet took a turn for the worse as he self-medicated with unhealthy foods. She was also to find him a nutritionist who could prepare meals for him. His pity party was over and it was time to get back on track.

She was also to let Katherine know that he would agree to an interview with the CBS *Sunday Morning* program. They were doing a special on honesty and wanted to talk about his stepping down from the line. This would be the only interview he would do, and chose this outlet because the demographics of the show were older and more mature than standard entertainment programs. This would be helpful because he wanted to be exposed to a greater audience than teenage girls. The biggest task she was charged with was to arrange for a meeting with the talent agent Stephen Crane at Crane Entertainment. They were competitors of Coastal Talent, and had expressed interest in Caleb years before. He hoped they could now overlook his past to focus on his future. They held their actors to the same standards as Coastal Talent. Now that Amber and her antics were completely out of the picture he felt confident that he had a better shot.

Bruce had stuck to his word and left Caleb and Janice alone, but instead turned his lens on Amber in his quest for revenge on her, since his wife of 12 years was divorcing him. He kept his guys heavily on her tail with the sole purpose of ruining her career and running her out of town. He pounced on her as she came out of Models-N-More with puffy red eyes after they dropped her. Bruce's agency got a copy of her contract, which they published and highlighted the text next to the photo: *"Models-N-More reserves the right to revoke this contract between the talent, Amber Skye, and Models-N-More at any time for any reason if we feel the model is a) not living up to her promise in the business, b) is fired from a job for any reason, c) has a bad attitude, d) performs poorly on a job, and e) any other reason we see fit."* The subsequent shots he ran showed her parents arriving at her apartment and at LaGuardia where she was leaving for Chicago with them. The photographer overheard her mom tell her that her room was ready for her at home, and ran the headline: *"AMBER SKYE RETURNS HOME TO CHICAGO TO LIVE WITH HER PARENTS AFTER A MODELING CAREER FAILS TO MATERIALIZE IN NEW YORK."*

***

Janice didn't know exactly why Caleb had turned over this new leaf but she wasn't complaining. His focus seemed to return to his work, which pleased Trey. He even seemed to smile once or twice after he shot one of the scenes. The week flew by and on Friday after wrap, the crew boarded the party buses, ready for a night of debauchery. They were upset that Caleb couldn't join them, but he had a flight to catch and couldn't be late.

***

Collette missed Lou terribly and wished her friend was there to keep her company as she acclimated to her new place. With no one to call, she checked her email and extracted the messages from her trash bin that she'd received from Caleb while in Paris and London. They where the explanatory emails that filled her with sadness. It really did sound like Amber was crazy and that he had really been having a tough time. Oh well, she'd moved away now with the purpose of focusing on herself for awhile. Needing to get out of the house and do *something* to let off steam, she went on a long bike ride to unwind. She took a book and relaxed in a park for a few hours before returning home to prepare dinner. She ate in front of the television as she watched a few *Law & Order* reruns. Later when she was ready to turn in, she tried not to think about the time she and Caleb had spent in her bed. She tossed and turned and finally slept.

***

Caleb hadn't been to his parent's house in at least two years. When he told his mom that he was on his way home she was overjoyed and said she'd pick him up at the airport. He insisted it wouldn't be necessary because he was flying privately and had a car waiting for him on the other end. He was planning to land, drive directly to Boulder to see Collette, and hopefully get her to come back. Anna only knew what she read in the press in regard to his relationship, like everyone else, as he had not filled his parents in on everything that had happened. His mother was shocked when she learned of everything and sent her son all of her positive energy and love in getting Collette back.

Four hours later, landing at 11 p.m., Caleb jumped in his car and headed down the busy freeway. He hadn't been to Boulder in ages but had lots of fun memories in the college town. He laughed to himself as he imagined Collette there, fitting in but standing out in the hippie town. After sweating for 45 minutes in the car about what he was going to say when he saw her, he finally stopped over thinking when he got off at the 26th Street exit. He drove slowly and reminisced about his buddy's birthday party at a bar on one side of the street, and about a house party on another. He was calmed by the memories of the warm and welcoming people of Colorado and promised to get back home more often. Perhaps this was the balance he needed in his life that had been missing. It was important to keep in touch with his friends and family that always loved him no matter what.

He turned off the lights in front of the chocolate brown house with the enclosed porch at 655 Juniper Avenue on the cul-de-sac. The neighborhood children's bicycles in the various driveways, and opened doors and windows of houses, brought him comfort. He was reassured that Collette was in a nice neighborhood filled with families. All of the lights were off inside her house when he rang the doorbell. Looking inside the screened-in porch, he noticed a bike with one of her scarves tied to the handlebars. He found it endearing that she had branded the bike as her own in this way, adding her own personal touch. Another ring and no answer. He called her name softly only to be answered by an unleashed chocolate Lab who barked when he saw this stranger.

"You looking for the girl who lives here?" an innocent seven-year-old boy said. He appeared out of nowhere as he retrieved his dog.

"Yes, I am. Have you seen her?" he asked, smiling at the freckle-faced child whose face shone in the moonlight.

"She left about thirty minutes ago. I heard her on the phone talking to someone named Lou. Said she was going to Rhumba on Pearl Street."

"You heard all that?" Caleb asked dubiously.

"Yep! She also said she missed some asshole named Caleb and she sounded sad."

"TOMMY!" The boy's mother appeared from the house, and grabbed his skinny arm.

"Mom, ouch!" the boy said as the dog lay on the ground licking his leg.

"What are you doing out here talking to this strange man? You're supposed to be in bed young man," she said, eyeing Caleb suspiciously.

"My apologies ma'am. He was just telling me where my friend is," he said with his hands up as if she were pointing a gun at him.

"Well he knows better than to talk to strangers," she said, giving his arm a good yank. "I'll have your father deal with you."

"But I had to find Rusty. He was out here running around." The young boy tried to make his case.

"Damn dog. Gonna get you killed one of these days."

"He really was looking for his dog, ma'am, and he was nice enough to start talking to me," he said as he headed back to his car. "Good night to you both," He smiled at the boy as the mother looked at him with sudden recognition.

"Caleb Christopher? Are you *Caleb Christopher* the actor?" she asked dropping her son's arm and walking towards Caleb, her mouth agape.

"Yes, ma'am I am. Listen, you've got a great son, ma'am. I can tell he's a terrific boy. Bye, Tommy," he said getting in to his car.

"Bye mister!" he replied waving his arm enthusiastically.

"Oh my God, that was Caleb Christopher!" She grabbed her son and dragged him into the house, yelling to her husband.

At Rhumba, Collette was surprised at how young everyone was and felt old at 27 in this town full of college students. She waited in line to get into the bar for ten minutes, not too bad she thought, and maneuvered her way through the rambunctious crowd. She brushed past finely chiseled man-boys and beautiful girls and grabbed the one seat left at the bar. The girl who just abandoned the seat looked desperate to get out of there. She soon found out why.

"Heeeeey you!" a tall blond Adonis said to her.

"Hi." She smiled as she surveyed the drink list.

"Brock. And you are?" he asked, extending a hand.

"Collette." She shook his large hand feeling him hold on to hers for a moment too long. "Can I have a Stoli and tonic?" she asked the female bartender. Collette withdrew her hand and placed it demurely on her lap.

"Hey leave her alone, Brock. No need to scare all the ladies away." She winked at Collette.

"Thank you," she mouthed back.

"Sorry, babe, but you are smooooooookin'!" he said, smelling like he had one too many two hours ago.

"Is it always so crowded in here?' she asked, trying to change the subject.

"Maybe. But let's talk about you, babe. You must be new in town if I haven't seen you before."

"Umm," she said, accepting her drink. Realizing that it wasn't worth having a conversation with this bonehead, she pulled out her BlackBerry and began to compose a text for Lou.

"Don't wanna talk? That's okay babe. I don't wanna *talk* either. If you catch my drift." He winked as he leaned in.

"If you'll just excuse me," she said, turning away from him. She scanned the crowd for a moment, hoping he'd think she was expecting someone.

"Can I get another one over here?" he yelled to the bartender, waving his empty glass.

"Brock, it's time for you to settle your tab. I think you've terrorized us long enough," she said, glancing in Collette's direction.

"Come on, babe. Just one more. And one more for Collette here too. My new laaaaadaaay..." He leaned in close again.

"I'm all set. Thanks though. I will settle up with this if I could," she said, putting a $20 bill on the bar.

"Put that away, I got it, babe. Let's just get goin'," he slurred. "I don't live that far from here. Just over there." He squinted and pointed in a random direction. "Yup, just over there."

"Brock, knock it off before I call your dad to come get you again. You better hope he doesn't take away your trust fund this time. That'll be $7.50," she said, addressing Collette.

"DUDE! Do *not* call my pops! He was piiiiiiissssssed the last time you did," he said.

"Just get moving then and I won't need to call him. You don't want to embarrass him again, do you? He's like the police chief or something around here," she said to Collette.

"No," he pouted.

"Well go hop in a cab outside and get home safely," she said.

"Alright. I'll go but I don't haffta like it." He stumbled getting off the bar stool.

"I know, Brock. I'll see you later."

"Okay! I'm leaving now. Last chance for the Brock Brock train. Whoo hoo!" he said.

"I'm all set," Collette said, trying not to burst out laughing.

"You sure babe, cuz this train is leaving the station," he said, then howled.

"Brock!" the doorman screamed from the front.

"DUDE! What's up, man!"

"Out! Come on, buddy time to go."

"Whoo hoo! Brock Brock train! Ooooooooowwwwwww!" he said, as the doorman gently led him outside and into a cab. He continued chugging his arm out the window and howling as the cabbie drove off.

"Oh my God, what was *that*?" Collette asked the bartender.

"That was trouble, that's what that was. He's harmless but sure can be a jerk. This town is full of trust fund babies like him who do nothing but get wasted and stoned all the time."

"Really? And his dad is chief of police?"

"No, he's the mayor, but that's what I say to let him know I am two seconds away from calling him. He usually leaves after I say that. He got busted for a DUI a few weeks ago and his dad had to take out an ad in the *Daily Camera* apologizing for his son saying he was going to enter rehab."

"Wow."

"You must be new in town. I'm Karen."

"Collette, and yes, I am new," she said, introducing herself.

"Karen, I need those drinks!" A cocktail waitress called out from the opposite side of the bar.

"'Excuse me, Collette."

"Of course." Collette nursed her drink and tried to bob her head to the loud music while she pretended she wasn't tired or bored out of her mind. She left a ten on the bar and headed out.

Caleb had finally found a parking space after driving around for 20 minutes and walked down the rowdy street. Pearl Street was sedate during the day, but turned into its own version of the Vegas strip at night. There were young girls everywhere falling on their asses thinking it was funny and preppy boys who yelled "dude!" to each other so loudly it was as if they didn't realize they were standing right next to each other. As Caleb approached the bar, he had no idea what he was going to say or how he was going to say it, he just knew he needed to say *something*.

"...so there was this totally obnoxious asshole next to me at the bar and they had to kick him out! He was really cute but such an ass it was hysterical..." He heard Collette's voice say

this from around a corner. He froze in his steps and continued to listen. "...*I guess I like it okay, but I miss New York, but it's pretty here and I'm looking forward to starting school next week...what?...Caleb called you...what?...you TOLD him???....yes, I miss him but...he knows about Spencer?...oh my God!...Lou!...*" Caleb's legs felt cemented to the ground when Collette turned the corner and nearly knocked him over.

"Oh, I'm sor—*CALEB*?" she said. "Lou, I gotta call you back." She hung up the phone and threw it into her bag.

"Hi, Collette." He tried to speak but his tongue was heavier than his legs.

"What are you doing here?" she felt her entire body quiver and thought her heart was going to jump out of her chest.

"Um, I came to see you, Collette. I can't believe you moved here."

"Yeah, I can't believe Lou told you," she said.

"Um, I'm sorry for everything Collette." He was still unable to move.

"I don't know what to say, Caleb." She had played this moment in her head millions of times, and had planned out responses better than this. In those imagined moments she'd really laid into him and was strong in her delivery.

"Just please say yes," he said sinking to the ground as if he had no control over his body, limbs, or his speech. He was now on one knee and produced the ring out of his coat pocket. A tear rolled down his face as Collette inhaled audibly. The world around them stood still. Cars drove by and honked and drunk kids yelled "SAY YES!" as they flew by. Collette's insides turned upside down and inside out and her legs shook under her. She took a step toward him, and felt like she would topple over with each movement of her legs. When the proposal came again in her imagined moments, she grilled him hard about his indiscretions and made him practically beg her to marry him again. All that went out the window as her eyes filled with tears as a big smile spread across her face and she screamed to the top of her lungs *"YEEEEEEEEEEEEEEEEEES!"*

<u>46</u>

"Dude, isn't that Caleb Christopher!" a young kid asked as he emerged from a bar seeing Caleb and Collette kiss passionately, ignoring and oblivious to the world around them.

"Dude! It is!" said the friend who was able to get close enough to take a photo. The happy kissing couple did not budge as the flash went off and more people tooted their horns.

"What are you going to do with that, dude?" his friend asked as they looked at the evidence after having driven a block away.

"Duh! The *Daily Camera* is right there! I'm about to get paid," he said as they entered the newspaper building.

After a quick celebratory drink back at Rhumba where he was the subject of many pictures and autograph requests, they finally made their way back to Collette's place. They could barely keep their hands off each other, bursting through the front door, landing on the floor. They laughed and undressed each other and left a trail of clothes behind as they made their way to the bedroom.

"I don't know who that could be," Collette said as she put on a robe to answer the doorbell the next morning.

"Yes?" she said to the smiling woman.

"Hi, I'm Margie and I live next door with my son Tommy and my husband. Last night we met someone who was here looking for you." She flashed a toothy grin.

"Umm hmm."

"It was Caleb Christopher. The actor." She leaned in and whispered. "That's his car right there."

"Yes, it was me," he said, appearing in one of Collette's floral printed robes. He wrapped his arms around her from behind.

"Oh. My. God," she uttered. "MICHAEL GET OVER HERE IT'S HIM!" she yelled to her waiting husband on the side of the house.

"Shhhh … … " Collette giggled.

"Where are my manners! I'm so sorry, it's just that hometown boys that make it big like you don't really come back very often. This is Michael, my husband."

"Nice to meet you sir," Caleb said, shaking his calloused hand.

"Wow! Pleasure's mine, sir! Holy shit, Margie, it's him!" he said, tickled.

"Would you like to come in for some coffee?" Collette offered, opening the door.

"Why sure!" Margie said barging into the room. She noticed the clothes strewn on the floor. "Humph. My my. Someone had a good night." She nudged her husband in the ribs.

"Sorry about that. I haven't had time to clean up in here," Collette said blushing as she tossed the clothes down the hall. She felt Caleb's eyes follow hers, glowing brightly.

"Please have a seat," Caleb offered. They all sat down before Collette remembered that she didn't have any coffee.

"Do you like tea? I forgot I don't have any coffee," she said. She put on a pot of water and set out a few tea bags.

"Whatever you have is fine by us. We're the ones barging in on you at seven in the morning on a Saturday," Margie said.

"Where's Tommy?" Caleb asked seriously in Collette's rose-printed robe.

"Probably still sleeping. That boy is the only one I know who doesn't rush downstairs for cartoons on a Saturday morning. He always sleeps till nine."

"Oh, that's too bad. I had something to ask him."

"What's that?"

"Well, me and Collette are getting married today as soon as the courthouse opens, and I wanted to know if he wouldn't mind being my best man."

"Are you serious?" Margie said, feeling as if she just won the mega millions.

"Yes, I am. He was responsible for me finding Collette last night so it's the least I can do."

"Yes, we would love that," Collette said. She felt such warmth and affection towards this couple whose son brought them back together.

"I can't believe this. Yes, of course he'll be your best man," Margie said, choking up.

"But isn't city hall closed today? I mean it's a Saturday," Michael said.

"Normally, yes, but my new friend Karen who works at Rhumba called in a favor to the mayor last night."

"The mayor?" Margie and Michael said in unison.

"It sounds crazy, but she knows him personally from work, and after we became engaged we went in for a quick drink and Caleb told her how he wished we could just do it tomorrow, meaning today, if it weren't closed, and she said that maybe she could help us out. She called him right then and there. She woke him up! She said because she'd managed to get his son home safely, then he needed to marry hometown boy Caleb Christopher tomorrow at city hall. It was quite a night."

"Oh my God! I can't believe she called the mayor for you."

"Well, that boy of his does have a drinking problem, so I'm sure he owes favors all over town on account of him," Michael said.

"That's what it sounded like."

"Goodness, girl. You've got a wedding to get to in two hours. Let me see that ring!" she said, grabbing Collette's hand as she awed at the size and beauty of the Cartier ring.

"You have certainly got good taste," Margie said, looking at Collette as she smiled.

"I'm the luckiest man in the world and I'll never forget it," Caleb said.

Adorned in a white sundress with her Birkenstocks and a bouquet of daisies put together from Margie's garden, at 9:07 a.m. Collette Sandrine-Anais Smith became Collette Sandrine-Anais Christopher, while their witnesses, Michael, Margie, Dave, Anna, and Karen looked on as Tommy beamed proudly as best man. Caleb and Robbie wore matching Bermuda shorts and white button-down shirts as he hoisted his new little friend on his shoulders for pictures. Michael acted as photographer for the intimate event.

After the seven-minute long ceremony, Karen opened the bar where they convened for their private party, invading the walk-in coolers to scramble up eggs and bacon along with fresh fruit and toast. Rhumba did not open until 5 p.m., so they hung out all day enjoying each other's company, and invited any curious onlookers to join their celebration of love. By 11 a.m. word had spread like wildfire that Caleb Christopher was at Rhumba for his wedding reception, and soon both the *Daily Camera* and *Denver Post* had reporters outside waiting for him to emerge with his new bride. He and Collette happily welcomed them into the party and he signed numerous copies of the *Daily Camera* that featured him on page one kissing Collette the night before. He had no idea who had taken the photo or when, but simply said to the photographers, "Make sure you get this," as he planted another big one on his wife as the lenses snapped away.

47

"Ma, I know. I'm sorry you and daddy weren't there, but it just happened really fast. We decided to do it at like midnight or something the night before," Collette explained to her mom in the car on their way back to Caleb's plane the next day. "Please don't be upset, we're planning to come back here soon when you get here to celebrate with you and Lou…yes, I'm sure what I'm doing…Spencer? I was never in love with him, Ma…I have to go…yes, I'll call you later so we can finish talking. I love you too."

"What'd she say?" asked Caleb.

"The usual mom stuff. You know, how she's so upset that she didn't see me walk down the aisle, and how could I do this to her, and whatever else I tuned out," Collette said taking his free hand as he drove.

"I'm sorry C, I wish they could have been there."

"It's alright. I wanted to do it so I did. A drawn out engagement and all that planning was never for me. It was perfect the way it was. No interference from anyone. Just me and the man I love."

"I love you, Mrs. Christopher."

"I love you too, Mr. Smith," she said, as they broke out in laughter.

"So, are you pissed at Lou for giving you up?"

"How could I be? I was hoping that you would figure it out sooner or later."

"It wasn't easy. She's a tough one that Lou."

"That's my girl," she said, smiling to herself.

"But she did tell me about Spencer…what do you think he's going to say?"

"What do you think Amber's going to say?"

"I don't give a shit what that girl has to say. That was a mistake from day one and she did nothing but ruin everything. I mean, that photo when she ambushed me? Unbelievable. She's back at home in Chicago if you haven't heard."

"Good for her. I hope she gets the help she obviously needs."

"What about Spencer? Your little Roman holiday? Hmm?"

"Like I told you, I doubt I will ever hear from him again. I felt so bad the way everything went down, but I guess having a casualty or two from our whole crazy love story isn't a surprise."

"Yeah, guess not."

***

Collette missed her first day of class at the university. She was sad when she had to withdraw, but was elated when she attended her first day of class at Columbia University in New York three weeks later. For a continuing education class, the course load was heavy, with lots of reading in addition to the numerous writing assignments. She hoped she would have time to actually do the work since she had signed on with a top modeling agency. She had modeled again for Joe a week before her course started and he showed the photos to an agent friend who loved her instantly. He definitely wanted to represent the girl who had just married mega star Caleb Christopher.

During Caleb's interview on *CBS Sunday Morning* he gushed about Collette. He said he learned the value of being honest from Collette, one of her greatest virtues, and he couldn't explain how much he loved her because of it.

While planning her trip back to Colorado with her parents to retrieve her things, she also started brainstorming redecorating ideas. Although she loved Caleb's loft as it was, she wanted a fresh look and feel that reflected their new lives together. She received no resistance from Caleb. She called Margie to tell her she'd be back in a few days to get her things and to see if she knew anyone to rent Abigail's house. Margie told her not to worry, that'd she'd take care of everything. She had a cousin moving to the area with her small child who needed a place, and since Abigail had met her before, she was sure she wouldn't mind. Margie worked out the details with Abigail directly, and sent her a slew of the wedding photos with THAT *Caleb Christopher* (!) and her son Tommy. Abigail couldn't believe that a celebrity like Caleb Christopher had stayed in her house and promised to refund her prepaid rent as soon as she received it back from Margie's cousin, which was more than fine with Collette.

Collette, Lou, and Caleb flew to Denver to visit the new home of her parents and for the formal celebration Collette promised them. Caleb's parent's home was the perfect setting to welcome Hampton and April to Denver, and to celebrate Caleb and Collette's marriage.

Karen, Michael and Margie showed Collette's parents photos from the wedding day, and they were smitten with Tommy as he repeatedly recounted his story of how he told Caleb where to find Collette. He was proudly the man of the hour as they celebrated far into the night.

__Epilogue__

Collette didn't know when she was going to be able to finish her latest assignment for class. She was in the home stretch of her program and it seemed the more intense her course work got, the busier she was with work. The first course she had taken nearly two years ago had basically been a practice run for her to prepare for a full MFA in Creative Writing, for which she was close to finishing. If only she could magically have more hours in the day.

Midway through the beginning of her master's program, they finally got around to redoing the loft. They had to design a style that represented them both, somehow integrating her eclectic pieces and style with his more contemporary preferences. It wasn't an easy feat, but in the end they were very pleased with the result.

In the past year she had also been very busy as a working model, and had secured a contract as the face of the new *RJ* (as in Roberto and Julien) clothing line. The winners of last year's *Real Runway* program had joined forces to create a line, and were ecstatic when Collette arrived for the casting.

None of the other models stood a chance as they reminisced about the good old days. As spokesperson, her agency had negotiated a very sweet deal for her where she was only required to work 48 days out of the year at the hefty sum of 2.8 million per year. This sum, along with her earnings from other modeling jobs, allowed her the freedom and independence to finance her education, and time to represent the beauty and skincare site, Lovehue.com. The site, created by another former celebrity personal assistant friend of hers from college, was the best online beauty store to have come along in years and Collette was happy to be a part of it.

The next year flew by and soon they celebrated her master's degree at their second home in Denver. Over the past year they had made a point to go see their parents more often, and during one trip they impulsively bought a home there. Tommy, now almost ten, was thrilled at the news and was happy that he was going to be able to see his friend Caleb more often. One of the reasons they fell in love with the house, that took three months to renovate, was because of its central location between the home of Caleb's parents and the home of Collette's parents.

Collette, now 30, was four months pregnant when they packed up and headed west. Caleb's agency, Crane Entertainment had been finding him better material which allowed him to be more selective in his roles, so he had been around a lot more and would be more present as a father. Collette renewed her agreements with Roberto and Julien, while the agency made sure the pot was sweetened—requiring her to work less for more money—as she continued her relationship with Lovehue.com.

Required to now work only 45 days a year, she used her free time to write a novel about a young woman's experience as a personal assistant to a celebrity. The name of the heroine was *Trin*ette, which many people thought was her, *Coll*ette, and although those who knew her knew that they were not the same person or shared the same experiences, she was always humored when they thought it was. The success of her novel, *Trinette and Tristan*, remained on the *New York Times* bestseller list for 18 weeks straight, the only greater success being the birth of their baby girl, Chloe, further solidifying their trilogy of love, happiness, and honesty in life.

<u>Acknowledgments</u>

I would like to thank my editor, the wonderful Kara Storti, for guiding me through this process and making me a better writer. I would also like to thank my mom, Allan, Gina, Madear, David, Kelly, Rachel, Maureen, Melissa, Barbara, Kara M, Kate M, Lesley, Dawn, Lynne, Natalie, and Anne for their constant unwavering support and love. A big thanks also to Sarah L and Jennifer M for their formatting wizardry, and to Harper's Bazaar and Estée Lauder for their role in making my dreams come true.

Cover photo © Trinette Faint
Cover design by Jennifer McCabe
(mccabephotography.com)